DEADMAN'S CHANCE

A Chance Adventure

Robert Knox

RevPhule Puplishing

Thanks to my amazing wife. She not only supports me everyday but this is the first book she also helped me edit. Words cannot express my appreciation and love for her.

PREFACE

When I started writing this my intent was to work on Book III of the Stone Cold series. After I wrote the first part I know the main character wasn't JC. I tried to put it aside but couldn't. Thats how we eneded up here.

I hope you enjoy the story as much as I did. For those of you waiting on the next Stone Cold, its coming. I need to edit it and then let my wife fix my mistakes.

Thanks for reading this and any other of my work, as always please leave a review. They not only insipre me and the many other indie authors but they help us in our writing. I read every one of them, good and boad. If you've left me one I thank you for it, all of it helps.

Prologue

Well damn. That hadn't gone according to plan, not one bit. It had been a simple plan, there was no reason it should have been hard to execute. Really simple, ride into Denver and get a room not end up shot to rags in a ditch. Nevertheless, here I am with three holes leaking blood around the moss I'd managed to pack them with. It had been a rush job since hiding in a ditch from the last two back-shooters took priority. They were searching the woods for me now but soon enough they'd find my trail. I'd rolled in the mud at the bottom of the ditch trying to hide where I fell. Even in the dark they'd be able to see the disturbance but maybe they'd look past it for a minute. That minute might be just enough to give me an edge.

My left arm was useless which made reloading my Colt a pain in the ass. It didn't feel like any bones were broken from the slugs that had ripped through my body. There was a neat hole through the skin and muscle and the bandanna I'd tied around it after packing it with some moss seemed to staunch the bleeding. It was much the same for the one through my thigh.

Luck saved my life by an inch there. The bullet had passed through the muscle, missing the artery. If it had hit an inch over, I'd already be dead. Binding that one had cost me a sleeve. After ripping it off it and packing both sides with moss, I used it to bind the wound tightly. The last wound was just a graze along the my right side. It hurt like hell and might have nicked a rib, but it wasn't anything to worry about right now. My biggest concern at the moment were the two men coming in my direction.

"Charlie, where'd that puncher go?" His high nasal tone was annoying. Even through the pain it made me want to punch him in the nose.

"Shut up ya damned fool!" His companion's sharp whisper carried even further then his pard's. "Ain't no way I know more 'an you!"

"He's got some holes in 'em. Gotta be leak'n, might be he's dead?" They were closer now, maybe twenty feet away and heading my direction.

"Ain't that lucky an ya know it Hank, ain't neither of us at lucky." He was still hissing out a loud whisper. I was not dealing with experienced hoot owls, these two were the bottom of the barrel.

"Y'all said he was jus some kid. That damn kid took out Quince and Tommy like they was nothin'. Still think he's just some kid Bodey?" There was a certain 'I told you so' tone in his response. It found its mark and pissed off his buddy.

"Shut the hell up! All we can do is find 'em ta make certain he ain't still breathin'!" Bodey snapped.

I eased back into the mud a bit further and waited. I had to calm my breathing and try to focus. Hopefully they'd walk right up to me soon because I didn't know how long it'd take them to find my trail. The fading light of dusk helped hide me in the mud but the growing chill wasn't doing me any favors. My only hope was that they wouldn't see me until it was too late. Thankfully, that's exactly what happened.

A shadow moved in front of me and I got ready for the end. One of them nearly stepped on my boot just before he died. My Colt interrupted, fire stabbed through the darkness. The slug sped out of the barrel and punched through the bottom of his jaw. It exploded out the top of his skull, spraying his pard with bone and brain. Charlie jerked back splluttering in shock. He was most likely blinded, either by the sudden bright light or blood and brain.

I didn't give him a chance to recover. My next round punched through his chest just about the same time he broke his own nose. He had raised both of his hands trying to wipe the brain matter out of his eyes and had bashed himself with his pistol butt. He fell into the mud, dead and unconcerned with any further injuries. My stunt had worked and both of them lay dead or dying. The second man's body jerked in the mud for second before it stilled. Silence returned, even the insects took a moment before they started back up.

I had survived these skunks but it still left me in a bad spot. Never mind bleeding from a few holes, the first man seemed intent on exacting some additional punishment for his demise. His dead body fell across my wounded leg making me cry out in pain. The edges of my vision started to close in, making me fight it back before moving. Why did it have to be the bigger one? Evidently I'd pissed off fate again.

Nope, this was not at all what I had planned for my day, not one damn bit. After collecting a nice bounty from the last job, I just wanted a bath and a real bed for a few days. The last thing on my agenda was facing a gang, one who didn't even know who I was. These fools just wanted my animal and guns. My mind flashed back across the last hour trying to figure out what had gone so wrong.

CHAPTER 1

I'd been just ambling down the trail, my mind focused on making the city before nightfall. Or I would have if not for the three men with guns out sitting in the middle of the road. They had appeared after I swung around a tight turn. I didn't remember seeing them on the map when I checked it, you'd think someone would have noted it. They were looking down at two bodies laying in the road. They must have had a map that didn't mention strange travelers because they obviously didn't expect me either.

Credit where credit's due, they adapted pretty damn quick. Even as my thumb flipped my thong off, the first one leveled his pistol and fired. He was the one who'd hit my thigh. Thankfully, I managed to stay in the saddle and get my pistol out despite the pain. My first shot was thrown off from the impact of his bullet. Luckily, it didn't save his life. The jolt pulled my aim up off the center of his chest. The speeding lead ball took him in the left eye, knocking him out of his saddle and startling his horse. The dun wasn't pleased by the noise or the sudden shift in weight.

The horse jumped, throwing off the next man's aim. It saved my life but not Chief's, his barrel dipped down and shot my horse out from underneath me. Thankfully he fell away from my wounded leg, so I managed to roll out of the saddle. My Colt spewed flame again even as I fell, hitting the slowest of the three just left of his breast pocket. I'd have been proud of that if I hadn't been aiming at the other one. The man slumped in his saddle like he suddenly fell asleep. His pistol tumbled to the ground but his well-trained horse just stood in place, waiting for a rider that would never give another command.

I turned toward the last man just as a round from the brush on my left punched through my arm. It fouled my shot and spun me around on shaky legs. My right boot caught on Chief's bridle, tripping me across my dead horse. Before I could get my bearings, a bullet punched into him just to the side of my head. I jerked back and fired on reflex at the last mounted man. My 44-40 slug shattered his shoulder and his pistol went spinning off into the darkness.

His horse wasn't as well trained. It bucked, dropping him from the back of the saddle. His right foot hung in the stirrup and the man had just enough time to scream. His horse took off at a full gallop, dragging the man with him down the road. There were two more screams, and half way through the third it cut off. He was out of it, dead or not the man was no longer a threat.

Two more rounds whined by my head from across the road. The flash of light from their barrels gave me my first glimpse of those two. When I stood up to return fire, one of them got a quick shot off that burned along my ribs. It was a quick and efficient reminder that I wasn't immune to lead poisoning myself. I let my body spin with the force before falling on the other side off the road. Chief's body was momentarily blocking their line of sight.

Common sense and a few seconds to think convinced me to crawl further back, packing my wounds as I went. I grit my teeth to keep from screaming while I stuffed moss into my arm. Finally I managed to get over the rise and roll down into a mud filled gully on the other side. I quickly packed and bandaged my leg before crawling up the other side.

With the last two dead, all I needed to do was not die myself in the muck. There were at least two horses standing in the road. It meant crawling up the other side of the gully but it was the only way to survive. First things first, this corpse needed to be moved off my legs. After that I'd worry about getting back to the road and onto a horse. If I managed those two feats then maybe I wouldn't die like some mud-covered crazy man. There was a small town of some sort about ten miles down the road. I had seen a doctor's sign outside of a small ranch just this side of it. Getting there should be simple, right?

Getting the corpse off my leg was miserable but fairly easy. Crawling up the far side of the ditch was another matter entirely. By the time I could see the road, my head was spinning and spots were flashing in my vision. Could be blood loss or just exhaustion, truthfully it didn't matter which because either one could kill me. Rolling more than crawling down the small hill, I finally came to rest against my dead horse. Chief had been a good mount for the last year and I was more then a little annoyed about his being dead.

I ignored everything but my Winchester, the rifle didn't matter but having a crutch to stand up with did. There was no way any of these horses would let me crawl up to them. Using the rifle to get my right leg under me, I finally managed to stand up. I swayed precariously for a minute before my body found enough strength to stay upright. Staggering like a drunk trying to make it out of the saloon, I managed a few stumbling steps toward the grey mouse. The animal stood amongst the bodies, cropping grass at the side of the trail. I have to give that horse credit for patience, it hadn't shied away in the slightest.

He was going to be my new mount, if I survived this that is. Despite being a stallion, he hadn't moved a muscle when his rider slumped in the saddle. The corpse must have fallen out of the saddle while I was killing the last two. The most important thing was that he stood stock still as this body-shaped lump of mud and twigs slowly climbed into the saddle. Even though he could smell the blood the animal stood still, eyeing my approach. I hissed with pain as I levered myself into the saddle and flicked the reins.

Thankfully he set off at a smooth, even trot. We covered ground just fast enough to keep me conscious, and those ten miles felt like they took an hour. Most of that time I was fading in and out of consciousness and didn't really notice much around me. The fact that I noticed the soft glow of light through a window was pure luck. Adrenaline made me just alert enough to see the house when it came into view. It was the one I'd spotted earlier, the sign swaying in the soft breeze.

Maybe I wouldn't be shot out of hand for riding up in the dark. It seemed a safer bet than trying to ride for a city in my current state. It was doubtful I'd make it to a city before dying, not to mention my appearance. Most folks would probably shoot me on sight, mistaking me for a demon. Well maybe not on this horse, no animal this good would let a swamp monster climb on his back. He proved his worth again by following my lean and turning into the yard.

"Hello the house!" I managed to yell. It was all I had left in me. Force of will was all that kept me in the saddle until the door opened. My body slid out of the saddle and landed in heap in the dust. The last thing I remember was screaming when my wounded arm hit the ground under my weight. The darkness I had been fighting off won the battle and whatever happened next was beyond my control.

Waking up was a much more pleasant experience. I found myself tucked into a bed, clean and bandaged. It felt like a different world and for the briefest moment I thought maybe I'd died. The pain that ripped through me when I tried to move cleared up that misunderstanding. I wondered who washed off the mud but before I went too far down that path my brain decided it wasn't important.

I slowly took in the room while my mind tried to piece together what had happened after I fell from the saddle. It was too pleasant to be hell and there was no way they'd let me in the other one so I must not be dead. The lack of cell bars or handcuffs helped narrow my circumstances down a bit further. Best guess was I was in the house I'd fallen in front of. The bandages were another clue, they were done by someone who knew their craft. A doctor was a likely guess but what would they be doing living out here in the middle of nowhere?

That mystery would be solved shortly as I heard steps echoing on the hardwood floor outside of my room. They were coming closer in slow, even strides. Seconds later, the door opened to reveal a man in his early forties. He was just starting to grey around the temples, and the ring of black hair surrounding his bald pate made the grey stand out. He was a tall, thin man wearing a black vest over a crisp white shirt.

"Good to see you're awake young man." he said, breaking the odd silence after a minute. "You've been unconscious for two days from blood loss and infection. You might have avoided the last if you hadn't wallowed in mud."

"Seemed like the thing to do at the time." We weren't exchanging names so I did away with the idea. "Since a few folks decided to use me for shooting practice."

"Figured it was something like that." He paused before continuing, like he was debating something. "Name's Moses Blanchard. Wasn't sure ya was human when we found ya out front. Once we realized it was a man underneath all the mud we cleaned you up and I plugged the holes."

"Appreciate that. Name's Chance McElroy, just call me Chance." I nodded my head in thanks then winced at the pain. "Pretty sure you're understating your medical training by calling what you did plugging holes."

"Was a medic for the Union, 'bout the only thing I can do is treat gunshots and cut off limbs. Thankfully you didn't need the later." A crooked grin split his face. "My boy found a dead horse and three living ones surrounded by dead folks back up the trail. Your handy work?"

"Yeah, I came around a bend and found them standing over two dead bodies." I chuckled, remembering their surprised looks before continuing. "Reckon they hadn't planned on my arrival. They fired fast enough though, after that there weren't many options."

"Makes sense, they were all wanted men. Sent the boy to notify the sheriff, his deputy came by yesterday. Their horses and rigs are in the barn and the bounty is waiting for you, think it's a bit over four hundred dollars. Deputy dropped off the drafts the other day."

"That's a pleasant way to wake up. Figure I owe you something for helping me out. Split the bounty?"

"That's too much and I have some issues about taking bounty money. Call it forty dollars. My boy had fun bringing the horses back, said he was playing cowboy but he wouldn't say no to a bit of it. Do me a favor and keep it around ten dollars? He don't need more than that. He brought back the saddle off the dead horse too, said something about it looking different."

"Tell him wranglers deal with ponies, not punchers. Also, cowboy's kind of a bad word in some places, I'd watch claiming the title." I chuckled thinking about Arizona territory. "It's a Colorado saddle, had it for a while now. Tell him I appreciate it and will settle up on the tab when standing isn't a losing battle. That thing is about the most comfortable style I've ever found."

"Sleep, it'll be a few days before you can be up and about. Blood loss is slower to recover from than the holes that caused it." He left a pitcher of water within reach just before I dozed off.

CHAPTER 2

I slept for two more days, only disturbed by occasional breaks for food and short conversations. I'd met both his son and daughter when they brought me food. Grace and Bernie, short for Bernard, respectively. They were both adults and Grace was older by a couple of years at 24. During one meal, I discovered she had a magical ability. She could talk non-stop without breathing. Over dinner, she spit out a constant string of words and I was amazed she did so without taking a single breath.

Bernard was quieter. I don't think he said more than ten words and those ten words formed questions about what had happened to me on the road. The two were a study of contrasts in manner and appearance. She was lithe and graceful, pretty in her way but full of far too much energy. He was shorter than me, square and built for hard work. There wasn't a bit of fat on him and even though his sleeves were down I could see the steel corded muscle underneath. Their father came to see me again on the third day, carrying some clean clothes. They were mine, probably from my saddlebags.

"Took a guess these were yours." He smiled at my surprised look.

"Good guess, figure this means I'm not going to have my comfy bed anymore?"

"True enough, the bunk house is empty and the beds are good. Sorry, I can't take another night on the sofa." He smiled when he said it and I felt a bit bad for putting the man out.

"Just need to check those wounds first. Don't want them to spring any leaks. If they look good you can try getting up and moving."

"Really do appreciate everything, sorry about putting you out."

"You needed the bed more than me when you came in, 'sides you're paying me." He checked my wounds before re-bandaging them without much fuss. "Your boots are at the foot of the bed and the rest is already in the bunkhouse, including your gun belt, Winchester, and the rest of the guns from the road."

"Thanks, I'll see how getting dressed goes before I start strapping on my guns." I laughed. It had been a long time since I'd been unarmed this long and the truth was I didn't mind it for once.

"I'll leave you to get dressed. Just holler if you have problems, especially if the pain spikes."

He left the room and ever so slowly I stood up. I was surprised that I didn't feel weak or unsteady on my feet. After getting dressed without any difficulty and stomping into my boots, I grinned. It took longer than normal but the pain hadn't flared up too bad. My injured leg still hurt when I put my boot on but that was it. With no severe pain stopping me, I stepped out the door mostly steady. Moses was waiting for me when it swung open. After passing another inspection, he decided I was fit enough for the move.

"Blood loss is a funny thing. Once you recover it's like nothing ever happened. You're healing those bullet wounds like you've got experience. They were all clean wounds with no ragged edges that I saw once the mud washed off."

"I was wondering 'bout that, don't feel as weak as I expected."

"That's the way it works with blood loss. Come on, I'll show ya to the bunkhouse." He turned, leading the way out of the house. "If you're up to it you're welcome to join us for dinner. It'll take at least another week before you're ready to travel."

"Think you can stand to feed me that long?"

"Forty dollars remember? That'll cover plenty of feed." His smile was filled with laughter.

We walked slowly across a decent sized yard toward a squat, low building next to the barn. If I had to guess this place had been a horse ranch a while ago. Now it looked like just a decent place to live with no more stock than a family needed. The buildings were maintained well but you could see they weren't in use.

The only horses in the corral were my four and two others that I guessed belonged to Moses. They looked like a matched pair for buggy or carriage. Both were brown mustangs, probably some Morgan in their linage. They all looked well maintained and cared for. My horses had been curried after their tack was removed and none of them looked like they'd missed a meal.

Taking a moment to study the four I now owned, I leaned on the fence rail to ease the pain. One was obviously a Morgan, chestnut brown with a clean white star on her head. The two others looked like good animals too, a paint and a big red roan and both were geldings. None of them looked older than five or six at a glance. There was no doubt the best of them was the grey with the roan coming in a close second. That was one thing you could count on, outlaws always had good horses. More than once, I'd gotten more for their horses than the bounties on their heads.

There was time to really look them over later, right now I was out in the open and unarmed for the first time in years. A cold chill ran down my spine at the thought. After years of living with my Colts at hand, it was unnerving to suddenly realize what an easy target I was. The thought made me pick up the pace until I got under the overhanging roof of the bunkhouse.

Moses paced me easily, opening the door in front of me into the dark room. When I hesitated, he turned to study me before shrugging and walking inside. A minute later, he struck a match to light the lamp inside. The soft glow revealed a neatly kept and maintained bunkhouse. Six sets of bunkbeds, two tables and a simple stove filled the room.

It was obvious someone had recently cleaned the place, there were still a few streaks of dust from a broom marking the floor. My gun belt and rifle were laid on a bunk with four other rifles and three gun belts. I'd have to clean and inspect them all later but it was obvious someone had at least cleaned off the mud and dried them. I still had the feeling that cleaning them all would be a long process in my current state.

"Little skittish?" Moses chuckled, interrupting my study of the room.

"Just careful, it's a habit that's hard to break."

"Never asked what you do."

"Bounty hunter last few years, started out working with longhorns in Texas when I was a kid."

"Was a kid?" He studied me and I knew the look. I had seen it so many times now it didn't even surprise me anymore.

"Younger if that makes it easier." I liked this man and owed his family, there was no need to be rude. "I've been on my own since I was nine."

"Nine? Mind telling me why?"

"Folks died. I left out before the locals could throw me in an orphanage." There was no reason to tell the man all the details.

"Bet there's a story or two on that trail." The older man shook his head, the idea was just unbelievable to him. He let a few seconds hang in the air to see if I wanted to tell him the story. When I didn't elaborate, he left me in the bunkhouse to get settled in. "Plenty of wood an I bought some coffee over earlier."

Moses just couldn't imagine a boy left alone like that. It made me laugh, having seen such shock more than once. It never ceased to amaze me, the stories people made up in their heads about how I must have managed it. They never guessed the truth. Of course, the truth was usually simpler and more deadly than they imagined. I still remembered it all clear as day.

CHAPTER 3

Father passed away first then Mother followed him two days later, both died from smallpox. Not that I knew that at the time, to my child's mind they just got sick and died. I wasn't strong enough to dig graves in the hard-packed west Texas soil and didn't even bother trying. Burning the house down with them in it after taking what I could carry was the best I could do for them. It was also why no one came looking for me since they all thought I was dead. Everyone just guessed it was a raid or some such tragedy.

I'd love to tell you how rich my inheritance was, but like most dirt farmers wealth wasn't something we had. The old mule had died two weeks before and that limited what I could take. Three days worth of jerky, Dad's small trail coffee pot, a cap and ball Colt Navy, and a Bowie knife were the extent of my worldly possessions. My personal wealth totaled one dollar and sixty-five cents. That was it except for my slouch hat, long handles, boots, and patchwork clothes.

I made the jerky stretch seven days before it ran out and five days after that they found me. A hunting party of Lipan Apache found me half dead near a watering hole. Later, I learned the only reason they didn't kill me was my fighting spirit. When a brave walked toward me with the intent of cutting my throat, I buried my knife in his stomach. Before they knew it, another one died from a thirty-two-caliber ball.

They decided anyone with that much fight would be

amusing to torture. One of them knocked me out before I could cock the hammer for a second shot and everything went dark. They took me back to their village, half-starved and trudging behind a pony. I walked when I could and they dragged me when I couldn't.

First, they staked me out with rawhide under the sun for three days. I never said a word, not once did I beg or ask for water. The only reaction they got from me was a hate filled glare when they came close. On the fourth night, the bindings on my right arm finally snapped since I'd been slowly working them against a rock the whole time. Killing the three who had tormented me the most was easy. They died choking on their own blood without ever waking up. I escaped with their knives and the few supplies I could carry.

They caught me two days later and would have killed me then if it hadn't been for one of the older braves. His son had been one of the three I killed and he wanted me to suffer and die slowly. His plan was to beat me to death with a mesquite branch he'd picked up for the purpose. The look of surprise on his face when I caught the stick and spun the broken end around was priceless.

Before the others could do anything I stabbed it through his throat. At the time I was probably mad from pain and thirst, the only thing I remember was the look on his face. The medicine man watched me, laughing as the man's blood sprayed across my face. He told them I was touched by the spirits. How else could a boy kill so many of their warriors?

For the next three years they kept me with them. I wasn't a slave, they mostly let me do what I wanted. They didn't exactly take care of me but there was always enough food and water to keep me alive. My mind cleared over time but even my child's brain knew not to tell them that. Keeping up my act just made sense, all the while I was learning everything I could from them.

My young mind and body absorbed everything there was to learn, from skinning and using the hides of animals to surviving on what little the harsh southern Texas land had to offer. By the time I was ready to escape I had no doubt I'd be successful. I could run, hunt, hide and survive as well as any brave in the tribe.

When I escaped the last time, I was far more prepared for what lay ahead. It was easy to gather up my Bowie knife along with some supplies before I left. Sadly, the pistol wasn't worth the effort since it had long ago run out of shot and powder. My ragged clothes had gradually been replaced over time with tanned skin and buckskin britches.

It took every trick I knew to stay ahead of them. They tracked me for weeks, hunting me like an animal. But unlike other prey I struck back, killing them in their sleep and taking their supplies. I chased off their ponies, making them run with me through the Nueces Strip. I set simple spike traps, deadfalls, and anything else I could think of to make them pay. One night, I dropped three diamond backs into their camp from the cliff above then I showered them with as many rocks as I could while they tried to escape the vipers.

I wasn't always successful, they were hardened warriors. My body still bears the scars of those weeks. By the time a cavalry patrol found me, I had been on the run for three weeks. The large slash that ran from my left ear down my cheek to my lower jaw told the soldiers I'd had a rough go of it. It looked worse than it was after I packed it with a mixture of herbs to help it heal, yet another trick I learned from watching the Apache. My belt had four knives and seven scalps hanging from it.

They didn't know what to do with me at first. I looked like a half wild Apache myself but finally the lieutenant decided to me someone else's worry. They took me back to Fort Clark and made me the commander's problem. It took a week to remember how to speak English and longer still to tell them the story I made up. They might believe I was being hunted but that didn't mean they would believe the rest.

The first lie I told was swearing up and down that I was thirteen because that was the most important thing they needed to believe. After that I let the commander fill most of it in, if my story readily fit his assumptions he'd easily believe it. My family had been killed by the Apache years ago and they had kept me as a slave. Finally I escaped using skills I'd learned from them. That there had been fights wasn't a debate, the scars and scalps hanging from my belt told that story well enough. I didn't feel a bit guilty about putting the commander in a tough spot. Technically, I was too old for the orphanage but not old enough to stay at the fort alone. Both things suited me and it was why lying about my age was so necessary.

I got lucky while the commander was still figuring out what to do with me. A local rancher happened to be dropping some horses off the day after I arrived. No one was paying attention to me, I was perched on the corral fence just watching everything. There was a big paint stallion in the herd that was going to be trouble, I could see it in his eyes. Sure enough, as soon as one of the hands looked away he reared up and tried to knock the wrangler out of his saddle. Before the man even noticed the movement he'd been knocked off his horse and the big stallion was turning to stomp him before he hit the ground.

Cat quick I was off the rail and moving. I stepped across the backs of two surprised horses and before anyone could react I jumped for the stallion's back. By the time they turned their heads I was gone. Landing on the horse's back and wrapping my hands in his mane got his attention on me instead of the wrangler. That split second of distraction was all it took for him to scramble out of the way. To this day I've never seen a man scramble under a fence that fast.

The stallion cleared the area around him, bucking and

spinning. To his credit, that horse did everything he could to get the annoying thing off his back. None of it worked, I clamped down and hung on no matter what he did. It seemed like hours but in reality it was probably less than thirty seconds before another man pushed his way next to the stallion. He grabbed me off the horse's back and blocked the paint with his black gelding.

Once the weight was off his back the animal calmed down. The man swung me to the saddle in front of him and I glared back at the big paint. We locked eyes for minute in unspoken respect before he ignored me and turned back to his mares. The man behind me in the saddle watched all of this without saying a word, he just studied me. Thinking back, I must have been a sight. My hair was so matted and dirty you couldn't tell it's real color. I was rail thin and wearing nothing but a pair of worn-out buckskin pants and a lot of scars. Later, he told me that the challenge in my blue eyes flashed when I met the stallion's glare. I wanted another round with him and it made the man laugh.

His laughter broke me out of a staring contest the stallion had already disregarded. When he finished laughing, he rode out of the corral and dropped me off at the fence. He didn't stop laughing until he stopped in front of the commander. They spoke for a few minutes before both men stepped down from their horses and walked toward me.

"Boy," the commander spoke as he approached, "this is Thaddeus Martian, he owns the Double T ranch."

"Pleasure to meet ya son." His voice was friendly, the laughter still echoing in it.

"Same. Names Bini... ummm, I mean Chance." I had started to introduce myself by what the Apache had called me, Bíni' ádįh. It probably wasn't an intentional naming and I was trying to break the habit of using it.

"You want to stay here at the fort or come with me to my

ranch? Major Nelson says it's up to you."

CHAPTER 4

That was all it took. I spent the next three years working on the Double T. They taught me everything from working cattle to playing poker, including how to spot a cheat. Thad and the other hands also insisted I learn to read and do numbers. They quickly discovered I had a passion for reading and was passable with calculations. When Thad let me have access to his library a whole new world opened up to me, world of far away countries, pirate adventures and great military tacticians. If I could find something to read around the ranch, I usually read it more than once. With the eclectic nature of punchers, this led to a very diverse education.

Thad started teaching me how to shoot on the way to the ranch. After the first lesson, he told me I had a natural inclination for shooting. It surprised him how quickly my body seemed to memorize the habits. Before we got back, I was easily out shooting him with a rifle despite my age. When one of the hands had me try his quick draw rig it shocked everyone. I was fast and accurate, two things that usually don't come without hours of practice. From then on he had me work every day with the guns.

He advanced me enough of my wages to get a new Winchester 44-40. Two months later, he gave me two Colt conversions in .44 caliber. We took them to a local gunsmith before leaving town that day. Following Thad's recommendations, he removed the front sights and adjusted the trigger pull.

It took me a while to stop wearing one on each hip. Youth had convinced me that eventually I'd become as good with my left hand as I was my right. Accepting the truth took longer than it should have, but once that foolish notion was gone I was able to use some sense. A right-hand hip draw paired with the second gun set for a border draw was a better choice. Both were right handed, and with some work I was just as fast with the border draw as I was with the hip.

I still had a thing for knives and kept a Bowie on my belt and another knife tucked into my boot. I could get the pistols or knives out faster than anyone else on the ranch. My confidence about throwing the knives was enough to make people place bets on it. That stopped when I took out a rattler that was set to strike one of the other hands. It had only been a foot away from his leg.

The first man to die by my hand lost his life in a showdown that same year. It was in Laredo over a card game. He was cheating and couldn't believe a kid had caught him. When he realized the other men at the table believed me he only had two choices: leave his money and tuck tail or draw on the mouthy kid. He chose poorly and wound up on Boot Hill. The men who witnessed it told Thad about how calm I was in the situation. After that, I wasn't allowed into Laredo unless I was with him.

After turning fourteen, I rode the line for the first time that winter. I'd never bothered to correct anyone about my age and folks still thought I was older than I was. It was a long, cold few months stuck in a cabin with a surly old hand who spent most of the time drunk. When the weather finally broke, we expected the rest of the hands to show up and start the gather. When they didn't turn up I knew something was wrong. A day later, I was sitting on my horse looking down at the burnt out remains of the ranch. Thad and the rest of the hands were hung from the gate.

What followed was the beginning of my career as a bounty

hunter. It wasn't my original purpose, at first it was an act of revenge. That was where it all started though, if not for that attack I'd have just been another puncher. That one event changed the path of my life. What might have been a fairly simple and peaceful existence turned into one where hunting men became normal.

After burying my friends and the closest thing I had known to a father, I rode into Eagle's Pass. Five days later I rode out leading a string of eleven horses, each with a body draped over the saddle. Thad hadn't interfered with the outlaws crossing his land and it had cost him his life. I wouldn't make that mistake. If a bounty said dead or alive there would only be one option for me.

Those eleven corpses made me $1,350 in Uvalde. The Texas Rangers couldn't believe I had ridden in and out of Eagle's Pass alive. They were more shocked when I told them King Fisher had not only allowed it but helped identify the men who had raided the Double T. I hadn't known it but he and Thad had a sort of friendship. Of course he couldn't go after the men for raiding a ranch, not if he wanted to stay on top of his little empire. But that didn't mean he would stop me from doing it.

I used the bounty money to get a new horse and supplies. My biggest purchase that first trip was the new Colts. They'd finally released the 44-40 model with a five-and three-quarter inch barrel. I put the old ones in a safe deposit box in Uvalde. Thad's memory was tied up in those two guns. The new ones took about a week to get modified to suit me. While I waited for them, a leather worker made me a new belt and holster set up.

I kept a few hundred in cash and the rest went into a bank account. That account and my reputation had grown over the last few years. True lawmen usually didn't care for me, but they left me alone to do my business. Outlaws had developed a strong dislike for me and more often than not tried to kill me on sight if they got the chance. A few different handles had become attached to me, mostly by the men I hunted. Deadman's Chance was the most artistic, but No Chance was a strong second runner.

There were a lot of bodies behind me, the ones who'd most recently tried to kill me didn't even earn a mention. My body was covered with scars but the most prominent was still from the Apache. The raised skin looked like a jagged bolt of lightning splicing my face. It marked me more than any feat I could have done myself. It also kept me comfortably away from polite society. People were uncomfortable around me, they either wanted to ask but were afraid to or just blatantly stared.

I had been unpacking while my mind looked back over the past. My story had never bothered me much, most likely I'd tell Moses if he asked. Then would come the debate about morality, good folks never could understand the type of ruthlessness it took to do the job. Not to mention the look of horror that would pass behind their eyes when they heard about my reputation.

It's not that bounty hunters were particularly hated but most people thought they were only slightly better than the men they hunted. They saw them as drifters who valued nothing but money, men with no roots and low morals. It would surprise most of them if they knew the truth about me. Most of my money was in a bank, probably more than enough to live comfortably on for the rest of my life. At this point, it was at least enough to easily buy and stock any large spread if that's what I wanted. Telling them about it probably wouldn't help, they'd wonder why I was still chasing men.

I was well aware of the hypocrisy of those who looked down on me. The same men who condemned me without knowing anything would gladly befriend me if I was their neighbor. Money had a funny way of affecting folks' morals. They might hate what I was now but if I started spending money? They would happily claim their share and proclaim my better qualities. It was funny, the men I hunted weren't much different than the good churchgoing men they robbed. They used violence to get their wealth while the man standing proudly in church would use twisted words to get his.

Money changed folks for good or ill, it just never made sense to me. I'd seen a minister in Arizona Territory disappear in the night with every dime from the church to go chase gold in California. He left his wife and two kids penniless, dependent on the very same congregation he'd stolen from. All to chase some mythical rock buried underground. When I finally caught up with the man he was nothing but a stumbling drunk. His claim was busted and there was nothing left except a hollow man.

I'd started reflecting on what I was doing. What was I risking my life for? It wasn't the money, that didn't mean anything to me. It was some twisted personal crusade, trying to bury my pain in seeking justice. The idea of grieving had been lost somewhere between my parents' death and the Apache. It was a lie, a lie I was living every day. When I realized the truth it hit me like a mule kick.

I was no better than some of the men I brought to justice tied across my saddle. I was caught in the same cycle of violence they were, hoping that someday it would fix something. It was a day that would never come. You can't fix the pain of loss, you can only learn to live with it. That was what had led me to Denver. I needed a place to figure out what to do now.

CHAPTER 5

While I had been lost in thought, my hands automatically went to work lighting another lamp and starting a fire in the stove. When my mind came back to the present I was most of the way through making coffee. I quickly cleared the table before laying out the guns with my cleaning kit. The first order of business was my Colts. They looked clean but I could feel the mud grind in some of the mechanisms. Someone had cleaned off the mud but hadn't cleaned them properly. Next up would be my Winchester then maybe I'd start on the other weapons.

The process gave my hands something to do while my mind was struggling with my personal problems. That is, if you considered having too many options and not enough drive in one direction or another personal problems. I wasn't ready to start my own ranch yet, that was still several years off if ever. Hell, I'd only figured out that was possible a few days ago. I didn't even know if it was a true want or just a return to the familiar. What the hell could a seventeen year old do if he didn't want to be a bounty hunter?

Go back to punching cattle? That wasn't what I was looking for. I'd end up a gun hand no matter what I wanted. Being a gun for hire wasn't any better than bounty hunting. Maybe I'd just drift for a while, let life come as it may. That was the best I could come up with, maybe finding my place on the trail somewhere. My hands had finished my guns. The light dancing on the smooth blue metal drew my eyes for a minute before I broke the trance.

Four more Winchesters, two Colts and three Smith and Wessons still sat waiting on my attention. There was no rush to finish and my body was still healing. I already felt the drain pulling on my energy. Maybe listening to the doc wasn't a bad idea. For the first time in a week, I took out my pipe and packed it. I walked slowly to the chair I had seen outside under the overhang, carrying the coffee pot and a tin cup with me. It felt good to relax with a good pipe and hot coffee after so many days stuck in bed.

The sound of horses' hooves broke my peaceful reverie. They were still a ways off but there was no mistaking their direction. I slipped back inside to sling on my gun belt and check their load. Levering a round into the Winchester, I eased the hammer down with my thumb leaving a round in the chamber. It sounded like they'd be here soon and I needed to find a good vantage point.

Outside, I slipped into the shadow of the barn and watched the dust cloud approach the ranch. By then I could hear the men as they turned onto the access road that led to the house. It wasn't long before I got my first look at them. Six men riding tired horses, each one looking trail worn and exhausted. One man rode in the middle of two others and it took me a minute to figure out why he sat in his saddle so awkwardly. His shoulders weren't moving right and that's when the realization hit me, he was tied to his saddle horn at the wrists. It made him look uncomfortable every time the horse moved.

The afternoon sun glinted off the star on the lead rider's chest. So he was a lawman, probably transporting a prisoner to Denver. Something about the way they rode told me this wasn't a thrown together posse, these men spent their lives in a saddle. They moved like they were extensions of the animal below them. When they reined up in front of the house I could make out the star. It was a U.S. Marshal's badge and the four with him were his deputies.

"Hello the house!" the leader called out in a clear and commanding voice. "Mos' you in there?"

"Quit your yelling and get off that damnedable animal, Reese. No one with any sense will go near that monster." Moses called back stepping out onto the porch.

"He ain't mean so long as I'm near him." Reese laughed before stepping down off the large black horse he was riding.

"Rest of ya step down with him. Figure you got someone in need of care cause you never stop by just ta be friendly."

"Now that's just mean Moses." Reese protested innocently.

"So that man doesn't have some lead in him somewhere?" Moses accused, but I could hear the good-natured tone.

"Didn't say ya was wrong, just said it was mean." Reese shook Moses hand before turning to his men. "Ya'll get the horses taken care of. Matt, get him off that horse an inside so he don't die before the hanging."

"Ya'll hold up a second." Moses stopped them before continuing. "Chance, we got company. They're friendly enough for lawmen anyways."

"Chance?" Reese asked looking toward the bunkhouse. His eyes caught movement when I stepped out from beside the barn. To his credit he didn't draw his pistol but a couple of his men leveled their rifles in my direction.

"Rode in here half dead last week, seems to be recovering well enough." Moses laughed when the deputies jumped at my appearance. "I have a feeling ya might know him, or at least his reputation."

"Howdy" I said, walking forward. My Winchester sat cradled in my arms while I tried not to wince.

"Holy shit!" One of the deputies exclaimed when he got a good look at me. "That's Chance McElroy."

"What the hell are you babbling about Tom?" Reese

demanded. I just grinned and kept walking forward. The man had been one of the deputies in California who watched me turn in the Bondit gang. Guess a lone rider leading in five horse carrying six dead men left an impression.

"Remember me telling ya 'bout that run in California?" Tom asked his boss. "The guy who took out them three vaqueros. The ones 'at had me cornered, that's him."

"Good seeing you again deputy." I smiled, but truthfully I had forgotten about that situation.

"Same, wondered where ya disappeared to after that little fracas." Tom was stepping toward me smiling. "Never did get to thank you for saving my bacon. Them three had me dead to rights. If it hadn't been for you stepping in, well things wouldn'ta gone well for me."

"Glad I could lend a hand." I took the man's extended hand, smiling at him as we shook.

"Seems I owe you my thanks too." Reese said. The man was studying me carefully. "Appreciate you saving one of mine's bacon. Reckon I've heard of a bounty hunter that matches your description. If I remember right, there's a less then flattering name associated with him."

"No Chance or Deadman's Chance?" I asked curiously. Tom's eyes locked on me before the full weight of it hit him.

"The latter." Reese admitted with a devilish grin.

"Damn, that's you? Never put it together, but I reckon I shoulda." Tom laughed.

"Don't matter, both apply to me." I smiled, knowing the reputation that went with those names. "Earned both of them and make no apologies for it."

"Sounds 'bout right." Reese said noncommittally then he did the strangest thing. He smiled and stepped forward to shake my hand. "Any man who the owl hoots fear more than us is okay by me. Besides, from what I've heard most you go after are the worst of the worst."

"They usually have the bigger numbers." I grinned. It was a lie. The truth was I picked them for their crimes. If I was going after someone I wanted to be damn sure they were guilty. You couldn't apologize to a dead man.

"That's true." The marshal admitted but something in his eyes said he didn't believe me.

"Boss, this polecat's bleeding on me." The deputy who was holding their prisoner complained.

"Shit, forgot 'bout him! Alright ya'll get it done, we can jabber later. Get him inside, Joe. Mos' will get him sewn up." Reese snapped back into commander mode and got everyone moving. "The rest of ya get the animals taken care of. We'll be staying here at least a day so find yourselves space in the bunk house."

He turned on his heel to follow Moses and Joe into the house with the prisoner. I grabbed their horses and walked with the rest toward the barn. I didn't notice the shocked look on the faces around me when Reese's black followed me without arguing. They watched me carefully but when I started stripping off the animal's tack and he didn't try and kill me they got to work on their own animals.

We got the tack off and the horses brushed down before feeding them. Each stall had its own water bucket and they all got filled so the mounts would have whatever they needed. When that was done they followed me to the bunk house.

"Traveling pretty heavily armed there." A deputcalled Rusty laughed. He was admiring the guns laid out on the table, most still waiting to be cleaned.

"Came from some friendly folks I bumped into on the road." I grinned. "They just donated them to me along with four horses and tack. Said they didn't need them anymore."

"Uh huh, sure they did. Guessing there's more to that story." A short deputy they all called Pug laughed.

"It's how I ended up in Mos's front yard looking like a pile of mud." That was all it took to get them staring at me.

Lawmen were the same across the country, tales of danger ranked up there with fish tales. Leastwise that's what I'd found. We all sat around swapping stories for the next few hours. Some whiskey showed up and it was passed around with the coffee. I passed when it came my way, already struggling to keep my exhaustion at bay.

Men who did the things others wouldn't or couldn't sharing their own stories of both good and bad times seemed to help in some way. It didn't have a logic to it but no one else really understood. I was by no means exceptional, everyone here had been in shoot outs, had caught bullets and thrown their own back. We shared the dark sense of humor that went with our professions, and it was on clear display.

CHAPTER 6

After awhile they wandered off to find a bunk and grab some sleep. By the time it was full dark, just me and Tom were left. I was half asleep but managing to keep up with the conversation. We sat out on the porch holding coffee cups, just relaxing and enjoying the quiet. The man had wanted to say something all night but hadn't gotten the chance.

"I got a daughter," Tom said breaking the silence, "she's a year old now."

"Congratulations, it's good to have family."

"You're missing the point. She wouldn't have a father if you hadn't stepped in. There's no way to thank you enough for that." I could hear him choke up a little as he spoke.

"It was just luck but I'm glad I was there to lend a hand." It took me a minute to collect my thoughts before I continued. "Somehow knowing that makes what I've been doing for the last few years feel worthwhile."

"You don't know do you?" He chuckled, breaking the tense cloud that hung over us.

"Know what?"

"You've got a reputation with the marshals and the rangers. You'd never have a problem from either group or catch them letting others disparage you." I could see his smile in the moonlight. "You could walk into any marshal's office or ranger station and they would do everything they could to help you out. Most of us wouldn't even ask why you needed help."

"Why? I'm just a bounty hunter." It just didn't make sense to me. These men were the real law, they helped shape the country as it grew.

"You're one of the few who'll go into the Nations after someone. You'll follow a man into an outlaw town despite the odds and bring out more than you went in for." He laughed loudly and added, "Hell, they have three dime store novels 'bout you."

"They aren't about me." I said defensively but knew the ones he was talking about. I'd hired a lawyer to make the publisher pay me royalties and that was only after he told me I couldn't stop them from being printed. Making them less profitable was all I could do and it hadn't seemed to make much difference.

"Oh? How do you figure?"

"Never been to New York."

"Suppose you don't know anything about the publisher having an account for you? I met the man in Frisco, said twenty percent of sales were in an account for you. Something about lawyers an such."

"Was hoping to making it less profitable so he'd stop writing 'em."

"That's free money, don't know why you're complainin'. No one I know has a bad word to say 'bout you getting paid. Ya ought to go see him. He'd love to get the stories straight from the horse's mouth."

"Not sure the money is worth it. 'Sides my horse got shot." I grumbled. My mind contemplated how many young gun slicks had tried pushing since those came out. All trying to earn a name for facing me down.

"You've managed not to get a name as a gun fighter. That's despite how many high noon showdowns the books say you've had. Whole lot of bad men ain't on the trail anymore because of you, even the young fools don't want to tempt that."

"That's only cause I don't hire out as a gun. An there's been enough men who challenged me for the name." I said thinking about the last one, a kid in San Saba. I'd tried everything I could to avoid that fight but he just wouldn't let it go once he heard my name. "Got two things that keep them away though."

"What's that?"

"Well, first I'm hard to find. I'm not sitting in some town wearing a badge or at a poker table playing cards."

"That's fair, what's the other?"

"The books describe my scar right but they always say I'm older. Most of the young toughs never look at me twice." I laughed.

"That's true, didn't expect that myself." Reese said walking out of the shadows to join us. "How old are you anyway?"

"You won't believe me." I said with a crooked smile.

"I'm guessing twenty." Tom said.

"Close to what I'm thinking." Reese added.

"Seventeen." That left the two men stunned.

"That means you started…"

"Fifteen when I walked into Fisher's place and killed the men who raided the Double T." This was the first time I could remember telling anyone about that.

"You knew Thad? That's why you went in there?" Reese asked, something in his tone saying he knew the man.

"Took me in after the cavalry found me."

"You had that scar even back then." Reese said calmly. There was a dawning realization filling his eyes, this man knew me. Tom was lost and just sat there listening.

"How?" It was all I could say.

"I was on that patrol, a green private on his first assignment in Texas. We found this half dead half wild kid laying near a watering hole." He made a choking sound as the memory fully came back. "You had four knives and seven Apache scalps on your belt. Even tried to cut Sergeant Fin when he picked you up. He had to knock you out 'cause you wouldn't stop."

"That part's always been a bit hazy." I admitted.

"Jesus." Tom finally managed to get out. "You killed seven Apache? At fifteen?"

"He was thirteen then." Reese said. "At least that's what he told the commander."

"Too old for an orphanage." was all I said but he caught it.

"How old were you?" Reese's voice was surprised and curious.

"Not sure, even now I'm not positive how long I was with the Lipan. Maybe a year younger, not much more I think."

"Can ya tell it from the start son?" Moses asked from where he stood. He had joined us not long after Reese did.

"Might as well." I laughed. "It's not really a secret."

So, I did. For the first time in my life I told the three of them the full story, the man I'd saved and two others who had helped save me. I told them everything up until the Double T was wiped out. They'd all heard the stories after that, they were probably exaggerated but close enough. They knew enough to filter out the tall tale from the truth. Then I talked about my current situation, how I wasn't sure what to do now and I was struggling to figure out my next step. When I was done there was a heavy silence. Reese broke it first after studying me for a few minutes.

"Come work for me."

It was all he said, but it offered something I was afraid to risk. People to care about again and that meant the pain that would come if they died. Folks like Tom whose daughter I had never met but now felt connected to in some way. Could I take the loss again? Everyone I'd ever cared about had died. I didn't know how much more of that I could take. It never really went away, their faces still flashed across the darkness when I closed my eyes.

Could I afford not to? That was a far more terrifying question. I had been hollow so long that even the faint connection to Tom's daughter had sparked something long forgotten inside me. It wasn't love, I didn't even know the girl. Still, it was some connection to the world around me that I'd been avoiding. Something that tied me to people again. Now it was too late, it had found a way in. I couldn't help feeling that the empty space, the void that had been so comforting, now haunted me.

"Can you make me a deputy at seventeen?"

"According to some military document you're close enough to eighteen." Reese grinned as he spoke. "Besides, I think you need this. I'll be damned if I don't make it happen. The new training program should cover enough time. By the time it's done you'll be eighteen. You understand I'd expect you to bring men in alive if possible?"

"I knew there was a trap in this somewhere." I laughed, sipping my coffee.

CHAPTER 7

It took eighteen weeks of official training for me to become a deputy marshal. Most of it was in classrooms, studying law and folks' rights. Reese didn't think I needed the field training and the man in charge of the academy agreed after testing me. For me, having access to the library was enough to keep me happy but my instructors wanted me to take more formal classes. That changed when they started testing our class. They stopped worrying about the savage bounty hunter after they saw my high marks.

I spent hours reading law and studying its application. At graduation, one instructor did his best to get me to me clerk for a judge saying that after a few years I would become a lawyer. Part of me struggled not to laugh but I have to admit it was tempting. There was something so fascinating about the way it all worked. It was also a living thing, growing and adapting as needed to the changing world.

Reese pulled some strings and got me assigned to his command. Unless I got promoted or asked to move this is where I'd stay. Currently, we covered the Colorado territory with fifteen deputy slots and only ten were active right now. I was number eleven until something changed. Each deputy was assigned an area to work except for three that Reese kept in Denver. They traveled to support the rest of the territory as needed.

I rode the train into Denver the day after graduation. After picking up the grey mouse from the stock car, I wove through the crowded streets toward the office. I made a quick loop over the hitching rail out front of the office which gave me a moment to look around. Part of me couldn't believe how many people were here. That also made the back of my neck itch, it was too many. I opened the door to escape the crowd. The man behind the desk looked up when I walked in.

"Here to see Marshal Reese." was all I said. He studied me for a few minutes without saying anything, like he was trying to decide if it was worth disturbing the marshal for me or not. He looked to be in his late twenties, a bit shorter than me with close cut brown hair and ugly green eyes.

"Why ya wanna see the marshal kid? Something I can help ya with?" Evidently he decided I wasn't worth it.

"Nope, just the marshal." I knew I could have explained it to him but something about the man was bothering me. He wasn't wearing a star. Either he wasn't a deputy or he didn't care enough about the job to wear it.

"Look kid, ya can tell me, or I can run ya outta here." He snapped, starting to rise from the chair.

He made it about halfway up before I kicked the front of the desk. It slid back into his hips and pinned him to the wall with a soft cracking sound. Before he could recover I stepped toward the desk, keeping it braced with my knees. The move effectively trapped him against the wall. Pain flashed across his face first, followed by shock then it slowly turned red with anger and shame. I'd humiliated him and done so in the marshal's office. The noise must have been loud enough to get Reese's attention because I heard him stomping up the hall.

"What the hell are you doing up here now?"

"Boss, this kid's starting trouble." the man whined. His tone was wheedling and it grated on my nerves.

"That kid is Deputy US Marshal McElroy. My first question would be why does he have you pinned against the wall like a bug?"

"Deputy? That kid?" Whoever the guy was it seemed to be beyond his belief that I could be a deputy.

"Harvey, tell me...no never mind. Chance what happened?" Reese finally turned to me, ignoring the man.

"I asked to see you, he called me kid and said he could handle whatever I needed. When I refused, he threatened to throw me out."

"Harvey? What the hell made you think you could handle something when they asked for a marshal? Much less The Marshal?" Reese's face changed, I could see it coming before he spoke. "You know what, never mind. You don't seem to get it, you're a jailor and that's all. I'll never make you a deputy, don't know why you can't get that through your head. I gave you this job as a favor to your mother and now it's become a problem. Get your shit and get out. You're fired."

"But Boss I can't..." Reese cut him off.

"Nope you're done. You just ain't suited to this type of work. It isn't the first time I've had a problem with you and that's not even mentioning the way you treat prisoners." Reese turned to me and continued. "Chance, let him go. Sorry for the rough introduction."

I stepped back from the desk, letting it slide out a little. It was enough so that Harvey could move. The man stood there for minute glaring at me. He blamed me for this, I could see it in his eyes. He wasn't wearing a gun but that didn't mean he wasn't dangerous.

"Harvey, old man Miller was looking for help at the smelter. Tell him I sent you." Reese offered, trying to soften the blow his words had landed.

"Ain't going to work at the smelter, it won't suit my constitution." His voice just got worse the more he spoke.

"Won't suit your laziness you mean! Get outta my sight and the next time you get into trouble don't call me." Reese had lost his patience.

"I'll see you around." He snapped, glaring at me.

"You probably shouldn't." was all I said. The last thing I wanted to do was kill some kid just because his pride was hurt.

"Chance." Reese had a warning tone in his voice. "Harvey, I'll say this just once. You decide to get in a fight with this one an' you'll be ten toes up on Boot Hill."

"Ain't afraid of that kid, be him that's buried if we fight." He slammed the door before either of us could say anything else.

"Damn it! Try not to kill him, it just won't be worth the headache." Reese said shaking his head. "Come on back an we'll get ya sworn in."

I followed him down the hall and into a small office. We left the door open so we could hear if someone came in. There were two chairs in front of a desk that were covered in papers. Reese dropped into the larger chair behind the desk with a heavy sigh. After a few deep breaths, he started searching through the drawers. Finally, he tossed a star onto the desk in front of him. The star was missing the tip of one point, like someone had clipped a quarter inch off.

"Interesting design." I said, picking up the star and examining the missing point.

"Shit, sorry give me that one back."

"Naw I like it. Know the story with it?"

"Dodger, one of my first deputies wore it. That point got taken off when he was dry gulched. Sad thing is, I know who did it but can't arrest the skunk. Lack of evidence and witnesses."

"Think I'll keep it if you don't mind." I pinned the star on my vest and waited for him to continue.

"Baxter, he works for the J Bar ranch but he damn sure ain't a ranch hand. He's the reason we can't get his boss Carter under control."

"Tell me about it." Now he had my curiosity piqued.

"Sure, you're a new enough face. Maybe ya can get somewhere with it. I'll tell ya straight, it's a dangerous job. Two deputies have been killed trying to deal with it and a third was shot to pieces."

"Ain't saying I'll do it but fill me in." I wasn't going to jump into a den of rattlers blindfolded, but if it needed doing there was no reason to avoid it.

"Small town down near the Nations called Carterville. Yes, it's named after the ranch owner. He claimed land back when it was all rough country and later founded both the ranch and the town. Figures that makes him exempt from the law. Baxter and the useless sheriff make sure it stays that way." I could tell from his voice this was a burr that had been worrying him for a while.

"Carter's no slouch in a fight but he tries to stay out of the mud nowadays. Thinks he too good for such things now that he's considered wealthy." Reese's face fell before he continued. "I sent Dodger down there to remove the sheriff from office. Someone shot him on Main Street. Looked like a rifle shot, maybe a Springfield. The mayor told me it was Baxter but couldn't or wouldn't swear to it in court. The man's got a family and Carter's been known to have everyone killed if a man crosses him."

"But he told you about it?" That didn't make any sense to me. Why take the risk if you won't see it through?

"He told me what was going on down there from the start. He's a good man and believes in the town but none of that makes him brave." There was a pained smile on his face as he spoke. Part of me understood what he meant but it still bothered me. "Anyway, once he told me the story I sent two deputies to get Baxter and the sheriff. One came back shot to rags and he left the service once he recovered. He said Smitty, the other deputy, got a Dutch ride. What was left of him after ten miles wasn't fit to be seen."

There was anger in his voice now, understandable rage that simmered just under the surface. Being dragged to death behind a horse was a bad way to die. For it to be done to a deputy marshal without someone being held accountable was absolutely unacceptable to Reese. It made my decision easy. This was the type of thing I pinned on a badge for.

"I'll go. Am I right in thinking you're not going to question my methods too much?"

"You gotta follow the law but outside of that you'll not hear anything from me about how it gets done."

"I'll keep it legal." I assured my boss before asking, "So, this swearing in?"

"Short or long?"

"Short."

"Swear to uphold the constitution and laws of the country to the best of your ability?"

"Yeah."

"Done. There's a room for you at Miss Molly's boarding house, pay's fifty dollars a month plus expenses. If you don't have a receipt it ain't an expense. You turn those in to me every month." He reached into another drawer and retrieved a small black notebook. There was a short pencil stuck in a space at the top. "Take notes, you'll have to write full reports when you finish an assignment."

"Got it." I tucked the notebook into my wallet, knowing it would never get used. My memory had always been good. There were two things I still needed to know. "Boarding my horse? And where's Miss Molly's?"

"Elwood's livery is out back, it fronts on the next street over. He's still got those other two horses over there. Wants to buy 'em both, I'd trade for a pack mule if it was me. Molly's is three blocks down from the stable, turn left down Fifth Street. You'll see her sign in a few blocks on the right. Big grey house, she's expecting you and already has the rest of your gear in a room."

"Thanks, I'll come by tomorrow before I leave for Cartersville."

"Take a couple of days before you go. Sell what you have to Elwood and get the mule set up. You're also going to need to do some shopping. Doubt you have any clothes other than what you're carrying."

"That should be plenty." I was curious why I needed more clothes.

"You'll need to get a suit for court. The judge won't allow range clothes in the court room." He smiled before adding, "They also help if you want to eat at some of the better restaurants."

"Great!" I commented dryly. The last thing I wanted was to eat in a fancy place full of people.

"All part of growing up, can't live in jeans all the time." he laughed. "Take a couple of days to figure out the city and get settled. Hell, normally I make new deputies work the desk here for a month then only send them out with experienced deputies for next six months."

"Yeah that's…"

"I said usually. Even if I didn't know your past, the letters I got from your instructors made it clear that's pointless."

"Nice to know they thought highly of me." I laughed.

"According to what I read, that's because they had to reinvent half the course just to keep your attention." he said with a chuckle. I hadn't known anything about that. It didn't seem right to ask if he was serious so I let it drop.

"Fine, I'll take a couple days and get everything set up."

I looked down at my clothes and figured it might be time for some new ones. I'd keep these for when I was out on the road but they were starting to look a little too frayed for wearing around town. I'd replaced my slouch hat with a Stetson while at school but I was still wearing long handles with stitched up bullet holes.

"Good, meet me at the diner across the street for breakfast if you want. It's free with your room at the boarding house but the eatery puts on a good spread for cheap." I took his tone as dismissal and headed down the hall. His annoyed words followed me out the door.

"Damn it! I need a new jailer." I heard his chair squeak when he got up.

I walked out the door gathering my horse's reins from the hitch rail. Cutting down the alley next to the office, I started thinking maybe the grey had earned a name. I was planning on keeping him and doubted I'd find a better one anytime soon. By the time the livery was in sight, he'd been branded Miz (short for mizzel) since his color reminded me of a drizzling rain. He agreed to it by nickering when I asked what he thought. True, he might have been talking to the mare we just passed but I took it as approval.

CHAPTER 8

I came up behind the livery and spotted the paint and the red roan in the corral. I'd given the Morgan to Bernard for fetching my gear. They both looked up when they recognized Miz's scent and trotted over to the fence to greet their one time companion. All three were geldings so there was no challenge among them. The former owners must have traveled together awhile for these three to have bonded like this.

"Reckon ya must be Chance, 'em ponies seem familiar enough. " a weathered old man said as he walked out of the barn. He looked older than the mountains, lines crisscrossed his face as he squinted in the sun. Half of those lines were hidden by a beard that reached down his chest. Despite his age, he was still a big man standing six feet tall regardless of being stooped. There was two hundred pounds at least walking towards me on those bowed legs.

"Got it in one. Ellwood I'm guessing?"

"Nope 'at fools been dead fer ten years. Bought the place off'n his widow and never bothered to change the sign. Name's Rusty, though some still know me by Beaver Bob."

"Beaver Bob?" I had to ask.

"Been up here since beaver trap'n was a thing. Folks seemed ta sprout up like trees one day an I figured I'd have ta adjust to city livin'."

"When did ya come out here?" He opened a side gate and let

me lead Miz into the corral.

"Reckon it were back in 1830ish, I was still a snot nosed kid back then." He turned, leading me into the shade of the livery. "Bring him in here, we'll get the tack off 'n turn 'em out. Figure after that we got us some dickerin' ta do."

"Heard ya wanted those two. Need a pack mule as part of the deal."

"Figure y'all be want'n a pannier ta go wit 'em. Oughta work out cause I'll want that tack that came with those two, I'll even take that extra one that showed up."

"Sounds like we got some trading to do." I smiled, noting the smirk on the man's face.

I knew it was going to be a long process. This was a man who loved dickering, probably more than the actual deal itself. We had been working to get the tack off while we talked, and after a quick brush down Miz went to join the others. Rusty promised to curry him proper and check his shoes later on.

I spent a few minutes in the tack room studying the three saddles, mostly because I needed some idea of their quality before we started trading. While we were in there, he showed me the best pannier set up he had. It looked almost new and well cared for. After that, he led me out to a side coral that had six mules loafing around in it. They varied in size and color, from a little molly that could have been a pony to a jack that was easily 19 hands.

"If'n it were me, that buckskin would be the one. Trail trained an better than any watch you'd ever set."

"How old?"

"Five, broke ta pack an saddle. Raised him up myself, that's why I know'd he's been taught right. Trained him like one of my mules to be silent 'round horses but call out if'n something wanders close ta your camp at night. Does it quiet like too." He let out a sharp whistle and the mule walked over to us.

I had to admit he was a beautiful jack, standing 14 hands with a dark mane and socks. His temperament seemed pretty even, once Elwood introduced me that is. Until then he was eyeing me with more than a little suspicion.

"Sounds good, guessing he's got a name?"

"Well now, I don't know if you ever been round folks like me afore but our sense of humor can be a bit odd."

"Give it your best shot, doubt you'll surprise me."

"Name's Meat." He sounded a bit ashamed when he said it. I stared at him for a second then doubled over laughing. Once he realized I wasn't offended he joined me. When we finally got ahold of ourselves, he slapped me on the back and spoke again. "Think we'll get along just fine."

I'd been right, the next three hours were spent dickering. In the end, I left with $243.67 along with Meat and a nearly new pannier with all the associated tack. Rusty kept the two horses and all three of the saddles. I ended up giving him back twenty dollars when I spotted a beautifully made six braid riata hanging in the tack room. There was no way I was leaving without it, you just didn't see them very often this far north.

I escaped before he started trying to sell me a fur cap he'd noticed me looking at. I finally made it to the boarding house and stopped to admire its crisp appearance. It was immaculately maintained and the flower beds out front spoke volumes about its owner. This place was truly a home rather than just somewhere to stay. The lady in question opened the door when I stepped onto the porch. She looked me up and down for a second before speaking.

"Rooms are four dollars a week or fifteen dollars a month." Her voice was sharp and precise but her eyes never left the scar zig zagging across my face. That's why she hadn't noticed the badge pinned on my chest.

"Marshal Reese said you already had a room for me Ma'am." I

smiled, trying to be pleasant. "Name's Chance."

"Deputy Chance then, yes you do. Mind your feet, I just finished cleaning my floors. Follow me."

That was that and she spun on her heel and walked away, expecting me to follow. I wiped my boots off on the mat before stepping inside and following her retreating form down the hallway. She took out a key and unlocked a door at the end of the hall near the kitchen.

"I keep you all on the first floor since your hours vary. That key is for the room, the back door is always open so if you come in late please use it. Meals are at six and six, coffee is always on in the parlor. Stay out of my kitchen and don't come home drunk. No women, bawdy or otherwise, except in the parlor or on the porches. I can't stand a slovenly man so don't come sit at my table smelling of horses and sweat. Privy is out back and there's a washing table by the pump. Laundry can be arranged with the celestials, it is not a service I offer. Chin's is my recommendation, it's nearby and they do a good job. Anything else?"

"No ma'am, if I have any other questions I'll ask."

She handed me my key and stalked away. I had no idea what I had done to offend her but it must have been something terrible. Taking a look into the room gave me somewhat of a clue. Having a small arsenal laid out on the bed might have put someone like her off. Three gun belts, five pistols, three Winchesters and a Sharps big fifty were all neatly laid out on the bed cover.

Four sets of saddle bags were stacked at the end of the bed and three bedrolls leaned in the corner near them. I knew the guns were all clean, but I hadn't gone through the saddle bags aside from dumping the clothes and food they contained before I left. The Sharps had been traded for before I left, Reese had two of them and wanted one of the Winchesters.

It was just heading toward noon so I should be able to sell the guns today. The saddlebags would go to Rusty as agreed once they got sorted out and emptied. Searching the saddlebags didn't yield much, some piggin strings, an extra fire kit, a bottle of clear shine I would use to clean wounds and some d-rings for repairs. Mostly the usual items men who lived in the saddle always had around. The lucky find was a small coffee pot. They were easier to carry and you could also use them for cooking. Once they were sorted, I rolled the pistols into one then rolled the three Winchesters into the worst of the bed rolls. The Sharps I would keep, they were damn good long range rifles and I'd never had one.

Rusty had given me directions to a gunsmith, it was only a few blocks down from the boarding house. I wasn't impressed with the kid working the counter but they bought everything for a decent price and I left with another $180. I needed to swing by the bank since walking around with this much cash was never a good idea. First, my body told me I needed to eat something. Last night's meal was long gone and waiting until six for dinner wouldn't be much fun. My stomach was already nipping at my spine.

When I dropped off the saddlebags with Rusty, I asked him about a place to eat. You can always trust an old man on where to find good food. He recommended a restaurant just up the street, it was on the way back to Miss Molly's and near a barber shop. He strongly recommended a bath before sitting down at her dinner table. According to him, the woman had no tolerance for the scent of man or beast.

The eatery was decent and I had a good fried steak with some fresh green beans and potatoes. It put a dent in my empty belly but I passed on the pie. It looked good but there were only a few hours until dinner and something told me Miss Molly's pie would be better. Next was a trip to the barber which involved the same old argument. My long hair suited me just fine, all I wanted was a bath. While washing off three days' worth of dirt and scrubbing my hair clean, it occurred to me what might have bothered Molly.

I had planned ahead enough to bring my saddlebags with me. They held my last set of clean clothes and all my dirty ones. On the way back, I stopped by Chin's laundry to set up an account. They promised to drop off my clean clothes at the house tomorrow but they didn't think the long handles would survive the washing. When I walked back into the boarding house I was greeted by a slightly happier Miss Molly. She found me in the parlor getting myself a cup of coffee. Evidently, my clean clothes and freshly scrubbed face was enough.

"I appreciate you bathing, it makes dinner more palatable." She said primly. "I must apologize for the way I stared when you first arrived. Marshal Reese did warn me about the scar, but it still caught me off guard."

"Ma'am, folks have been staring at that scar since I was a little one, you've nothing to apologize for." I did appreciate the kind words though. "I got rid of almost all the stuff that had been stored in my room. 'Bout all that's left is the bedrolls."

"I doubt anyone will buy them but if you'd like I can air out the tarpaulin. The blankets might be past saving though." It was a peace offering and I took advantage of it.

"Thank you ma'am. I'm not sure what to do with the blankets but I do agree with your opinion on them."

"Call me Molly please. I'll burn what can't be saved by some fresh air." She thought for a minute before adding. "Or donate them to the poorhouse."

"That'd be perfect Molly, and please call me Chance." We shared a smile, putting the animosity to rest before I took my coffee to the back porch.

Dinner wasn't far off, there was just enough time to enjoy a cup of coffee and a pipe of tobacco. The rest of the boarders met me at the table, at least the ones present. There were three other deputies boarding here but they were out of town. The others were a mixed bag. There were two drummers, a hostler and two clerks from the bank. Their ages varied from late twenties to early forties. They were all nice enough but not the type of men I spent much time around. They were respectful of the badge, but one and all thought I was just a kid with a rather unfortunate scar.

Only one of them mentioned my scar and he was the youngest at the table. He was in his early twenties and a teller at the bank. The glare he got from Molly shut the conversation down before I could answer but his eyes told me what he really wanted to know. This was someone connecting the dots between me and those dime novels. Not that I cared, but I would prefer to dodge that line of inquiry if possible. The food was good, I had to admit the woman could cook. We enjoyed a spread of chicken, mashed potatoes, fresh corn and biscuits. Dessert was apple pie, probably the best I'd had since childhood.

Afterwards, I sat on the back porch smoking a pipe while my eyes took in the sunset. My mind was contemplating everything ahead of me when I heard the door open. Molly stuck her head out before venturing all the way to join me. She had a cup of tea in a delicate China cup and I had to stifle a laugh when I saw the cigar in her other hand.

"Shush, young man." It didn't sound harsh but the upturned corner of her mouth gave away her amusement. "We all have our vices, and my Charlie left me with this one."

"Your secret is safe with me." I smiled and offered her a match.

After I finished my coffee, a deep yawn escaped my mouth and I excused myself to bed. It had been a long couple of days and I still had shopping to do tomorrow. Just being around this many people was hard enough. The constant hum of voices filled my ears and no matter where I looked there was always someone there. After so many years in open country, it was hard to get used to. Shopping was a completely different nightmare involving hot, crowded stores and people talking to me. I wasn't looking forward to it.

CHAPTER 9

I met the dawn sitting on that same back porch, and oddly enough Molly joined me again. She got up shortly after I arrived and went into the kitchen, mumbling something about breakfast needing to be ready soon. Her singing softly carried through the through open door and the scent of bacon wafted out with it. I couldn't catch the words but I thought she was singing an old Gaelic tune I'd heard before. My stomach complained about waiting but there was still an hour before the table would be set.

Thankfully, breakfast was served before my stomach climbed out my throat and went hunting for food on its own. Again I was reminded why the marshals used this boarding house. The food was amazing and it never seemed to run out. When I finally managed to push back from the table, my belt felt snug around my waist. There wouldn't be any need for lunch and my stomach might not fight me about it.

Not long after that, I strolled down Main Street looking into various clothier's shops. Most of them were much fancier than I wanted, Denver was a wealthy town and these shops reflected that. Luckily a mercantile sprouted up and I headed that way. My list here was longer but they had some clothes too. Some of what I bought would be delivered later today to the boarding house and I'd pick up the trail supplies tomorrow morning before leaving town.

I loaded five new trail shirts, two sets of long handles and two pairs of jeans onto the counter and placed a new pair of boots on top of the pile. The boots were a lucky find, the shopkeeper had bought them off a drummer and the quality impressed me. I also bought some new bandanas, socks and a few other unmentionables. A new bedroll, camp grill, decent sized coffee pot, a good Barlow knife, and a seasoned cast iron skillet rounded out my order. Some of them were luxuries but if I was taking a pack mule there was no need to go without.

All totaled with the food and supplies I spent just under fifty dollars. The shopkeeper promised someone would be at the store first thing tomorrow to help me load the trail goods and the rest would be delivered later. I wasn't looking forward to breaking in the boots but my current pair had been close to done back at Mose's place. I'd limped them through school out of necessity but it was time to pay the piper.

Next up was the clothiers and the shopkeeper had recommended a place close by. He promised that the owner was quick and used to dealing with people who didn't care for fancy clothes. Thankfully, he was right. The man got me sized and helped me find a simple black suit. The jacket was longer than normal so it would hang over my guns and it came with a vest and tailored white shirt. I had two stops left and it was just passing noon. The problem was, I needed a break and that's when I remembered the saloon I'd noticed on the way here.

I took a seat at the bar a few blocks off Main Street. The name of the place was what caught my attention. Fiddler's Ride wasn't a normal name for a saloon. Thankfully, the bar was mostly empty with just a couple of miners and one lone drifter sitting in the back corner. It gave me a break from the press of humanity. The man behind the bar was short with heavy sideburns, his eyes took me in at a glance.

"What's your poison friend?" The bartender asked, tossing a clean towel over his shoulder as he approached.

"Cold beer would suit."

"Be a dime." He smiled while pulling a draft.

"Thanks." I slid a dime to him as he set down the beer. It was cold as promised. It was also a damn good brew. "Good beer."

"Name's Jacob Coors, the secret is in the water." He smiled at my compliment.

"Didn't realize it was your own brew." I raised an eyebrow in surprise.

"I supply a few of the local places, mostly the higher end ones. They'll happily pay for the quality."

"I'll remember that, have to ask if I sit down in one of them." I smirked while taking another sip.

I took my time drinking the beer and chatting with Jacob. Bartenders never seemed to wear on me like other folks. Maybe it was the ability to have a conversation about nothing without it sounding like wasted air. Sadly, I couldn't put it off any longer. There was more shopping to be done. Rusty had recommended a nearby leather shop and a new set of chaps, a saddle sheath for the Sharps, and new rain slicker were must gets. The mercantile had them but I'd always found leather shops had better quality. Fortunately, the man there seemed to hate talking about as much as I did.

I managed to make it to the bank and deposited most of the money into my account and got a few drafts just in case. That was it, everything was done and my brain was screaming for me to get on Miz and run for the hills. For the rest of the afternoon, I organized my purchases and got my saddle bags packed for tomorrow. I kept my worn trail clothes for now but swapped out one of the shirts for a new one. The same with the jeans but I had to trash my old socks and such. They'd fought the good fight but it was time for them to go. I had already tossed the stitched long handles after Chin's said they wouldn't survive a cleaning.

I wanted to see more of the town at night now that I'd hidden for a couple of hours. Maybe some poker and a few beers would help me get to sleep. The first saloon was on the higher end, I picked it because I wanted some decent food. The steak dinner they offered was pretty good and the beer was cold but the ambiance was a bit too rich for my blood and I couldn't relax. The next place I found was closer to my speed and I spent a few hours there playing poker.

My last stop was a return to the Fiddler's Ride, it was a familiar feeling place. Punchers, drifters, and miners packed the place. I'd tucked my badge inside my new wallet before walking in, this wasn't the place to flash a star around. Levering my way to the bar, I found a space to occupy that was mostly out of the way. Jacob slid a beer to me before I even spoke and waved off my dime, putting his finger to the side of his nose. The man had a good memory and appreciated me putting the badge away.

I made it halfway through my beer before someone pushed into me. When I spun around to see who was pushing, I came face to face with the last person I wanted to see. Harvey was standing there fixing me with a drunken stare. There had to be ten thousand people in Denver and I had to run into this guy. There went my night.

"You!" He snapped when recognition broke through his drunken stupor.

"Don't do it." was all I said but sadly it didn't stop him. The fool went for his gun.

Before he could get it halfway out of his holster my right cross slammed into his jaw. We'd been standing almost chest to chest, too close for gun play. This man was truly a fool. I felt his jaw break when my blow landed and I cursed under my breath. He dropped to the sawdust floor like a puppet with his strings cut. The crowd had stepped back when he went for his gun and now they stood around his crumpled form looking shocked. A big man was pushing his way through the crowd using a club to clear a path.

"What the hell's going on here?" He asked when he finally made it to the clearing.

"He went for his gun. I didn't let him get there." My answer was short, but I didn't think this needed a lot of explanation.

"That's your story, huh?" The big man was casually smacking his club against his palm.

"No, that's what happened." I said simply. If this man thought I'd be cowed, he was about to be sorely disappointed.

"Look boy…" There it was. I cut him off before he got the rest out.

"Call me boy again and it'll be the last thing you do."

"Joey don't…" Jacob tried to stop him, but it was too late.

He didn't bother with any more banter, he just swung the club at me. He was fast for a big man, just not fast enough. I ducked under the swing and grabbed his wrist. With a quick turn, I used his weight to help launch him over my shoulder. Instead of throwing him like usual, I kept a hold of his wrist and slammed him into the ground. His shoulder took most of the impact but enough went to his neck and the lights went out.

My blood went cold when I heard the twin hammers of a double barrel come from behind me. I spun left before the last click sounded and my Colt came level with Jacob's face just as he tried to readjust his aim. My finger already had the trigger pulled and it was just my thumb that kept it from firing.

"I don't want gun play. Hell, I didn't want any of this. Nothing's broke other than that fool's jaw." My voice was calm and carried over the silence that filled the bar.

"I got you dead to rights with…" Jacob started but another patron cut him off before he could finish the threat.

"Jacob, he's already got the trigger pulled and the only reason you ain't dead's cause he didn't want it that way. You pull that trigger now and you'll both be dead." His face went pale at the realization and slowly his eyes met mine.

"That fool on the floor started this, not me. Your bully boy thought he'd be tough and call me a kid. That's his fault not mine."

"That true Ken?" Jacob asked the man who had spoken earlier.

"Every word, Harvey bumped into him then went for his gun. Stranger could've killed him then but didn't. When Joey swaggered up, well you know how he is." The aforementioned Joey groaned from the floor, starting to come around.

"How's about I call it a night and head to my bed?" I asked, my eyes never leaving Jacob. I watched as he swung the sawed off up and eased the triggers down. "I'll be out of town awhile, no reason for me to come back in here."

"Nope, you come back whenever ya have a mind. I trust Ken, if he says you didn't do anything wrong it's enough for me. I'll talk to Joey. Hell, maybe he can learn something from this." He looked down at Harvey's crumpled form. "Him though? Hate to say it, but you'll probably have to kill him. Just not in here."

"That's fair." I said, easing the hammer down and sliding my Colt home. "Sorry for the trouble."

"I betcha that was him, gotta be with that scar." Just as I reached the door Ken's voice carried over the crowd.

Another man in the dispersing crowd asked, "Him who?"

"Deadman's Chance, that's who…"

The rest of their conversation was lost in the noise as I made it out the batwing doors and into the cool night air. The walk back to Molly's gave me time to calm down. It wasn't that I regretted what had happened. Harvey was going to be a problem no matter what and bouncers were never particularly smart. Thankfully I was done with big cities for a while. Leastwise, any I had to be nice in. Getting out of town tomorrow and back into the tall and uncut sounded better and better.

CHAPTER 10

As I sat in the saddle watching Denver slowly fade from sight, my body seemed to relax the further down the road I went. It was nice to be away from civilization and riding into the foothills again. Rusty had helped me get Meat loaded this morning and he assured me the mule had a good temperament. He and Miz had managed to get it worked out between them without too much debate. There was a nip from Meat that got him kicked and that seemed to decide it. The one thing I debated was the location of the Sharps.

Keeping the Sharps on Miz meant I had ready access to it. But having two rifles in sheaths got in the way, especially when one was the long barreled big fifty. It wouldn't be something I could get to fast but a Sharps wasn't meant to be used quickly. The reality was simple, the big rifle was something you had to set up to fire. It wouldn't be much use in an emergency. Its sole purpose was to reach out and touch someone long before they thought you could. It got packed on Meat along one of the panniers.

Winding my way down a switchback, I watched the various failed mining sites roll by. They were hidden back in the trees and my eyes scanned them for any sign of movement. They always made good hideouts or places to set up an ambush but the stories they told of gold rushes interested me far more. Each one represented lives and fortunes won and lost.

Those relics spoke of the men who built them. How sturdy

was a cabin built and did the sluice still carry water? That same sturdy construction had been translated into building civilization out of the wild. It had been their ambition that had made it a territory. If the rumors were true statehood wasn't going to be long in coming.

'Course judging by the way things looked, statehood was going to spread across the country soon. Ever since the war ended, Americans had spread past the Mississippi building towns, bridges, and railroads that connected it. Populations that used to be counted on one hand now numbered in the hundreds or thousands. They were backed by the military who kept the tribes at bay by wiping them out or driving them into reservations. It essentially equaled the same thing, once they moved to the reservations death was inevitable.

For them, becoming dependent on someone else equaled death. That truth drove more and more braves to choose death in battle. They would rather raid the settlers and be killed than become farmers or "toothless old men." I could understand their way of looking at things more than most. Living free and by your own hand wasn't something you could easily give up. Hell, joining the marshals had been a tough choice because it meant answering to someone.

The only reason I'd done it was because I glimpsed the future. There were no old bounty hunters, not that there were many old deputy marshals. Maybe it was just knowing that if I disappeared as a deputy someone would take note. If I'd been killed before, no one would have even noticed. Part of it was wanting something in my life that was more than nothingness and death. It still didn't make sense to me but I knew there had to be more. I needed to feel something. Being alone had been my armor but it was becoming a trap, and one I desperately needed to find my way out of. The problem was I didn't know how.

There was something to be said for being a part of

something again. It gave me a very tenuous connection to humanity to start with. I'd have to get used being around people but that was a fair trade. I was learning to do it in small doses but just being in Denver for three days had almost been too much.

The marshal's school had been a challenge but it was maybe a hundred people rather than thousands. Most of them were in some way or another like me. They were used to being alone and tended to avoid inane babble to fill the silence. That was the main reason I took this job. These men made sense to me. We shared similar traits that led us to the marshal service.

But not all of us were the same, even if we did share some traits. Most were western men used to stomping their own snakes. All of us had already faced death more than once and most had lost family or loved ones to violence. That altered a person, it fundamentally changed you in ways that were hard to explain. It had made me who I am, there was no doubt about that. I was honest enough to recognize my place in the marshal service. They probably wouldn't be sending me to pick up a con artist or petty thief. The murderers, rapists, and rustlers? They would be my missions. Men and women who killed without remorse or cause.

That suited me just fine. Understanding violent men and knowing how to hunt them was something I'd learned long ago. They were simpler in a way, not dumb like some people assumed but more direct and it tended to make them predictable. If a man's answer to every problem was a hammer they left a clear trial to follow. Less direct criminals were more challenging but I'd learned how to handle them too. It was tedious, you need patience to find them. If you got on their trail you had to watch it every step of the way or it would disappear. Catching them was a challenge but most of the time when you did they'd fold. Unlike the hammers, they'd take a shot at prison.

I had three waiting for me in Cartersville. The man himself was most likely a hammer who'd learned to use other men. Baxter was the mystery out of the three. He might pick a fight with me as soon as I made it convenient, or he could stalk me and wait for his moment to try and shoot me in the back. It was just as likely that the man would cut and run in the night, leaving me with nothing.

The sheriff would probably be easy, if I pushed he'd fold. Most lawmen who went bad did so out of fear, either of death or old age. If you were a local sheriff who knew your time was limited and knew they'd replace you soon, what would you be left with? That was where the greed came from. There was no way the sheriff was getting away only to do the same thing somewhere else.

I started planning. I'd ride in, confront the sheriff first then Baxter would likely come for me. Knowing that fact gave me an edge. I'd just have to hope he did it head on and not from the back. Carter would come in once Baxter was gone. I wasn't dumb enough to think Baxter was his only gun hand, he was just the one I knew about. There would be others before Carter faced me himself. Men like him were always happy to let others get their hands dirty. That meant after Baxter was gone I'd have to go on the defensive and wait out the gun hands. There were a thousand holes in my plan but it was a start.

It was going to take three days of hard riding to make it into the town, that's if I went directly. A man like Carter wasn't stupid, there was a good chance he had someone watching the marshal's office. He had to know killing a deputy wasn't something that would just go away. The first part of my plan was looping down into the Nations. If anyone was trailing me, they'd guess I was heading after an outlaw. Since I was so new they might assume I was assigned to the Nations and ignore me when I didn't turn toward Cartersville.

If I got lucky they wouldn't mark my animals, neither of

them had a particularly unique look. To be safe, maybe I'd set up a camp on the outskirts and ride Meat in to town to deal with the sheriff. Men like Baxter weren't known for their patience, he'd come at me as soon as the sheriff was locked up. Then I could bring Miz in and the game would really begin. I'd deal with his men until I got Carter to tip his hand. I didn't think it would take long, men like him couldn't tolerate even the slightest loss of power. Any threat to what he saw as his land or property would have the man snarling at the door like a starving wolf.

Five days later, I turned into a small box canyon. It was familiar to me, there was a small cabin in the back of it next to a good source of water. The spring was year-round and there was decent graze for a few animals. It was an old hideout, so there might be someone already using it. My badge was tucked in my wallet out of sight just in case the current occupants weren't good law-abiding folk. Rounding the last bend I sighed with relief, the place looked deserted. I still called out before getting too close, but when no one answered after a few minutes I knew that it was empty.

After checking everything outside first, I finally opened the door and walked inside the cabin. It looked like it had been empty for a while and dust layered the table and beds. My plan was to stay here for a few days, giving any potential watcher time to get bored. If they were stupid they might ride in here after me. The Nations were a mess to track in but I made sure not to obscure my tracks for the last two days. If they were so inclined, why wouldn't I make it easy for them?

It took a few hours to get the cabin cleaned up before I lit the stove. After getting some coffee on and my two companions turned out, I sat down to catch my breath. So far my plans were pretty simple and had worked out. Now I just had to relax for a couple of days while watching for any signs of someone on my back trail. The soft clip of hooves on stone coming up the canyon told me that might not be necessary. It was either another outlaw coming in or someone foolishly following my tracks.

CHAPTER 11

The mouth of the canyon was two hundred yards from the porch I sat on. The Sharpe's was already balanced on the rail aimed at the opening. Listening to the soft clop of hooves as they got closer my mind focused down the sight waiting. The outlined shape of a man on horseback slowly resolved from the shadows. That set off warning bells on its own and motivated me to leave the porch. The porch was too open, too exposed to return fire. About fifteen feet from the porch was a heavy log, obviously put there as a firing position by someone. The last time I tracked a man here he'd used it for that purpose. Some of the holes that peppered the front of it were from me.

Laying behind it I rested the barrel in a nook that looked carved for the purpose. Slowly centering my sights on the approaching shape. The big fifty caliber round was already chambered and ready. Watching as the shadows slowly melted away revealing the man and his horse for the first time. He paused when the sun filled his vision blinding him for a second. I could see him blinking, his eyes slowly adjusting to the bright light. He wasn't used to this type of work. Anyone who was would have pulled their hat down to keep their eyes protected out of habit.

The soft click of the first trigger setting sounded like music to my ears. Now the primary trigger would fire with the slightest touch. The man was about what I expected. Tired looking and covered in dust from a long days on the trail. The most important thing was the second mistake he made. Another telling hint that he was no real outlaw. He rode a horse that stood out too much. His paint was almost solid white with one brown sock and a matching patch on one eye. I recognized it from Denver and that told me everything.

It was hitched outside of a saloon across from the marshal's office. Always the same place and ready to ride. There'd always a good amount of droppings behind the animal. Easily telling anyone with sense how long it had been there. That was what originally made me notice it. Leaving your animal tied outside all day while you drank was just wrong. You depended on your horse far too much when you left a city. Treating it like that might lead to your death if you weren't careful.

The next day when I noticed it again. That time my suspicion stopped me from finding the owner. Whoever it was made it obvious the horse was waiting for something or someone. My first thought was a robbery or some other criminal act but then I thought about Carter. A wealthy man wouldn't hesitate to spend the money. The owner might be watching for a deputy or team to leave.

My eyes followed his slow approach adjusting the sights as he moved. He would either back out or approach and call out. By now he could easily see Miz and Meat grazing, so he had to know I was here. At a hundred yards pulled his horse to a stop before he calling out to the cabin.

"Hello the house!" His voice echoed around the box canyon. I let it fade before answering.

"Yeah, what can I do for ya?" I spoke in a normal tone. Turning my head allowing the canyon to disguise my location.

"I'm friendly just needing some water an maybe some of that coffee I smell."

"That's a good thing cause right now my Sharps is trained on your chest." I watched the panic spread across his face, even this far away I could see his skin go pale. "So, step out of that saddle easy and if that Winchester moves it'll be the last mistake you make."

"I'll just move on if …"

"I don't remember giving you a choice. Do as I say or die in the saddle, your choice friend." He sat in the saddle for thirty seconds before making a decision.

"Fine I'm stepping down." He shakily stepped down from the saddle doing his best to keep his hands away from his guns.

"Go ahead an drop that gun belt real slow."

"Look I …" I cut him off.

"Wasn't a question. Drop it where you stand and walk toward the porch." He cringed but did it. When he got about ten feet from me I gave my last command. "Turn around and don't move."

He didn't debate me this time and did it without question. I left the Sharps leaning on the log before stepping over it and drawing my Colt. A quick search found a holdout pistol in the right boot and nothing else. I tied his hands behind him with some piggin strings and jerked him to the porch. After tying his boots to the porch rail I went to get his horse and gun belt. Using the dry grass to rub him down before turning the paint out in to the small corral. Slowly walking back I studied the man before taking a seat on the log.

"Let's save time, I'll tell you what I know then you fill in the blanks. You've been on my back trail since Denver. Please don't waste my time denying it, I don't have much patience."

"How'd you know?"

"Your horse, shouldn't use one so unique." I grinned down at him before continuing. "My guess is you're working for Carter."

"Who?" I could tell by his voice he was lying.

"I did warn you about lies right?"

"You're a marshal, what're you going to do?" He snorted a

laugh.

"You know I remember seeing a notice about a stolen horse that matches yours. We'll have to take him back to Denver to be sure." I spoke casually, like I was just talking to the air. "You look resourceful enough. The nations aren't a bad place to survive. Might be hard with no guns but I can't risk someone shooting me in the back."

"You can't leave me out here with no horse!" He finally caught on to what I was getting at. "That'd be killing me."

"What? Not at all, I'm sure the tribes would help you out." I grinned happily sipping my coffee. "I think this is Cheyenne country, they ain't to hostile."

"Baxter, not Carter. Had me watching for any law that was headed his way." The thought of being left to the mercy of the Cheyenne with no horse or supplies was enough to get him talking.

"Did you let him know I was coming?"

"No, didn't get a chance. I was going to send one when you stopped at a town, but you never did." That had been intentional on my part. I wasn't going to make it easy for anyone on my back trail.

"Well, that means you're still useful to me. Do they expect you to check in?" He hesitated before answering so I gave him some incentive. "You can help me an ride away or not and walk."

"No, I only contact them if someone was heading that a way. You turned into the nations, so I didn't know what you were up to."

"Ain't going to be comfortable traveling, but you'll ride." I watched his shoulders relax at my words.

The next morning, we left the canyon. Him trailing me sped up my plan but only by a day or so. Two nights later I left him tied to a tree while I scouted for a good camp outside of Cartersville. It didn't take long to find one. It had good cover with fresh water and plenty of graze. The surrounding copse of trees would hide a fire and disperse the smoke. Camp was easy to set up and after feeding my prisoner I went into town on foot. He didn't like being left tied between Meat and Miz. Even my promise that if he stayed still they probably wouldn't trample him didn't make him relax. Which was exactly what I wanted.

The town wasn't big, there was the typical Main Street lined with a few shops. The livery was at the western edge of town, the blacksmith conveniently located next door. The east end was two saloons with rooms attached for the soiled doves. In between was a general store, feed and grain, eatery and the sheriff's office. The last one held pride of place right now but something about the way it was laid out bothered me. It was too open, that's when it hit me. Someone had planned this, they had allowed for additional buildings.

There were only three cross streets right now but I could see where the rest would go. Even the ones now where divided by some sort of wealth. Each street had a few houses, totaling maybe twenty houses. The largest of them stood at the end of Center street, there was even a sign naming the street. There was only four other houses on that street and they were obviously the largest in town except for one. It was a small cottage near the large house at the end, maybe a servants house.

The big house at the end was set far down the street with nothing but the cottage around it. My guess was to allow for more houses to eventually fill in the gaps. It was a two-story place that someone had spent a lot of money building. My intuition said it was Carter's luxury home in town. The mayor's house was the next nicest but didn't come really come close in grandeur. I did chuckle at the sign out front announcing whose house it was.

Back on Main Street I stood in a shadow watching the door of the sheriff's office. Light split the shadows as the door opened revealing a scarecrow of a man. He strolled down the boardwalk toward the saloon with a shotgun over his shoulder. The sheriff obviously doing his last walk through town. This might be a good time to deal with the man. My guest, I hadn't bothered to ask his name yet, said the sheriff spent most nights in the Lazy Ace. It was the nicer of the two saloons, both owned by Carter. He would wander back to his office around midnight, usually drunk.

If I locked him up when he returned it would give me five hours to get the horses taken care of and prepare for Baxter. That was plenty of time, it might even let me take a nap. Moving from shadow to shadow I made my way to the door, no sense in delaying. The longer we were camped outside of town the more risk of discovery there was. Besides the sheriff was going to be the easiest to deal with no matter how I did this.

Baxter would be more of a challenge. Maybe the man would come at me straight up but I didn't believe that was likely. I'd have to predict his shot and get it right the first time. There wasn't likely to be a second one. Taking a few minutes to study the street, trying to puzzle out where he would shot from. The saloons were too far away without enough cover. Everything except the livery was single story so there was no elevation on Main Street. The man would want a higher vantage point to shot from. It really only left one option and that told me something else.

Carters house, it had to be. If I was a betting man he lived there too. Looking back at the house I noticed a crow's nest off to one side of the roof for the first time. From there someone could see the entire town except for very few places. I doubted Carter built it as a shooting platform, most likely he built it as a place to sit and look down on his kingdom. That didn't change the fact that it was the best place to shoot a man from in the entire town. Then I looked up at the roof of the sheriff's office, it was just as I expected.

Most sheriff's offices were the toughest buildings in a town. Constructed from heavy stone packed with adobe, the roof almost always had a chest high wall around them. This one was no exception. It wouldn't give me absolute cover but I should be able to get off the first shot. It was a good idea but no longer an option. Legally I couldn't just shoot him on the assumption of guilt.

That meant I had to be sighted in and waiting for him to find me. Or maybe find who he thought was me? He'd shot the tip off a badge, I just thought it was luck but now maybe not. If I was right and he was shooting from up there? Maybe he used the shine off the badge to aim. That explained the mystery much better and told me two things. One good, one bad.

The good was I might be able to get away with a decoy, like a scarecrow. The bad, it meant the man was a damn good shot. If he hit the star from that perch it was easily 500 yards, shooting down at a small target. He had to be using a Sharps or a Springfield, either of which had the range and damage to kill at that range. I wasn't going to have an advantage other than surprise.

What I needed was a way to get him there at a particular time, knowing when to expect him was the only way this would work. I might have to use a pawn and it would still be risky. Luckily there was always one thing you could bank on with his type. They always looked to have an edge. Maybe my guest would take part in this charade without knowing it.

Shaking off the planning I turned to the door. Of course it was locked, thankfully that had never stopped me. I had it open after a bit of fiddling and slipped inside. When the door closed I struck a Lucifer to have a Quick Look around. With the windows shuttered there was no chance of anyone seeing the light. There was a simple clean desk, the ever-present rifle rack, and a map of the area. What caught my attention about the map was a note pinned to it.

To Sheriff Cartersville.

Twenty-five men to Circle J arrive Wednesday. Stop.

Drovers for next drive, five as guards. Stop

J. Carter

That meant the ranch was full of men. Men I didn't really want to tangle with, punchers and more then a few gun hands. I did some quick math and at a rough guess it meant that there was probably forty men at the ranch right now. If they were gathering a herd most of them would be out on the range but that wouldn't stop them from coming if called.

The drovers probably wouldn't go to far once they learned it was against a deputy marshal. Just his regular hands plus the five or six gun hands, it was still too many. Even as my mind worked this out I was closing the door behind me and moving out of town. There was no way my quick little plan would work now. I owed the sheriff for keeping that telegram. If the man had a better memory and had tossed it out things could have gotten bad for me fast.

70

CHAPTER 12

Walking back into my small camp I found my guest glaring at me from between Meats legs. He didn't look happy, probably due do to some rather fresh droppings sitting nearby. I'd say I felt bad about it but that would be a lie. I did need to figure out what to do with him though. This job wasn't going to be quick and he didn't serve any purpose aside from wasting my time. After cutting him loose he sidled in closer to the fire. In the back of my mind the answer regarding him was already there. There was just no reason to warn him beforehand.

Three days later I left a rather unhappy guest with a Cheyenne I knew. Black Owl wouldn't let him go and he was far to green to take the cagey old man. Black Owl might drive him insane but he'd keep him there. I met him not long after he found this place. He'd been forced out of his tribe because he was spirit touched. They left food and clothes for him outside his little canyon and made sure no one bothered him. In fairness to them he was bat shit crazy. I'd watched him talk to a rock wall for most of a day once. That seemed odd but later that night when he was telling me what the rock said it went from odd to full blown crazy.

You could count on him to keep his word though. He'd promised the tribe to stay here and he hadn't left in twenty years. I'd asked him to hold a man for me before. Kept him for two weeks while I chased his partner. The man was so happy to see me when I came back it shocked me. Black Owl just said he was a good listener as if that explained everything. I don't remember his name but he told me that the old man had talked to him for the first day and a half without taking a break. The problem was he never bothered listening to your response. He just talked non-stop about whatever he felt like. The problem was he didn't do it in English but in a language only he understood.

I always felt some sympathy for whoever stayed with him. I knew first-hand what it felt like. Black Owl had nursed me back to health after I showed up with two holes in me. He knew his medicine and brought me back to life but that week had been rough. Still, he'd keep his word, when I came back my guest would still be here. He'd promised and only asked for some tobacco in trade. It might not be a legal jail, if he wanted to the man could leave anytime. He'd just do so with no mount, weapons, or supplies.

Riding a wide loop around town this time let me enter the Circle J range before town. My plan was to wait for the herd to leave, taking most of the hands with it. There were too many men working the drive for me to do anything before they left. That meant finding the herd then waiting for it to hit the trail. The place good-sized ranch and despite knowing what I was looking for it took time to find them.

Watching from back in the woods that bordered an open pasture I got comfortable. A few hundred yards away the herd started, it looked to be fifteen hundred head or so. There was a chuck wagon set up on the far side, past that was the remuda. Punchers worked cutting cattle, branding some and others were run off to other parts of the range. Those would be the base beef's that any good ranch kept. Young steers that hadn't put on enough weight yet and quality breeding stock. Earlier I'd pasted another field, this one was fenced and kept the bulls separate.

The punchers wove through them almost casually, not showing any concern for the forest of horns milling around.

The herd was trail broke and almost ready to go, it wouldn't be long before they left. Soon they would start them toward the rail head, probably Dodge City. I could wait, there just wasn't a reason to rush this. If giving them a few days to clear off would make my life easier that's what I was going to do. That made far more sense than facing a bunch of gun hands.

The next day I moved back to my original camp outside of town. While scanning with my field glasses I witnessed something that changed my plans. Stalking down Main Street I got my first look at Baxter. The way he looked it could only be him. A bit over six feet with the paunch but not enough to disguise the muscle under it. A Springfield casually draped over his shoulder was my biggest hint regarding his identity. If not for that I would have guessed he was just another saddle tramp. The self-satisfied look on his face said this was Baxter. He was half dragging half leading a woman down the street toward the sheriff's office.

She was pretty, mid-twenties with auburn hair. It was struggling to stay up in what was once a neat bun. Her dress was form fitting enough to be flattering but not revealing. She wasn't a saloon girl, that much was obvious. This woman looked like a proper lady. There was just something about her, an aura of propriety that she had. It made you pay attention but not in the way you did a doxy or simply beautiful woman. Maybe this was what folks meant when they talked about nobility, the right to rule nonsense.

It was the oddest thing, watching someone being yanked down the street but still looking regal. While the man who looked like he'd just left the trail, filthy and unshaven. Something about her just naturally pulled your attention to her. She was stunning but that wasn't it, there was something ethereal about her. I couldn't take my eyes off of her. That was until Baxter pushed her toward the door the sheriff's office. Thirty minutes later he walked out followed by the sheriff. They had a brief conversation and Baxter walked away smiling.

I didn't know what they said but knew it didn't bode well for the girl. I'd have to move tonight. Some part of me couldn't let anything happen to any woman, especially not that one. Watching Baxter turn up the center street, casually walking to the big house at the end gave me some ideas. Minutes later he appeared on the crow's nest carrying the Springfield and a coffee pot. He was planning on staying there for a while. If he stayed long enough I'd be able to loop around and get behind him. If there was one thing I'd learned from the Apache, it was how to move unseen and unheard.

Three hours later I was creeping up to the back door of the house. Moving under an open window, I heard movement inside. My luck held when the maid collected their things to go home for the evening. The house was empty ten minutes later when I slipped through the window. Laying there on the floor behind a desk, my ears searching for any signs of life. I'd left my boots outside and now crept across the finished floor sock footed. Moving from door to door listening for any sound that would give away his location.

It didn't take long to get up the stairs. Just outside the door in front of me was a ladder hanging down from the roof access. Above me I could hear him humming some familiar tune, then the sound of an empty coffee pot rattling. The sun was fading from the sky, slowly covering the land in shadows. Hopefully he would be coming down when the light faded. With all the patience I had learned from hard won lessons my body stilled. Even my breathing turned shallow and silent.

Every fiber of me wanted to slide my Bowie into this man as soon as he appeared but knew I couldn't. I wore a badge, killing men without giving them a chance wasn't an option. But there was no way I'd be dumb enough to announce myself and give him a chance. With a quick silent swing the barrel of my Colt went across the back of his skull. He crumpled to the floor out cold, his rifle clattering beside him. I hogtied him before the man had a chance to fight me. When he was secure my hands explored the back of his head, there was a little blood but not enough to worry me. I breathed a sigh of relief, the last thing I wanted was to cave in his skull. There was still some pressure to show Reese I could operate within the law.

After searching him and taking both pistols and three knives I did the only thing left. Pulling off his boots, I stuffed a sock in his mouth then used his bandanna to gag him. It wasn't my fault he didn't bath or wash his socks. Taking my time to search the entire house, I found another Springfield, a collection of pistols, and a few Winchesters. Probably taken from whoever he had killed. There was also $3467 stuck in a box under the bed. Unsure what to do with that I took the money belt and put it on. I'd have to ask the boss about what found covered later.

Now it was time for the sheriff. The sun was setting fast casting everything in deep shadows. Usually, he'd be off on his rounds about now but I had a feeling he was waiting for Baxter to return. I left through the back door to retrieve my boots. Then went back in to lock Baxter in the cold room for now. He wasn't keen on that but being hogtied and gagged limited his powers to object. This man deserved far worse than he was getting but that was for a judge to decide.

Leaving the houses I casually stepped onto the boardwalk. Walking like I belonged there, just strolling to the sheriff's front door. It was locked so I rapt on it and waited. A man grumble on the other side of the door as he stomped toward it. I couldn't make it out what he said but I'd bet the man was ready for his evening drink. When the door opened he stopped, frozen in place staring at me open mouthed.

"Carter sent me, came in for the drive. He wanted me to give you a message." This still didn't stir him to movement so I pushed my way into the office. The sound of the door closing seemed to finally jar the man into action.

"What's the message?" He was studying me, trying to decide if I was a drover or a guard. My guns seemed to make the decision for him.

I reached into my vest with my left hand casually. The move didn't seem to bother him since it wasn't near my guns. The man wasn't cut out for this line of work. A gun hand would never use their dominate hand to reach in a pocket. They might need to move fast and you learned to use the other one. His eyes were fixed on my left hand as it moved, completely ignoring my right.

He was either a fool or thought his place in Carter's schemes held no risk for him. His eyes tracked my left hand while my right snaked around his gun hand and yanked him down. My knee came up hard and fast. There was an audible clack when it collided with his chin. The man half flipped backward and landing on the floor, out cold.

Working fast I stripped off his guns, knife and badge. Using the keys that hung on the wall I locked him in the back cell after hand cuffing him to the bars. Taking the extra time to use the same trick from earlier. Gagging him as I had on Baxter. That's when I heard a gasp from the cell next to me.

"Who are you?" The female voice demanded.

"Depends on who you are." I replied simply.

"Miss Gardner, I teach at the school."

"There's a school? Isn't this place a bit small for that?" I couldn't imagine there was enough kids here to justify a school yet.

"Not yet but the mayor plans on one." She added quietly then in a sharper tone. "Not that he told me that in his correspondence."

"What'd you do to end up in here?"

"I did not do anything! The idea that I have committed some crime is insulting. That vile beast of a man Baxter just took me from my room. He claimed to have other plans for me." I could hear the fear in her voice behind the anger. Worse still we both had a pretty good idea what his plans involved.

"Stay here and be quiet. When I get back I'll cut you loose." I said turning toward the door and stepping through it.

"You never …" the door closing cut off her next question.

I was out the door and back at Carters house in minutes. There was a small stable out back that held a black gelding, it had to be Baxter's. After tossing a blanket across its back I led the animal to the back door, looping its lead to the railing. With a lot of grunting and more muffled cursing I managed to drag the man out the door. I did my best not to bounce his head off every step, it was mostly successful. Using some creative knot work had the man bound across the back of his horse. By then it was full dark, the half-moon gave me just enough light to see but left plenty of deep shadows. Luckily no one paid any attention to what was going on outside their homes. Either they didn't notice or recognized the horse and didn't want to deal with the owner.

After more cursing and a few muffled cries, I managed to get the big man into the same cell as the sheriff. Neither of them looked happy about it but the gags still kept the complaints quiet. The teacher had watched the whole thing in silence. I did notice the look in her eyes, it didn't promise anything good for the man if she got a chance. When she spit at him, nicely hitting his face, I knew that letting her near him would be a bad idea. It'd be a lie to say I wasn't tempted but the man was now my prisoner. If he didn't do something stupid I had to protect him.

"Five more minutes and I'll let you out." I told her after cuffing Baxter to the bars opposite the sheriff.

"Maybe leave me a knife to watch them?" The tone of her

voice confirmed that would be a very bad idea. She probably wouldn't kill him but might be mad enough to remove a few parts. To tell the truth it made me smile, you had to respect the strength it took to say that.

"Sorry ma'am don't think that'd be wise." I grinned, closing the door again.

Getting the horse back without being seen wasn't any more difficult than the reverse. It made me wonder about the folks in this town. How long had they been turning a blind eye? Baxter had dragged a woman down Main Street without anyone speaking up. It didn't bode well for the quality of people living here, at the very least it proved a lack of will. After putting the gelding back in the stall I spotted a set of saddlebags. Back in the house I loaded them with food and coffee from the pantry. There was probably some in the sheriff's office but if I was going to be stuck in there, more was better.

Fifteen minutes later I was back in the office. Locking the door behind me before walking back to the cells. I put my badge on before opening the door, it should get some interest reactions. They didn't disappoint me. The sheriff looked like he might cry, Baxter glared and tried to curse me through his sock. Miss Gardner was shocked but quickly replaced that with anger.

"How dare you keep me locked in here! You're a lawman!" She demanded.

"Cause it was the best way to keep you safe until I got these two locked up."

"Let me out of here!"

"After you calm down because I need some help. I need a message delivered to the mayor."

"Fine." She glared waiting for me to speak. Unfortunately, I got lost in the most beautiful green eyes I'd ever seen. They stole my voice despite her glare. Sucked me in to them like deep emerald pools that shimmered under the flickering glow of a lantern. That is until she snapped her finger in front of my face.

"Uh sorry, yeah um." I stammered, my face burning in shame. It took me a minute to collect my thoughts. "Just tell him that a deputy marshal has taken control of the sheriff's office. The sheriff and Baxter are already locked up. For now, I just need him to send a telegram to Marshal Reese in Denver. Tell him I'll be needing a jail wagon as soon as he can arrange it."

I was unlocking her door as I spoke trying not to get lost in her eyes again. The sharp sting of her hand when she slapped me took me by surprise. The taste of blood on my tongue was another shock, she knew how to slap someone. I caught her wrist when she went for my gun, that wasn't going to happen. I'd take a hit but she wasn't going to kill my prisoners.

"That's enough." I said calmly. "You're not killing anyone. Get yourself under control before I put you back in that cell."

She tried to kick me but I spun her around, pushing her out the door into the office. It wasn't intentional but she stumbled into the desk and fell across it. When she stood back up and spun to face me her face flamed with embarrassment and anger. Her hair had come loose from the bun in our scuffle, it fell down her shoulders. Soft curls cascaded down framing her face, it nearly let her catch me off guard again. The only thought I could manage at that moment was 'damn she's beautiful.' It must have showed on my face and didn't make her happy. With a screech that would satisfy any banshee she stomped out the office and down the boardwalk.

I could only hope she'd deliver my message. With her temper it wasn't a comfortable bet but it was what I had. An older woman stood in a doorway across the street watching the scene. She wore a knowing smirk as she studied me for a minute. Tipping my hat in response I started walking across the street toward her. I couldn't help but chuckle at what she must be thinking. It also made me wonder how much of tonight's activities she'd witnessed.

"See ya met li'l Miss Hellcat." She laughed when I stepped on to the boardwalk.

"Yes ma'am, seems I made an impression. Just hope she remembers my message for the mayor."

"She will, once she calms down most likely. Saw ya cart Baxter in there, sheriff dead or locked up?"

"Both of them are locked up. I might need some food tomorrow morning."

"We can work that out. 'Bout time one of y'all come ta deal with these fools."

"Have to get one more before it's done."

"Going after king rat huh? Brave, course ya know the difference between bravery and stupidity?." She smiled before turning back inside. "Bring breakfast over for the three of ya about dawn. If you're not dead of course. If ya are I'll just bring two."

"Fair enough ma'am, names Chance."

"Everyone calls me Bess. Don't die marshal, getting tired of this bunch. Hate ta kill them, you'd have to arrest me then." Her laugh was real and honest but there was something about it that told me she wasn't really joking. "Timed it about right ta stop me too."

"Yes ma'am." I smiled at her back. When she closed the door I walked back over to the sheriff's office and locked the door. That was when her last comment finally made sense. She'd been planning on doing something, probably because of the school teacher.

The two in the back were trying to have a conversation of sorts. It was still muffled but guessing by the tone they weren't happy with their circumstance. I'd have to cut them loose from the handcuffs, unfortunately that meant no more gags. It would increase the noise but it had to be done. First the other cells needed to be ready for more company. Clean buckets of water from the pump, after thinking about it I filled all three buckets. One in each cell with a slop bucket. There were two bunks in each of the three cells.

One last search of each man let me find a hidden knife Baxter had tucked deep in one boot. The shackles were hanging on the wall, each man got leg irons locked on before anything else. They would still let them move but make it a bit safer when I had to deal with them. The most dangerous part would be changing the buckets. There would be a chance for one of them to cause trouble when I opened the door to get them and again when I put them back.

Finally cutting Baxter's bonds after freeing the sheriff. The old man wasn't jumping up to move. He was still rubbing his wrists staring at me with a mix of anger and fear. Baxter took a minute to get his circulation going which let me easily step out of the cell. Both men spit out their gags and started cussing me in turn. I leaned back on the wall just letting them vent. To their credit it took about ten minutes for them to get it all out. The sheriff calmed first and started the ball rolling.

CHAPTER 13

"Guessing I'm removed from office?" His voice was still cracked. He took a drink from the bucket trying to get some lubrication going.

"And charged with at least aiding in the murder of a deputy marshal. There's more of course but that one'll get ya hung." The man's face paled when I mentioned the noose. "Course your friend there will hang with you. For the actual murder."

"Ain't no one gonna testify 'bout that." Baxter's laugh was harsh and dry. He was still spitting lint from his mouth. "Sides you'll be dead an I'll be free soon as Carter gets here."

"What makes you think he'll even know?" I smiled coldly at the man. He had managed to get up and sit on a bunk.

"He'll know when I don't show up later, supposed ta bring that female to him." There was something in the way he said that, something off about it.

"Funny, she thought you were coming for her." I mentioned. The sheriff was leaning against the bars. The man obviously lacked the faith Baxter had.

"I might've forgot ta mention him when I escorted her." The man enjoyed people being afraid. Something in people like him was diseased, like a rabid cur. All you could do was put them down before they spread it.

"Looking forward to meeting the man. Having heard what a fine man he is, it makes me almost afraid he'll fall short of my expectations."

"He won't." Baxter's smile told me he absolutely believed that. "Course it won't be a long meeting."

"Probably not, course that might not be good for you." I said the last walking out of the cells and bolting the heavy door.

They were still talking inside but it was mostly complaining, nothing useful. Ignoring them I grabbed a towel beside the stove to pour myself some coffee. Carter probably wouldn't be here before dawn which left me a few hours to grab a nap. After checking the lock, I kicked my feet up on the desk and tilted my hat down over my eyes. Sleep came fast, my body long trained to take what it could when it could.

Someone banging on the door woke me up. I wasn't sure how long I'd been asleep but it would have to be enough. Easing my feet down to the floor, taking a moment stompingly feet to get the blood flowing before standing up. When someone kicked the door they followed it with a threat.

"Unless y'all wanna go hungry someone better open this door!" It was Bess, keeping her promise. I still checked through the slit in the door, just to make sure she was alone.

"Thanks Bess." I said opening the door, letting the woman into the office.

"Told ya I'd be here." Was her short response but she had some humor in her voice when she continued. "Sides I wanna see those two jackasses locked up."

"Well right this way ma'am." Bowing with a flourish before opening the door to the cells.

There was a table against the wall to put the trays on. She laughed quietly while setting them down, a real grin splitting her face. She picked up the top tray before walking back into the front office, I heard her set it on the desk. The trays fit through a slot in the cell doors. When they asked I agreed to bring coffee back in a few minutes.

"Worth the walk?" I asked after locking the door.

"Worth that'n more." She cackled. "Someone'll bring over lunch later, won't be hard to find a volunteer."

"Thanks, I'll settle up on the bill before I leave town."

"Ain't worried bout it, the town council'll get the bill. Probably won't even bitch bout it this time." She was still smiling when I opened the door.

She almost got hit on the forehead by someone reaching to knock. It was Miss Gardner, looking even more beautiful with the soft glow of dawn lighting the world behind her. Again, she stole my breath, luckily it took her a minute to deal with Bess letting my brain recover some. Stepping back, she let Bess pass by while she mumbled an apology. What was it about this woman that affected me so strongly?

"Deputy." She said politely when she stepped inside.

"Ma'am." The word sounded awkward but at least my voice didn't crack. "Please call me Chance."

"Yes ummm Chance, I came to apologize for last night." A faint hint of red flushed her cheeks when she met my gaze. "I shouldn't have struck you."

"It's fine ma'am I understand." I sounded like some foolish kid but couldn't help myself. "Can't say I would have reacted differently in your situation."

"Please call me Mary." Her voice fell on my ears like a cool breeze on a hot summer day. "Still, I wanted you to know I forgave you."

"Forgave me ma'am?"

"Yes for leaving me locked in the cell."

"Ma'am I didn't really ask for that. I just did what I had too and would do it again." The minute the words came out I knew it was a mistake. Anger flashed like lightning across those emerald skies and her eyebrows arched up condemning me to death.

"You don't feel sorry about doing it?"

"Sorry it had to be done? Certainly, ma'am wish you'd never had to deal with any of it. That doesn't change the fact that it was necessary in the..." her hand snaked out faster than expected, leaving another stinging print on my cheek.

"Barbarian!" She snapped before stomping out of the office and down the boardwalk again. The sharp stamp of each foot echoed down the street. Each step sounded like she was trying to break the boards under it.

Pouring two cups of coffee while the redness faded, I smiled remembering the way her eyes looked. Even after locking the door my mind was still in a fog. I just didn't understand that woman. Of course I had to keep her locked in a cell, couldn't let her run off and accidentally warn someone. Or worse run off and get hurt or caught again. How did she not see that?

Walking into the cells ignoring the complaints about the delay in bringing coffee. My mind was still trying to figure out what had gone wrong with that conversation. I'd been honest, even willing to explain why I had to keep her locked up if she'd let me. It just seemed to make her mad and I couldn't understand it. Sitting down to eat breakfast I finally wrote it off to my ignorance about women.

Miss Gardner outside the sheriff's office...

She was stumped at what was wrong with that man! Could he not understand how terrifying that had been for her? Of course he should have apologized for leaving her locked in with that bastard. What kind of man would do that? It was complete madness. Never mind the nerve of keeping an innocent woman locked up at all. What was wrong with the man!

Still there was something about him. Something that set her emotions racing every time she was near him. So far both times had ended with her hitting him, that probably wasn't the best way to express it. She wouldn't have hit him if he hadn't been so frustrating! That man was like some wild animal, it was the only way to explain it. Raised by wolves or some other wild group of animals that was the only way to explain it. A lack of proper upbringing, it had to be.

She spent most of her anger trying to break ever board on the way to the mayors store. Her emotions had mostly calmed down when she reached for the door. Even as frustrated as she was with the arrogant man she still remembered to deliver his message. She managed to knock on the door without breaking something, the glass did rattle in the pane a bit too much.

"Stop it before you break the door down!" A panicked voice came from inside.

The mayor's portly frame stood in door checking to be sure the glass hadn't broken. She always found it funny how the man resembled the typical mayors from various books. Short with a thin circle of grey hair wrapping around his head connecting to the mutton chops that met below his nose. He was trying to glare up at her and it only made her want to laugh. The man just didn't have it in his nature to be cross.

"Morning mayor, I have a message for you." She managed to stifle her laugh but couldn't help the smile. "A rather vulgar deputy marshal has arrested the sheriff and Baxter. He needs you to send a telegram to Marshal Reese, asking him to send a jail wagon."

"He's done what?!" The mayor spluttered, accidentally buttoning his vest wrong.

"What did you not understand mayor?" She didn't mean for

that harsh tone to be in her voice but there it was. She'd never learned to hide her emotions, they always came through in her voice.

"Miss Gardner let me remind you who pays your salary. Please keep a civil tone when we speak." He didn't quite match her tone but tried.

"Sorry mayor. That deputy is just infuriating." She tried not to sound annoyed but as usual it didn't help much. Men did not respond well to her sharp tone. It had been a problem more than once.

"I mean no disrespect Miss Gardner but are you sure that's what's bothering you about the young man?" The mayor cocked one eyebrow studying me for a second. She couldn't understand what he was thinking. Of course that was it, what else could it be?

"Yes I am, what else could it be? Never mind, I've delivered his message and want nothing more to do with the beast!"

"As you say." The mayor almost chuckled but caught himself. "I'll send the telegram immediately, then go talk to the man."

She turn sharply on her heels and stomped away. The echoing sound solved one mystery for the mayor at least. He knew what that hammering noise had been now. Her temper was impressive but the mayor had noticed the slight flush in her cheeks when she spoke of deputy. That wasn't anger making her cheeks pink like that.

The smell of bacon wafted down from the kitchen, blending with the smell of his tea. His wife was about done cooking, breakfast was mere moments away. He'd send the telegram before eating. Putting it off for the sake of breakfast wasn't worth the risk. They'd finally gotten someone to come, he'd do everything he could to help the man.

Marshal Reese

Denver

Deputy arrested sheriff and killer stop

Send jail wagon soonest stop

Mayor

Cartersville

After his hunger was satiated he'd go met this man that so bothered that she devil.

Outside of town near Carters Ranch...

Two miles out of town at the at the edge of the Circle J a man's head jerked up in surprise. It was far too early for the daily telegrams to start. That's why he was still in the other room eating breakfast. Lurching to his feet he raced into the main room of his small cabin. Just as he reached for the headphones the ticking noise from the telegraph stopped. He'd only caught the last few words.

Message received Denver.

That didn't make any sense. No one in Cartersville should be sending anything this early to Denver? The sender had to be the mayor since he was the only telegraph operator in town. But why would that old man be messaging Denver? It had to be special but was it enough to disturb Mr. Carter with. What if it was just some special order for the store?

That made the most sense, but why send it so early? Walking back to his breakfast still unsure what to do. Food would help him think, food and coffee. Slowly he finished breakfast and decided that it had to be just some weird order. It had to be made early in the day for some reason. Definitely not something to bother Mr. Carter with, not after what happened to Mark. He'd told the man about a telegram that turned out to be just normal business. Baxter had shot him dead, Mark never even saw Carter. Nope this was not something he needed to worry about.

CHAPTER 14

Back at the jail I was collecting the trays and getting ready for a long day when a knock at the door got my attention. Leaving the trays on the edge of the desk before looking through the slit to see who was at the door. A short man wearing a top hat stood outside, it could only be the mayor. The vest and dress coat he wore were clean and matched his pants, all a soft grey like his hat.

Slipping the bolt to open the door, I greeted the man with a Colt in one hand. It was probably the mayor but no sense taking a chance. The man almost fell over when he saw the pistol leveled at him. His owlish eyes blinked wildly behind the spectacles perched on his nose. There was intelligence in them under the fear, though right at that moment the fear was most noticeable.

"Deputy I am Mayor Kelso, welcome to Cartersville." His voice was formal and carried the weight of his office. The shaking tone might not have been what he wanted. The man studied me closely, it wasn't in a bad way. I. Watched his eyes trace the scar but that was normal. His gaze was trying to understand some mystery. He seemed to come to a conclusion and grinned. I had no idea why he was grinning but didn't worry about it overly much.

"Nice place ya got here, you send my message?"

"I did, not one minute after Miss Gardner left. We hope you're going to help make it a peaceful town or at least deal with some of the problems." He didn't like my directness but that wasn't my problem. "I understand you have Baxter and the sheriff locked up?"

"I do, figure Carter will be a long before too long. Baxter was supposed to be bringing your school marm out to his place." I smiled at the man's surprised look. "Figure he'll show up after a while wondering what happened to his pet killer."

"He was supposed to do what? That doesn't sound right. Carter maybe many things but assault or harm a woman? No that's not possible." The man looked shocked at the idea of Carter doing something like that. Then the last part registered and the fear took over again. His eyes darted around like Carter would ride up at any moment. "Well, I've sent your telegram. Please let me know if you need anything else."

Watching the heavy man walk back down the boardwalk made me frown. Any faster and he would have been running. He would only do what I asked if it didn't put him at risk. What did make me smile was Bess standing in the doorway of the eatery grinning at me. She was holding a double-barreled shotgun by her side. It was mostly hidden in her skirts but I could see it sticking out just a little. She would back my play, something about that woman just wouldn't bend. Tipping my hat to her before walking back into office, carefully latching the door behind me. The only thing left to think about was if Carter would arrive before lunch or after.

I sat sipping coffee for another hour before going to tend to the prisoners. I swapped out the buckets giving them fresh water and a clean slop buckets. They both bitched and moaned but for the most part did the same thing I was. Waited to see what would happen next. We got our answer around three in the afternoon. The sound of horses coming up Main Street echoed around. I figured it was either Carter or his hands coming to find out what was going on.

With a flick the barrels snapped closed on the shotgun. My thumbs locked both hammers back and I swapped it with the other one beside the door. After locking back those hammers I got ready to meet the local boss. They pulled up out front and my ears caught the creak of a buggy mixed in with the horses. So, the big man himself had come to deal with me. When I heard the first steps on the wooden planks outside I opened the door. My first meeting with the infamous Carter had arrived.

"Figure you'd be Carter." I said casually with both barrels pointed at the man.

Too say he was surprised by my greeting would be an understatement. He gapped like a fish for a minute before he managed to speak. This was a man that didn't like surprises and I wasn't the kind any man liked. He was tall, easily a couple of inches taller than me but age and a few years of easy life had packed some weight around his middle. I could still see the strength that had claimed this land in the way he moved. This man was no office manager. This was a wolf and I was pissing on his den. Powerful muscles played under the soft layers and every one of them was tense.

"Who the hell are you?" He blustered. Mind you his hands didn't go near the Remington he wore in a cross-draw holster. A couple of the men behind him seemed to think about it though.

"Mister you better tell your boys to give up on drawing them hog legs. Both hammers are back so even if they shoot me you'll be a deadman. Likely reduced to a fine red mist at this range." I said it calmly but there was ice in my words. He recognized the wolf facing him as one of his own kind and made the smart choice.

"No one move, he's right I'll die if any of you shot him." The man had regained his composure now and gave orders like someone born to it. "Deputy, my name is Jake Carter, what's the meaning of this?"

"Your imitation law man has been removed from office, Baxter's in the cell with him." I didn't say anymore, knowing his next words would get what I wanted.

"I need to see Baxter, he takes care of my home here in town. If the man has broken the law I expect he'll need a lawyer."

"That's fine, just hand over that Remington and I'll take you in to see him."

"Sir I'll have you know I am an upstanding citizen. The very idea that you would feel it necessary to disarm me speaks to your lack of understanding."

"Understand this, if you want in there it will be as an unarmed citizen."

"Very well." He went to reach for it and I stopped him.

"Nope, you an me will got inside. I'll close the door and you can give it to me then."

"Fine!" He huffed indignantly, then turned to his men. "You all wait here if I'm not back in their minutes, do what you have to."

I stepped back and to the right, giving him enough room to pass me. The shotgun never wavered, even as I kicked the door closed and threw the lock. The noise made him jump a bit but he didn't turn around.

"Use your left hand and set that Remington on the desk. I'm going to search you once that's done. So just keep those hands above your head." Swapping the shotgun for my colt before stepping behind the man. He tensed but didn't fight me as I searched him. I took a knife and a holdout pistol from his pocket. It was pure luck that I accidentally brushed his sleeve and noticed the metal under the jacket.

"Gambler's rig?" I'd heard about them but never seen one.

"Yes." His shoulders slumped a little when he admitted it.

"Keep your back to me and slip off the coat." When he did I studied the machine strapped to his arm. It had a neat little slide that held a derringer, the slide stopped just short of his wrist. "Unbuckle it and set in on the desk."

He grumbled but did as instructed, when he was done I told him to head through the door. As soon as he opened the door Baxter started talking, the sheriff just sat there looking glum. The man knew he was done no matter how this played out. I'd picked up the shot gun again, and used it to wave the men back from the door. When they were all at the back of the cell facing the wall I opened the door and motioned for Carter to step in.

"I don't need to go in, I just wanted to see my man."

"You misunderstand, you're under arrest right along with them. Charged with aiding in the murder of a deputy marshal."

The big man started to spin faster than I thought he could but the butt of the shotgun ended his spin. It also sent him stumbling back into the cell, which worked out nicely if I do say so myself. A swift kick shut the door and I locked it before Baxter had done more then try and catch his boss. Now all I had to do was let the ten or so hands waiting outside know their boss wasn't coming back.

Walking toward the front door I picked up the shotgun by the door and set it back with the stock up. It would give me a bit more speed if I had to grab it or it could fall over and shoot off my legs. I figured it was a 70-30 split on how it would work out. Swinging the door open I stood in the doorway facing the men, no one moved. It's amazing how looking down those two barrels made people awfully careful about moving.

"Well boys your boss decided to move in for a while. Sorry to say he was so broken hearted by Baxter's predicament that he feels obliged to stay an comfort the man." I grinned at the shocked looks that showed up on their faces. "Figure it'll be a few days before the jail wagon gets here. What that means for you is simple. Stay out of my town."

The declaration was greeted with stunned looks all around. After a few second one of the more intellectual types decided to voice his objection. They'd elected him to the job by not moving first. It always amazed me how the smart ones never managed to beat the fools to take charge of a situation.

"You can't run us outta town, this 'ere is our town." I was truly amazed at his lack of understanding.

"No son, this ain't yours or Carters. It's part of the territory of Colorado. That makes it part of the United States, that means I'm the law here. Now I'll give you this, I can't or don't want to hurt the businesses here in town. So, here's what I'm gonna do. Ten minutes from now there will be a firearms ban on anyone within the town limits. If I catch anyone carrying a gun on their person or saddle within town limits they'll be arrested. They'll be held for three days and pay a fine of twenty-five dollars." I looked at the ten men arrayed in front of me and finished the thought. "That means y'all have ten minutes to disarm or get out of town."

"That ain't right!" One of them cried. "How we opposed ta get from the ranch ta here unarmed?"

"Not my concern boys. Nine minutes."

"What if'n we don't?"

"Arrest you." I smiled knowing what was coming next.

"An if we don't wanna be arrested." The young one in the back seemed to be the slow one.

"If you resist arrest that don't leave me much choice." I swung the shotgun toward the kid and watched the sweat trickle down his pale forehead. "I'll kill you. Eight minutes."

"Forty and found ain't worth dying far." One of the older punchers said as he spun his mount and headed out of town.

That broke them, one by one they turned galloping out of town. By my guess there was still four minutes left when they cleared the last building. Two of them had jumped off at the saloons, probably telling them what was going on. Just when

I started walking that way they came racing out followed by five more men. They all mounted and rode out of town. I knew there was still probably one or two more in the saloons, might as well deal with those hard cases now.

CHAPTER 15

I made it most of the way down Main Street when two men walked out of the Lazy Ace. It was obvious they had no plans to leaving their guns or town. Probably also planned on killing me and freeing Carter. It wasn't unexpected, as a matter of fact I was waiting for it to happen. The herd being gone didn't mean all the gun hands had left. A big spread like his would always have a few that stayed at the ranch. They were a necessary evil for most spreads, the law just couldn't be everywhere and rustlers were an ever-present danger.

"Hey law dog, gonna take us without that scattergun?" It was a challenge, one he figured I wouldn't accept. The look on his face was priceless when I leaned the shotgun against the railing. Smiling while thumbing the thongs off my colts before stepping into the street. This wasn't how he'd planned it and his steps faltered for a second. His partner didn't seem phased, I recognized him at a glance. Matter of fact I recognized both men.

The loud mouth was Phil Bunker, wanted for robbery, assault and back shooting a man in Texas. His smaller frame and left-handed draw made him stand out in my memory. The man was no slouch with a pistol but was hell on wheels with a blade if you believed the stories. His demeanor wasn't a surprise, he had a reputation for his mouth and blade then his pistol.

The quiet one was Edmund Vayo, aka Eddie Peppers. He was wanted for murder in Arizona Territory. He confronted a gambler one night and the two punchers next to the man stood up when the gambler did. According to witnesses they'd only meant to move out of the area, their timing had just been off. Eddie wasn't one to take chances, he'd killed all three. The problem was the two punchers were unarmed. If he'd stayed and faced it most likely he could have beat the charge. There was just one problem with that idea and most people knew the story. One of the punchers had been a rich man's kid, he was the one offering the reward.

"Ed this ain't the fight you want." I said facing Phil. They were still too far for pistol work so I had a minute still.

"You know me?" He paused to study me for a minute. I could tell when his eyes noticed the scar, it always marked me. "Chance?"

"Got it in one." I smiled at the man.

We had crossed paths a few years back and somehow ended up on the same side. I was after a kidnapper and rapist. Ed had been after the same man for the same things. The difference was I wanted the bounty. He wanted the man dead and didn't care about the money. He knew the soiled dove the man had raped, she'd been a childhood friend. Ed made him dead, I collected the bounty and ended up paying him half of it. He wasn't a bad guy, just caught in a bad situation. Most everyone knew the bounty on him wasn't backed by the law.

"I took his money." It was all he said and I understood. You take a man's money, you do the job.

"You know this guy Eddie?" Phil's nasally voice interrupted. He sounded full of confidence, half of that was likely whiskey.

"Ever heard of a bounty hunter named Chance? No Chance or Deadman's Chance?" Ed asked without taking his eyes off me, he had stopped walking though.

"Nope." Phil's sneered at me. "Don't care other then I'll be able ta say I killed him."

Phil never noticed Ed had stopped walking. It was his way of telling me this would be one on one. He was also volunteering Phil to go first without telling him that. The man was so focused on me he never noticed. I dipped my head slightly to Eddie. He was a good man but would follow the rules we all lived by. He had taken Carters money, that meant he'd do the job. I understood that and wasn't offended.

"Ready to die Deputy?" Phil's annoying voice broke my train of thoughts. He was squaring up about twenty-five feet from me.

"You called this dance." Was all I said. After that I stayed focused on him. Waiting for the twitch or blink that would give him away.

We all had them and knew it was the signal. Phil's was a slight dip with his left shoulder, one I'd seen on most lefties. His Smith and Wesson made it halfway out of his holster when the first of two 44-40's punched through his breastbone. The first slightly flattened lead bullet exploded his heart, killing him instantly. The second round slipped past his ribs and cut through his left lung like it didn't exist. A sharp hiss escaped his lips then his body collapsed into a pile of dust and blood. Dead before his pistol fell to the ground.

Ed was walking forward slowly, giving me plenty of time to drop the two spent cartridges and reload. He watched me warily but there was enough history between us that he knew I wouldn't shoot him without a chance. About the time I dropped the still warm colt back into my holster he stopped. Standing about ten feet to the right of Phil's corpse, the smirk I recognized as friendly split his face.

"Amigo, there is one more who will challenge you from the ranch. Probably tomorrow, he doesn't like the night. Names Blake, you don't know him. Young kid likes the sound of his voice."

"The young ones always do." I grinned back at the man.

"I hate to remind you but you're one of those young ones." He laughed slightly.

"Ain't like them."

"Me thinks you protest too much." His laughter was honest and not meant to be an insult.

"Fair enough." I joined him in laughing at myself. "For what it's worth I'd rather have ya switch sides."

"If wishes were horses amigo." His poetic side was showing and it reminded me of nights talking around a fire. "We both know that wouldn't work out, even had I not taken his money."

"I could work that part out, told you that before. We both know it's not really the law after you."

"Still took the man's money."

"Fair enough, I'll see you buried proper if it falls that way." I knew there was no more putting this off. Not liking something had nothing to do with thing like this. We both had obligations to keep.

"Same amigo."

"You lead the dance my friend."

He moved without almost nothing giving up his play. The only warning I got was a slight tightening around his eyes. My Colt spit flame just a hair before his but it was enough. The impact of my round on his right arm threw his aim off. His bullet whistled by my ear instead of punching through my skull. His pistol fell from numb fingers and he staggered back.

"You aimed for my arm?" He asked through gritted teeth, the surprise overcoming the pain for a second.

"Hell no, you're too good for that. I had to rush my shot." It was the truth. There was no way I'd risk a shot like that on someone as good as him.

"Amigo if I had to lose I think this way is acceptable." He

laughed.

It was cut off when he suddenly collapsed to the ground. I had been reloading, hoping he would pass out before he died. Quickly jamming the Colt back into its holster before dashing toward him. I spotted the mayor peeking out from a doorway on my way to him.

"Get a doctor!" I yelled.

The short man dashed around the corner moving as fast as he could. With a quick twist my bandanna was wrapped above the still bleeding wound. A trick I'd seen years ago flashed into my mind. Using the barrel of his colt to twist the knot tight on his arm, cutting off the blood. If it was left like that too long he'd probably lose the arm but it beat bleeding out in the street. Picking him up only made me grunt a little then I started off the way the mayor had run. About the time I turned the corner an old man was stepping out of his house following the mayor. When he saw me coming he stepped back to hold the door open.

"First room on the left deputy, just put him on the table." He followed me into the room.

The man wasted no time talking, with a pair of scissors he cut off the sleeve. I waited for his say so to untwist the bandana. He nodded and my hand twisted releasing the knot. I kept the pistol and stepped back giving the man room to work. He was carefully peeling back my bandanna to check the wound. He grunted when he could make it out though the blood then quickly rolled up his sleeves. A woman came in from another door carrying a steaming bowl, she set it on the table beside the bed and turned to me.

"Out, let him work." She shooed me out of the room without any more discussion.

"Wait." The doctor spoke up before I reached the door. "Do you want me to save him just so he can face the gallows?"

"No, he was doing what Carter paid him for. I won't charge him, can't charge someone whose shared my fire that many times."

"Good I hate wasting my time." He said gruffly after studying me for a minute. He was trying to wrap his mind around what I said but eventually gave up. "Go, I'll send word when he can be moved but it won't be for a few days at least. If he makes it, you did well to stop the blood but he still lost a lot."

"Get undertaker to verify the dead man is Phil Bunker, there's a $200 reward on him." I told the mayor as we walked out and started walking back to the sheriff's office. "Have him bring the paperwork and his belongings to the office."

"I will Deputy, is there anything else you need?" I could tell he didn't want to be part of this but he had called us. That put him on the hook to at least some degree.

"No, according to Ed there's one more that'll be in tomorrow looking for me. He might have a back shooter with him but I'll deal with that." I stepped onto the boardwalk as the man turned into his shop.

"Thank you Deputy." He had said it softly but I appreciated it anyway.

"Have lunch over in a bit." Bess called out before I stepped into the office. "Figure there's three now?"

"Yes ma'am." I smiled before tipping my hat to her.

"Knock that ma'am nonsense off. It'll be over shortly." Even from across the street I could see the upturned corners of her mouth.

"Yes ma'am." I said as she turned her back to walk back inside.

CHAPTER 16

Walking back into the office I took a seat behind the desk after refilling my coffee. All I could really do now was wait. Wait for lunch, wait for the coming attack, wait for the jail wagon and wait on to hear about Ed's condition. You'd think hunting had taught me patience but somehow the lessons never took. Guess this was going to be another learning experience for me. It wasn't too long until one thing came to its expected end. Bess knocked on the door carrying four trays. She set the top one on the desk before turning to the door. Somehow I managed not to fumble unlocking it too badly.

"Very clever being smart mouthed to the person feeding you." She laughed.

"You might have a point there Bess." My grin said there wouldn't be any regrets on my part.

"Ought to remember that boy." She laughed while setting down the trays then stepping back out of the room. Carter couldn't let that happen without saying something.

"Bess you better be real careful about whose side you're on. I have a long memory."

"Carter I ain't ever given a damn 'bout you." She turned to lock eyes with the man "Your men don't pay folks, they just take an figure you'll deal with it. You never do, that's the real reason this little kingdom of yours don't grow. You robbing it blind before it can even take root."

It seemed to shock the man, because he drew back like he'd

been slapped. The look on his face wasn't that of an insulted man. It was like someone had just handed him the answer to a question he didn't know he had. I admit to some amusement watching the man realize that the town was failing because of him. It looked like no one had ever pointed this out to him. I couldn't help myself.

"Never crossed your mind did it? All the supplies that you just take have to be bought somewhere. Someone else has to pay for them. These folks paying your bills is why they can't grow." The man's eyes had glassed over, he really was stunned by the realization. I could just make out his mumbled response.

"Never thought about it. Why don't anyone tell me?"

That when I realized it, something I should have thought about long before now. The man was tough, probably tough as nails. He could fight bandits, Indians and all kinds of misfortune. He understood cattle, drought, disease, and managing his ranch. None of that meant he understood anything about how to build a town. It made perfect sense when I really looked at it.

He'd likely come out here alone or with a few pards. Carved out his place with knife and gun, likely marked its boundaries in his own blood. That took common sense and grit. Knowing how to help grow a town? That wasn't something he would have needed. Almost every puncher I knew was well read but most of them tended toward tall tales or things they needed to know. Ask a puncher to identify a plant that could make a cow sick, no problem. Ask him how to create a balanced tax system that encouraged growth in a community? He'd look at you like a third eye had just appeared on your face.

I looked at the man with new eyes, suddenly understanding him and his behavior completely. None of this was out of cruelty, it was done out of honest ignorance. He might not be the vile killer we'd been led to believe.

I bought the flash in Baxters eyes when he recognized the

change. However this all worked out there wouldn't be a place for him in Carters world. Not now that he was starting to realize his own failure. One of them would be dead if I left them to figure this out. I wouldn't take money on either man, they were both wolves but one had just lost his place in the pack. They needed to separate anyway, now was as good a time as any.

I put one tray in each of the empty cells. Two already had clean water and slop buckets. I left the door open before walking backing to get the shotgun before opening the cell. A Greener tended to stop all but the most foolish ideas. It was the preferred solution of law men across the country with good reason. I put Baxter in the far cell with the sheriff between him and Carter. After they were all locked back up I brought coffee for each man before closing the door.

Lunch was fried catfish with hush puppies and collard greens. It was easily one of the best meals I'd had recently, that woman could cook. I thought about Carter while I was eating. There was a lot at stake and more than one unanswered question. If he went to jail this town would probably fail. He was the biggest source of money coming into the town. Not only did he quite literally own the land but it was his ranch and hands who moved the economy. Being convicted wouldn't change the ownership but it would still hurt the ranch. Even if he had a good ramrod someone still needed to run the business end. If he was hung someone decent could take it over, then maybe it would survive. I'd have to ask the mayor about it, or maybe ask the man himself.

I knew from training that as a deputy, if the marshal approved I could lessen the charge a man would face. Especially if he helped us with testimony. I didn't know how Reese would be about it, or even if Carter would. It felt like I'd have to find out if this town wanted to survive this.

A loud banging on the door brought me out of my thoughts.

When I peeked through the slit Miss Gardner was standing there. She was tapping her foot impatiently and glaring back at me. Two thoughts ran through my mind instantaneously. My first thought was of course, damn she is beautiful. Followed closely with the second. Did I want another fight? Because it was obvious that's why she was here. Even knowing I'd be receiving another tongue lashing made no difference. I'd take it just to hear her talk.

"What can I help you with Miss Gardener?" I asked opening the door.

"You can tell me what your plan is!" She snapped.

"No ma'am I can't." I replied calmly. Why was this woman so mad all the time? It just didn't make sense.

"Why because I'm a woman?" I maybe be a clueless deputy but even I wasn't dumb enough to fall for that.

"No ma'am, it's just none of your business." I smiled at the flush that colored her cheeks. "I won't be telling anyone."

"So, you don't trust the stupid townsfolk, the ones who could help you?"

"Prefer they don't actually, less likely for them to get killed." It was my job to risk my life not theirs. Still, she just seemed to get madder the more I talked.

"You sir are a stubborn prideful fool." She stomped her foot to emphasize the point. It just made her more beautiful to me, the way her eyes flashed almost made me smile. Her body also moved in fascinating ways when she did that.

"It's been said before ma'am." Judging from the look on her face that wasn't the right answer.

She spun on her heels without another word and once again stormed down the boardwalk toward the mayors. If this kept up they were going to have to replace boards. The image of her legs punching through the boards made me blush but

I couldn't take my eyes off her. That woman was simply stunning, I also had to admit to being just a little afraid of her. Nothing would ever come of my infatuation, not for someone like me. Women like her did not socialize with scared face half wild bounty hunters.

Miss Gardner

That man was so infuriating! He was so stubborn and it was going to get him killed. Something about that idea made her gasp, it was like a sharp pain stabbing her in the chest. Why was she so concerned about that man? She could admit he was attractive but that didn't explain it. Ever since their first meeting she had felt a fire start in her but it kept turning to anger. That wasn't completely true, at times it turned to... her cheeks burned with shame at the thought and she quickly stopped that one of thought.

She had been headed to argue with the mayor about helping the lone deputy. That was a bad idea and a waste of time, the mayor for all his qualities was not a fighter. Turning sharply deciding to walk across the street to talk to Bess. Maybe another woman could help her understand what it was about this man. That and Bess never seemed to be bothered by her sharp tongue. Mostly the older woman just thought she was funny for some reason. It helped that she knew better then to turn that tongue toward Bess. That woman brooked no foolishness.

"Bess?" She called into the eatery.

"Back here Mary." She was in the kitchen of course. "Here 'bout the deputy?"

"How did you know?" She was stunned that the older woman knew.

"Poor girl, ya can't even put down that temper to see it." Bess laughed but not in a mean way, it was almost sympathetic.

"See what?" Mary fell into a chair near the counter where Bess was kneading bread.

"That you love him." The words stung like being slapped, instantly her mind denied it.

"I most certainly do not! The man looks and acts like a barbarian." Even as the words left her mouth she knew it for the lie it was. Even the scar down added to his good looks in her opinion. Those piercing blue eyes inflamed something deep inside her as well, something she'd long since thought dead.

"Deny it all you want girl but I can see it." Bess paused her work and turned soulful black eyes on her. "Girl if you don't put that temper down you'll miss what most of us dream of finding. A good man who loves you, someone who'll do everything he can to protect and provide for you."

"But …." Suddenly the last part of what Bess said hit her like a brick. "You think he loves me? But I've been nothing but mean to him."

"That's true girl, don't think you've said a kind word to him since he rescued you. Don't change the fact that he's in love with you. Has been since he first saw you."

Mary had to think, had she really never thanked him? No, she hadn't, instead she'd slapped him twice. Oh god her temper was going to be the death of her. She had always known that but the idea that it could cost her him? That terrified her more then she could admit.

She had always thought the right man would be riding in a beautiful carriage drawn by white horses. He would be dressed in the latest fashion and sweep her off her feet. It was a fairy tale, she knew that all to well. Still the idea of a dust covered deputy being the man she had always dreamt of didn't fit. Bess had to be wrong. Even as the thought crossed her mind she knew Bess was right.

"How could that be? Not that it matters to me be but how

could he love me."

"Girl I'll tell you this just once. Lie to yourself if you want but don't do it to me. I like you Mary, even admire that fearless temper but you're too smart to believe that lie." Bess's gentle smile softened the blow. "I can see you care for the man. Its just as plain to see he's fallen for you. The problem is both of you are too afraid to open your mouths."

"What do you mean?" Mary wasn't ready to admit it but she wouldn't argue with Bess. Mostly because the woman was right, acknowledging that did mean she had to say it.

"He don't think someone like you could even like him, much less love him. That man's had a tough life, even tougher than you think girl. I don't know the story but I can see the scars an I don't mean just the ones on his body. That man's known pain in ways most can't even dream up, an he's walked though it without becoming hateful. You can't help but trip over your temper, part of that's fueled by your fear. You're afraid of a man taking away your independence. Afraid loving someone will give them power over you."

"But it would." Mary protested weakly.

"Girl it never has and never will. Being part of something always makes you stronger." Bess stopped her work again and turned to face her. "When my Thomas died in the war, that weakened me. Losing him stole my independence more than marrying him ever did. Before he died? The two of us as a team were tougher than any one person. Our farm was wiped out twice, once by a twister an once by fire. It took both of us to survive and rebuild it. Just ain't no way one person could've done it."

"But you're so strong now." Mary tried to say but Bess cut her off.

"No girl, I'm not. You just don't see me late at night when I feel alone, more alone than you can imagine girl. You don't see the empty spot that losing him left inside me. I'd give everything to have him by my side again, especially on those long cold nights. That man knew how to keep me warm." A wicked grin split her face and Mary could feel the blush spread across hers.

"Oh, Bess what do I do?" Mary's mind gave up the fight and let her heart win.

She'd known it already but was so afraid to admit it, to risk everything for a man. Her pulse sped up when she saw him come into the jail that first day. Not because of fear, it was just his presence that lit a flame in her. She still remembered looking up from the floor and seeing him through the bars. He looked like warrior angel standing there with the light behind him. She could still see those blue eyes when they caught hers. Her heart had sung out in joy, but was that love?

"You let him love you girl, that's all you have to do. Well, that an stop yelling at the poor boy." She laughed returning to her work.

Was that it? Didn't she need to be demure and act like a proper lady? Her mother had tried to push her off on every wealthy man's son in Chicago before she finally fled. Her constant critique of Mary's behavior had driven her to go in the opposite direction. The more she tried to make her a proper lady in society, the less lady like she acted. Now she realized those habits were haunting her even here, over a thousand miles away.

Her mother and father were probably still looking for her. Not because they cared, that just wasn't their way. No it would be because she could be another rung in their social climb. They had never made a secret of their expectations. Go to school, meet the right kind of man and marry him. Of course, the right kind of man meant wealthy and from the right family. They would absolutely lose their mind if she married some frontier lawman.

Bess just kept working but out of the corner of her eye she watched the young woman sitting beside her. She knew the turmoil that was going through her, recognized it from when she'd met Thomas. He had been just a poor sod busting farmer, her blacksmith father had not approved. Luckily for her the amazing woman who had been her mother understood. She reminded her husband of when they met, of how they'd both just known.

It still took a full year of courting before her father grudgingly consented. Those fifteen years with him had been the best of her life. She often wondered why she had kept going after losing him. What was it that had called her to this town, looking at the girl she thought maybe it was fates hand after all. A soft smile crept on her face when she saw the girls face change, she was starting to let herself feel it. Thinking about Percy, maybe she should take her own advice. The nights were still awfully cold.

CHAPTER 17

The rest of the day passed peacefully. The Doctor sent word that Ed would make it but was still unconscious and probably would be for a few days. He'd lost a lot of blood but there wouldn't be any permanent damage to the arm. No one else from the ranch came into town. I even walked a patrol that evening before the sunset. Said hello to a few of the shop owners and tipped my hat to the ladies going about the last of the days business. Mayor Kelso joined me for a cup of coffee after I was done but he didn't have anything new to tell me.

I liked the man, he seemed driven but not in a bad way. He was ambitious but not in a personal way. The man wanted to build this town, wanted it to be his legacy. With plans for not only his business but the others in town I had to admire the drive. He was prepared for the growth and even welcomed it. After showing me a map he paid to have made there was no denying it. It laid out the potential growth with a good layout for traffic and even a railroad depot. It seemed like a bit of a dream but he argued that if Carter released some of the land for farmers and other small ranches it would work.

When Bess brought dinner over she lingered for a while over a cup of coffee. Grimacing when she informed me that my coffee was terrible, it made me like the woman more. I told her some of my story and she shared some of hers. The woman had grit, there was no denying that. I admitted my disappointment regarding the arguments with Miss Gardner. She smiled knowingly and assured me that everything would eventually work. There was no doubt she knew more but wasn't willing to share it. All she said was to be patient and grow some backbone. The last bit didn't make sense to me. How was my backbone part of the problem?

I still needed to collect the trays and take care of the evening chores. When I went back there to do it Carter asked me for a private word. The man wanted to talk to me about something and it must be important. He even offered to help with the slop buckets if I would spare him some time. Baxter didn't like it, that more than anything got my attention and made my decision. Before I let him out to help me I locked the front door and made sure everything was secure. My curiosity was piqued but not enough to make me let my guard down.

We didn't talk much while working but the look on his face when I offered him a cup of coffee afterward was pure appreciation. He sat across from me at the desk holding his cup, the man's face was creased in thought. He was obviously thinking about what to say while staring into his coffee. I let him take the time, there was no rush. When he looked up I could see a change come over him.

"Was Bess right do you think?" There was real pain in his voice. I recognized it, the beginning of recognizing how wrong he might have been.

"I think she was but I don't think what's been done was out of evil intent." I answered honestly.

"You don't think I'm a bad man?" There was hope in his voice now.

"Oh, you're a bad man in the same way a lot of men are. Especially those that came out here ahead of everyone else. You had to be." Then I thought about it and changed a word or two. "Maybe bad isn't the right word, maybe ruthless and hard. You had to be, otherwise you'd be dead."

"How do you see it so plainly and I couldn't? I honestly thought there was nothing wrong with what I did. This is all mine. Bought with my blood and sweat. I let those thoughts tell me it had to be held in a grip so tight I almost strangled it. That sense of mine took control, never thought about the rest of the folks."

"You're what, probably late forties?" I asked.

"Nearest I can tell forty-five, give or take." He acknowledged.

"You came out here at what twenty or younger?"

"Bought the land from a Don just before '48 when Mexico signed the treaty. Me and two partners knew him from buying cattle. We all knew he'd lose the land when they signed if he didn't sell. The price was cheap an as Americans we could keep it. Built our first cabin in 49. I was seventeen."

"What happened to them?"

"Chuck got killed by the Arapaho in '58, bought Jake out in 59. Fool lost it all on a mine during the gold rush and died in a bar fight. They're both buried at the ranch." He grimaced at the memories. "What's any of that got to do with it?"

"I'm guessing you've mixed in other breeds now but back then your herd was longhorns?"

"Now it's mostly Herefords, not as mean and more meat on 'em. Course that means they need more tending but we have plenty of graze."

"That's what you know. I could ask you anything about cattle or punchers and you'd have the answer before I finished the question." He nodded his agreement so I continued. "You also know how to deal with Indians, outlaws, probably even the military. You can barter with cattle buyers for the best price any day. Probably even deal with miners since I'm sure you drove beefs to the mines."

"All true enough, those early drives to the mines were how we built this place. Hell, I met Kelso at the mines up north, he was closing up shop and looking for a new place to build." I could see the memories again wash through the man's eyes.

"What you don't know is how to be civilized. It wasn't a luxury you could afford while carving this place out of the wild and uncut." That stopped him in his tracks. I watched the flash of anger, his pride wanting to argue with me. Then I saw the realization hit so I continued. "You had to sacrifice that part of you to build this place. Civilized men die out here even now, it only takes one mistake. None of them would have made it back then, much less build anything."

"I never thought about that." He nodded starting to understand my point.

"When you're the one who leads folks into wild country you have to be a part of that country. You have to be meaner then the country you're claiming. If you're not it'll kill you, the lands got no forgiveness or mercy in it. Yours is a story that's been repeated in this country time and again." I smiled and met his eyes. "Won't be too long an this country will have no use for either of us."

"What do we do?" He was genuinely asking. This ornery old bull was asking a kid for advice. Maybe there was hope for him and by proxy me in the long run.

"We adapt, get tamed down back into civilized folks. There ain't another way, it's either that or die." It was on me now, I had to tell him what I saw in my future. "I'm a new marshal, just finished school. This is actually my first mission."

"Hard to picture." He barked out in a laugh.

"Still true, I've been a bounty hunter since I was fifteen. Before that I was punching cattle down on the Texas border. Becoming a marshal was part of being tamed. Most of the bounties I brought in were dead, have a reputation from it. There wasn't a law or a way I had to act, the poster said dead or alive. Dead was just easier. The only thing that kept questions from being asked was that I went after the worst of the worst.

Men far worse than Phil Bunker and his ilk."

"Bunker wasn't that bad." He tried to defend, but when he read the dodger I set in front of him all the color left his face.

"He was, but to you he was a useful type of bad man, controllable mostly. Truth is he wasn't the type I would go after, bad but not bad enough. Most of the ones I chased were so bad they couldn't have worked for you. They would have tried to kill you and take your place. Some part of them was gone, that part that let them live around folks and not take everything they could grab."

"I've met a few of those, buried most of them." He knew the type I was talking about. All of us did, anyone who dealt with their own problems eventually met men like that. This close to the nations he'd certainly crossed paths with some.

"I'm trying to become civilized, because I want to be part of what's coming. Statehood isn't far off and things are going to keep changing. I don't want to be left behind like the bleached bones of the dead."

It was the first time I'd admitted my reasons for accepting the badge to anyone but this man would understand them. He would know exactly what I meant, at least he might. Bess had opened his eyes a little and he was smart enough to see it. If he didn't change there would be nothing for him. Eventually someone would kill him or the state would just come take his land.

"It's too late." He sighed with resignation. "I'm already arrested and likely to be hung."

"Maybe. Maybe not." It was time for the offer and I had a strong feeling he'd take it. "Did you tell Baxter to kill the marshal?"

"No, even I know thats a dumb move. Marshals never forget."

"What about the sheriff?"

"He got busted out of a shanty town when the dust dried up. I hired him because he was controllable but he ain't a killer."

"What was his part in the Deputy's death?"

"To shut up about it. The only thing he really did was listen to the folks around town and tell me about potential problems." After a moment's thought he added another piece of the puzzle. "He did take the body to Denver and gave a statement to the Marshal. I told him to return the body and leave, he decided to spin a tale for your boss."

"That'll probably be a charge but I think he'll be alright." I grinned and admitted the truth. "I mostly arrested you and him to get both of you out of play. Doubt those aiding charges would stick in a court anyway. Anything you can truly be charged with?"

"Not more than locally, a real sheriff could probably charge me with a few things." He snapped his fingers as a thought occurred to him. "A western union could charge me with tapping their line."

"Yeah I'd get rid of that." I laughed. "It doesn't intercept and stop anything does it?"

"No just listens and warns me. Mostly about rustlers or things along the trail."

"You didn't hear about me sending one to the marshal?"

"Not a peep, the old boy I got listening must have missed it." He laughed. "I did hire him cause he got fired by them."

"Good help is hard to find." We shared a grin before I continued. "I'm gonna keep you locked up until I can talk to my boss but I doubt you'll be charged. Might need a statement about the deputy being shot and who did it. What you do after that is up to you."

"Think I need to just let the mayor be a real Mayor."

"You ever see the plans he has for this place?"

"No, didn't know anything about it." He studied me curiously.

"I don't know much but the man has a plan. It'll require you giving up control and selling some land." I watched the man cringe at the idea but he didn't immediately say no. I'd call that progress. "I think though, if you do at least some of it, you could have a real nice town here. The mark you'll make doing that is going to outlast both of us."

"How in the hell did you learn this? About becoming civilized again I mean." He finally asked. I knew the question had been there for a while now.

"An old timer at the academy. He told me that's what I was doing. That old man had seen the world grow and learned to change with it. For whatever reason he taught me how to do it. I'm just sharing the education." I grinned wolfishly over my coffee knowing the man was taking every word to heart.

"Must 'ave seen something in you. You really think I could make something here?" Now he was really interested. The idea of leaving a true mark on the country wasn't a small thing. For men like him it was part of what drove them to come west, there was a desire to help create something. The price they paid for that was forgetting how to live in that creation.

"I do. Talk to Kelso when this all gets settled."

"I'm gonna have to talk to the entire town if I ain't in jail when this is done. I'm going to have to account for what's been done in my name. Best way to do that is own it an try to balance the sheet."

"From what I can see they'll listen. These folks want to build something. You may not have been overly friendly but you've kept the real outlaws out. That makes it easier, I've seen towns where they took over. Cleaning that up usually kills a town."

"Can't stand outlaws, not real ones anyway. Violent men I understand, the country almost requires them for now. But theft, rustling, rape I won't tolerate."

"What was your plan for the school marm then? Baxter said he was bringing her to you."

"What?" If he was lying it was a damn convincing one. You can't fake the look of horror that crossed his face. The idea of it repulsed the man. "I don't know anything about that."

"That makes me a bit nervous. What the hell was he playing at then?"

Not far outside of town…

Where the hell was Baxter? That useless piece of shit dragged them out of the nations with the promise of an easy town. Now the four of them had been stuck out here in the woods for two weeks waiting. He was supposed to bring a woman and some whiskey today but hadn't showed up.

"Levar, tomorrow ride into town an find out where the hell he is." Craig's voice held just enough anger to rile up Levar.

"You ain't the boss round here old man."

The tall youth snapped, his lean shadow crouched by the fire. Levar was the youngest of the gang. At just eighteen he had killed four men, two of them in fair fights. The other two were done with a knife in the dark. There was also more than one small farm along his trail where everyone had died. Kids, women it didn't matter to him, the man was a cold-blooded killer despite his youth.

"No, he ain't but we need to know an you're the least likely to be recognized." Patty said, trying to keep the peace. The bickering got on his nerves. "Just the way it is, I'd happily go if'n it was safe."

Patty had been on the owl hoot trail with Craig since they met up in '66 after the war. Both men had fought for the south and lost everything. They had robbed, murdered and raped their way across the country since then. Each of them had high bounties and hadn't been able to go anywhere near a town for years. They were getting to that age where living in the nations or wild country was starting to wear on them. More than one conversation had been about retiring to Mexico or someplace further south. Patty heard some of the rebels had made it to Brazil and where building a place there.

"That's just cause I ain't old like you two!" Levar of course took it as an insult.

"Just go find out what's going on." Big Jacks voice resonated from where he lay across the fire.

He was another killer, half black and half Cherokee he hated everyone. At twelve he'd been left for dead outside of Baton Rouge. A local group of concerned citizens had tied him to a tree and whipped him to within an inch of his life. They stopped just short of murder thinking the swamps would finish the boy off. It hadn't and that mistake had cost those men everything. Jack had spent five years hunting them and their families one by one killing them all. Not just the men, he exterminated their family line. Each of the men had been found whipped to death after being gelded. Most folks didn't know he still carried the knife he used.

"Fine since y'all don't want too I'll find out. Fools probably in bed with some whore an forgot 'bout us." Levar finally conceded the argument.

They all knew this was how it would go. To a man they were tired of this and ready for some action. Baxter had promised a lot but hadn't delivered anything but a worse place to camp. The last time they'd talked he wanted them to wait even longer. Wait for this Cater to get the money from a herd that just left for the railhead. Craig doubted that would happen. Asking them to stay out here another two weeks was likely to get Baxter killed. Then they'd rob the town and fade back into the nations. Depending on what they heard tomorrow that might happen anyway.

CHAPTER 18

The morning arrived far too fast. After putting Carter back in his cell I'd laid awake on the cot for a while thinking before sleep took me. I still managed to get six hours of sleep which was almost a record for me lately. Unfolding from the cot, stretching out sore muscles, it had been a busy few days. After adding some wood to the stove then rinsing and refilling the coffee pot I sat down to wait. The sun was still just a soft light in the distance when I opened the door to get a breeze in the office. The flickering flame on the lamp created dancing shadows in the office.

Soon I was sipping coffee and enjoying a smoke while the town woke up around me. I could smell breakfast drifting over from the eatery. Bess would probably be bringing it over soon at least my stomach hoped so. She'd want to get that done before her normal business started. With any luck Blake wouldn't interrupt my meal. I'd surely appreciate if he waited until around ten, enough time to digest breakfast still with plenty of time before lunch. I hated killing a man to early, it always felt like it set a bad tone for the day.

Sure enough Bess was walking across the street just as the sun fully lit the town. Shadows from the buildings still draped the street in darkness, the sun was slowly painting the sky blue. Gradually the darkness shifted through the hues from deep purple to light blue. Watching the woman step lightly around horse apples made me smile. As simple as that was it said so much about her. There was no back up in her, nothing and no one would block her path. She was also the type of woman who willingly pitched in at any task. A good partner for anyone, someone who'd stand beside you against all comers. It made me wonder why she'd not re-married.

"Morning Bess." I said standing to hold the door for her.

"Deputy, how's your guests this morning?" She asked setting my tray on the desk.

"Let's do this then I'll tell ya." I smiled at her while opening the door to the cells. It didn't take long to get them fed and pass around some coffee. Bess was still waiting when I closed the door.

"So, what's so all fired important that I had ta wait to palaver? You know I have other people coming that expect their breakfast."

"I wanted you to know that your words probably saved this town." The surprise on her face was easy to read.

"What?"

"You chewing out Carter, it made the man realize what a fool he's been. I think once the smoke clears you might see a different man on the other side."

"Believe it when I see it." She said with a snort but there was a little nugget of hope in it. "I'll hope you're right, still ain't betting one it. That's all later, right now I need to get back to my kitchen."

"And I need to eat this beforc it gets cold." My eyes had zeroed in on the breakfast in front of me.

"See ya for lunch boy, don't die before then." She said walking out the door.

"Yes ma'am." I said while closing and locking the door behind her.

The morning ticked by at its own pace. After taking care of the chores around the office I started on the stack of ignored papers in a drawer. When my stomach finally stopped trying to unbuckle my belt I got up from the chair, heading out to do the morning rounds. Maybe the infamous Blake would make his appearance along the way.

I made it most of the way down Main before the man presented himself. He was walking down the center of the road looking every bit like he was posing for a dime novel. I'd seen his type before, dressed like what they thought a gun fighter should look like. All black and shining silver, wearing two guns in a rig that probably cost more than my horse. A trouble hunter who liked to brag about the men he killed. The type always annoyed me, they talked to much. I'd bet a double eagle there was notches cut into his nickel-plated Remingtons.

A heavy sigh escaped my lips in frustration, another youngster who'd die before learning anything. Leaning the scattergun against the wall of a saddlery I almost reached to check my Colts. Then I stopped, changing my mind. This wasn't about some dual of honor or some other ridiculous thing from a book. It wasn't even facing a man down over a bounty. This was about the law and it didn't support killing if it could be avoided. Stepping into a shadow I locked the hammers back on both barrels and waited. I didn't want to kill him but that didn't mean he felt the same. If he pushed me to it, I'd cut him in half.

He never looked my way, his eyes stayed focused on the sheriff's office. The arrogant grin on his face made me laugh. This damn fool would end up shot in the back and never know who'd killed him. He got ten feet past me before I stepped into the street behind him. There wouldn't be any fair fight here, not if there was any way to avoid it.

"I got a shotgun aimed straight at your back, don't think about moving."

He froze, no expecting this. It didn't line up with the showdown he'd been planning in his head. I was still closing the gap between us, taking advantage of his hesitation. Before he could start his mouth going the stock hit the back of his head. He dropped face own in the street like a felled tree. His head would hurt but he'd live, probably mad as hell but still alive. A couple of gasps escaped mouths behind me. Two men were standing outside the Lazy Ace watching the action. After taking Blake's guns and the knife he carried my feet turned toward them. The fools never thought to move, letting me get close enough for the shotgun work.

"Guess y'all thought I was kidding." They both looked surprised when I leveled both barrels at them. "Now move real slow like an drop those gun belts."

"We didn't..." I cut them off before they started with the excuses.

"You two were with the bunch yesterday. Unless your deaf ya heard me say there was a ban on firearms within the town limits. Either drop the belts or draw an die." Something in my tone must have convinced them I was serious. They both slowly dropped their rigs to the boardwalk.

"What now law dog?" The one on the right growled.

"Were going to walk down there an you two are going to pick up your pal. Then we're going to see how crowded a cell can get." I stepped behind them and slung their belts over my shoulder. "Strip that belt off him when ya get there. Just leave it where it falls."

They did exactly what I said and after holstering his pistols I threw his rig over my shoulder with the rest. They half carried; half dragged their buddy into the office. He was groaning by the time we got there. Probably just starting to come around when I told them to drop him on the floor. They went into the cell with the sheriff after I searched them. Each man had a few dollars and a pocketknife. They were just punchers who came in to watch the show.

"Three days and twenty-five dollars boys, get comfy."

"We ain't got no twenty-five dollars marshal." The older of the two admitted.

"We'll figure something out in three days, you two don't seem like hard cases, just hard headed." I said smiling as I locked the door. "Maybe your boss will stand for it."

"Ain't but two beds in here!" The other one protested.

"I'll get it sorted in a bit." I said closing the door and turning to the young man who was trying to figure what happened.

"How did I get...where am..." I could see it when the fog cleared and he reached for a gun that wasn't there.

"Up here Blake." When he looked up it was into two barrels of my shotgun. "What else you carrying? Just drop it on the floor."

"This ain't no way to face a man." He protested but didn't move.

"I'm not here for that, I'm here as a law man. You broke the law, I arrested you." The confusion on his face was amusing to watch. He just couldn't fathom how it had all gone so wrong. It was too far outside of what he expected.

"But you're supposed to..." I just shook my head at him.

"I'm supposed to enforce the law, not get into some damn fool gun fight. Now dump it out." I knew there was at least one knife and probably a holdout pistol. He stared into those two gaping holes for a second before deciding it wasn't worth it.

"Fine, but I'll kill you when I get out. Goddamn your yellow hide." He cursed me before slowly laying a derringer and two knives on the floor.

"Come on." I waved the barrels toward the door and followed him into the cells.

He went into the cell with Baxter, let those two figure out who was the most dangerous snake. Before the door clicked shut I was out the back door moving fast. I'd seen a man ducking behind the cobblers and figured it was a back shooter. There was no way I was letting someone like that wander around freely. His horse gave away its position by nickering when I passed by. He'd left it just outside of town in a small grove of trees. No need to find the man if you knew where his horse was waiting. Kneeling in the shade of a pine to wait for him I checked the hammers, still locked back.

Was that really him.....

Levar couldn't believe his eyes. He'd seen the whole thing from his spot behind the cobblers. That marshal wasn't supposed to be here. Hell he wasn't even supposed to a marshal. His reputation as a bounty hunter was enough, he didn't need a badge to be more dangerous. Whatever plan the rest thought they had was finished now. No Chance wasn't someone he or anyone else wanted to deal with. More than one professional back shooter had said plainly they wouldn't even try the man. To say there was stories about him was an understatement. Among the outlaws he was the boogey man.

Bennet or Baxter as he wanted to be called now was most likely dead. That was almost certain if that man was here. The only thing he could do was get back to camp to warn the others. They needed to get out of here right now. Even if they didn't want to leave he was. There was no way Levar was going to stick around to face that killer.

He turned to move through the shadows back to his horse with probably more speed than was healthy. His heart was pounding, every man on the owl hoot trail knew that demon's reputation. There weren't many men he feared but that killer was one of them. Once he got on your trail he never let up, not once did he miss his man. The only thing hope you had was getting enough of a lead, that only happened if he didn't know the land. Just as his horse came into sight a shadow moved to his left. It was too late, the reaper was waiting.

CHAPTER 19

It didn't take long for him to get there, the man came at a fast walk. He dell on his ass when I stepped out of a shadow, his eyes going wide with terror. His hat fell off when he hit the ground and I recognized the man. Stoney Levar, wanted for murder in at least three states. There was a five-hundred-dollar bounty on him, dead or alive. Last rumor I'd heard said he'd partnered up with some other hard cases. Supposedly they were hiding down in the nations after a raid in Kansas.

"Levar, what the hell are you doing here? Last I heard you were running with a couple other boys in the nations."

"Don't shoot." His hands shot into the air.

"Then gimme a reason not to, it's been my experience dead is easier to deal with." Let's see what he offers, might as well get some use out of my reputation.

"Big Jack, Craig and Patty are at a camp about five miles from here. I'll tell ya where."

"And what exactly are y'all doing here?"

"Bennet or Baxter, that's what he's going by now, brought us in to rob the town an some rich rancher." I cursed myself for not seeing it, Baxter was Darwin Bennet. The man was wanted for more than the other four combined. He'd killed a family down in Texas and their grandfather was some rich guy in New York. The old man had put a three-thousand-dollar bounty on him, dead or alive.

"Figure that's enough to buy your life. Ease off that belt an drop the rest. Then get to your feet, don't think Bennet will be happy to see ya."

"What?" He'd dropped his guns, two knives and a hold out from his boot. He'd made it all the way to his feet when what I said hit him.

"Bennet, he's in the jail."

"Ain't no way."

"Badge means I can't just kill ya'll anymore." I smiled at how wide his eyes got.

To say it was a joyous reunion would be a lie, Bennet cursed a blue streak when Levar walked in. He went in the cell with Carter because I honestly thought Bennet would kill him right then. The man was that mad. I'd had him draw me a map to their camp before taking him to the cells. I'd go fetch the other three in a bit. That might kill Bennet, having his plan undone by sheer stupidity might just end him.

Back out front in the office I started rolling up gun belts and putting them away. I took a few minutes to study the fancy two-gun rig Blake had. The matching pistols were pretty, a useless waste of money to me but pretty. They got rolled up and locked in a cabinet with the others, my collection was growing quickly. Bess was at the door with lunch, it ended up taking two trips to get all the trays here. She wasn't happy to discoverer she was one short, I'd finally managed to slip one in without her seeing me. I counted that as a personal victory.

After lunch I dug out the posters on the gang, including Bennet. No sense risking the other three wandering off to find trouble or hurt other folks. I dropped the trays off with Bess on my way to get Miz and go corral the last of my charges. Three more were going to mean some folks got paroled from the jail. I just didn't have room.

Back at the outlaw camp…

"What the hell taking 'at kid so long?" Craig grumbled.

"Might'a found Ben..Baxter an he's getting stuff ready." Big Jack didn't get why they were such hard asses about Bennetts name. They were in the woods, it seemed stupid to use the man alias.

"Most likely half drunk." Patty would be if they sent him.

"Don't like it, Baxter's late, now Levar isn't back. Something ain't right 'bout this sit'iation." They had just finished the last of their jerky and hard tack. If supplies didn't show up today they'd have to go into town.

"Something need to happen today or I'm riding out of here." Patty had had it with this mess. He liked riding with Craig but the back of his neck itched and that was never a good thing.

I overheard their belly aching crouched in the brush at the edge of camp. Miz was a few hundred yards back, far enough away their horse couldn't catch his scent. The three of them were loafing around a small fire complaining. They didn't care about the two missing men, it was the lack of supplies that bothered them. Like all men of their ilk, they had no concern past their personal needs or wants. The friendly weight of the double barrel was in my hands with the hammers locked back. Seemed to be about that time.

"Let me reunite y'all with them." My voiced boomed catching all their attention. Course it might have been me stepping out of the brush with both barrels pointed at them that did it. "Nobody move, I got a shotgun pointed at you with both barrels ready."

It went about like I expected, Big Jack had his back to me and stayed where he was. The man didn't play fair and wasn't fool enough to buck a stacked deck. Unfortunately for him Patty wasn't that smart. He snatched at his colt with a wild look in his eyes. It was halfway out of the holster when I pulled both triggers. The roaring boom of both barrels going off silenced the woods around us. It left my ears ringing, I wasn't used to the noise a Greener made. Dropping the empty scattergun my right hand filled with my Colt before it hit the ground. That was when my hearing returned and the screaming started.

It was Big Jack, or what was left of the man. The double ought buck had blown most of his right arm to rags. The force launching the big man face down in the fire. Tiny embers scattered into the air followed by the smell of burning hair. Some part of my brain noted they looked like fireflies in the acrid smoke. The smell told a different story. If Big Jack wasn't dead, he'd be praying for it before the smoke cleared.

Patty caught one of the barrels in the chest, the force of it flipping him over the log he'd been sitting on. I didn't know for sure he was dead but he wouldn't be getting up anytime soon. The way his boots were kicking propped over the log said he wasn't long for this world. Seen enough men die to recognize that particular jig.

A bullet tugged at my collar when Craig fired, he'd rushed his shot and missed. Probably because his left arm was full of buckshot and bone splinters. My Colt spit out back-to-back lead slugs at nine hundred and fifty feet per second. They both hit him just to the left of his third button. Both holes fit under a silver dollar and either one was fatal. He'd managed to make it to his feet before taking a shot at me. Now both knees buckled, his brain taking a second to realize the cold hand of death was already reaching up to take him. He fell to the ground in a heap, partially on top of Big Jake.

The smoke from my colts joined the cloud slowly drifting in the breeze. Damn! I'd wanted to take them back to town sitting in their saddles not hanging over them. Reese was going to be annoyed but there hadn't been a choice. I'd take a pissed off boss over death every time. The good news was spotting their horses close by, already saddled with the cinch's loose. Big Jake would be a pain in the ass but the other two wouldn't bo too bad. Jake though, I was going to have to use a horse to pull him over a saddle. The man earned his moniker, he loved to be easily 300 pounds. Luckily I knew exactly how to do that, years of working alone required some creative solutions.

Rolling Jake off the fire rekindled it, which made getting rid of the trash easy. The heavy dark smoke from burning their filthy clothes didn't concern me. By the time anyone came to investigate I'd be long gone. Rolled gun belts went into the saddlebags with the more useful things. Ammo, piggin strings, matches and the few odds and ends that almost every man carried with him on the trail. I'd learned long ago that puncher or outlaw didn't matter, every man carried certain things everywhere. The rifles, two new Winchesters and a decent Yellow Boy I put in their scabbards.

I'd been using the housekeeping to calm down before loading the bodies. Now I was out of excuses. Looping a rope over a sturdy branch and tying one end to the big man's ankles. I walked back to the Morgan mare not looking forward to this. The other end of the rope was tied off at the saddle horn. The Mare was probably Patty's, it was the smallest of the three and a beautiful animal. She barely noticed the weight easily stepping forward lifting the big man slowly off the ground. It took some pushing and shoving to get him laid over the saddle, even with her doing most of the work. The other two went faster and thirty minutes later I was leading three horses behind Miz back toward town.

CHAPTER 20

The undertaker wasn't happy when I told him he'd have to do paperwork in all three but still took the coin. When I told him the whole story about Baxter and these three he suddenly changed his attitude. He was very appreciative and more than happy to help. Knowing that I'd stopped someone treeing the town usually had that effect.

It took both of us and his helper to lever Big Jake onto a table. I spent another ten minutes cleaning the blood off the tack and horses before heading to the livery. He wasn't happy when I claimed them all but knowing the bill would be paid by me and not by the marshals made him smile. On the way back to the sheriff's office I realized something. I needed a bath badly, there was blood all over my shirt, face and hands. That was of course when Mis Gardner walked out of a shop almost tackling me.

"Oh! Excuse …" she looked up in surprise. Her eyes taking in the dark red stains that went from my knees to my chest caught her attention. "Is that paint?"

"Pardon me ma'am." I tipped my hat. I did my best to step around her without answering the question. The last thing I wants was to get her started on another tirade.

"Wait that's not paint it's blood!" Her voice had become shrill and carried down the street. This of course drew the attention of everyone else in the area.

"Yes ma'am it is." I didn't like this kind of attention but it wasn't anything new. My eyes got lost in her emerald pools, the danced with curiosity and disgust in equal measure.

"Were you hunting? I've never seen anyone get so much blood on them hunting." Her mind was trying to fill in whatever mistake had led me to get this much blood on myself from hunting.

"Yes ma'am, hunting." I didn't want to tell her any more than necessary. Let her think I just didn't know how to dress a kill, that was better then the truth. Maybe then she wouldn't get that look in her eyes. She wasn't going to let me off that easily.

"No decent man would walk through town like that. Are you some type of savage?" Her temper was flaring up again but it just didn't make sense. Why was she mad at me this time?

"Yes ma'am I was going to get a bath and change clothes." Unfortunately, the undertaker picked that moment to notice me.

"Deputy, here's the paperwork on those three men." He held out the small stack of papers. I couldn't even blame the man, he had no way of knowing.

"Thanks." I said dryly before folding them into my wallet.

"That's human blood!" I had to give her credit, she caught on fast. She'd also found the end of my patience with that shriek.

"Yes ma'am, I'm a law man. I don't often get the opportunity to hunt for pleasure. Especially not with a jail full of prisoners in a town that stands around allowing them to freely take what they want." I snapped and watched her go from pale to bright crimson. "Never mind facing three men alone before they treed this town."

It only made her more beautiful but my temper was up this time. It wasn't dinner yet and I'd faced down a stupid kid, arrested one of a crew set on robbing this town then had killed the rest of them. Which would probably piss my boss off and convince him I was nothing but a killer. Now all I wanted was a bath and some clean clothes before Bess brought over dinner. Evidently that was too much to hope for. This woman had decided to make a scene in the middle of Main Street. She gapped like a fish, shocked at my harsh response. With a sharp tip of my hat for once I was the one who tried to stomp through the boards. Stepping around her before she could continue her diatribe I moved off toward the jail.

Miss Gardner...

You fool! Of course, that was human blood but you didn't need to scream about it like some silly child. Her internal voice was cursing her foolish behavior. She just couldn't believe she'd done something so stupid. When he snapped back her brain had literally locked up. That frustrated tone wasn't new, it haunted her almost every day. It was the tone everyone eventually used when they finally had it with her.

This time was different, the pain was in her heart. It was breaking with each step he took away from her. She needed to apologize, needed to stop him but it was too late. He hated her and with good reason. What kind of person behaved like she had? Finally she tried to say something, anything to stop him. It was too late, to late by far. He'd turned into the sheriff's office and slammed the door.

The undertaker was staring at her, there was some amusement in his eyes and that restarted her brain. Was this little man laughing at her? Laughing at her for hurting that beautiful man? The man who had up until now tolerated her temper. The one who'd seemed like an angel when she met his brilliant blue eyes that first night. Now just like everyone else he'd avoid her. Do everything he could to not be near her. Tears blurred her vision, slowly one then another trailed down her cheek.

"What?" She snapped at the man. "Was there something you wanted to say?"

"Yes ma'am, there is. He did bring in three bodies, brought them in alone mind you. They were part of a crew that Baxter had put together. Outlaws that planned on looting the town. The wanted posters I read said murder, robbery, kidnapping and rape." His tone was polite but held some strong opinions about her behavior. "Not that you allowed the man any chance to explain."

"What?" The realization was starting to sink in. Baxter had planned on looting the town and he had stopped them.

"For the second time in as many days that man saved this town. In thanks you made a scene in the middle of the street." This little man was right she hadn't even thought about that. Even if it had been hunting what business was that of hers.

"I didn't know." She tried to defend herself but knew it was hollow.

"No because the man didn't want anyone to know. I don't think he wanted to kill them, wanted to bring them in alive. Even though his jail already has seven men in three cells."

"Seven?" She hadn't heard anything about more arrests.

"Yes, Blake came in this morning to kill him with two hands from the ranch. He arrested all of them. Then he caught a fourth man skulking around town. He was spying for the outlaws."

"How?" She was lost. He'd arrested four more men today and killed three?

"Because that's his job ma'am. That's what he said when I asked him about it least wise." His voice had calmed and didn't have that cutting tone. "When I asked him why he didn't take someone with him. Do you know what he said?"

"No." She knew she sounded meek. With each word the undertaker spoke her heart broke into smaller and smaller pieces. How could she have been so cruel?

"He just stared at me for a second and asked 'who?' I knew exactly what he meant. who would he have asked? He barely knows anyone in town, much less someone he might trust. The town he's saved. That's the man you just humiliated." The man spun and walked away. She stood in the middle of the street with her mouth hanging open.

She felt someone put their arm around her shoulders and lead her away. It was Bess saving her from the humiliation. Slowly she led her into the restaurant, patiently guiding her to the kitchen. Bess acted like she didn't see the tears streaming down her cheeks. The warm tea that appeared in her hand helped but it wasn't nearly enough. Her temper had once again cost her more then she could imagine. Utterly destroying any chance she had with the first man who ignited any feeling her since that day.

Stomping into the sheriff's office I headed to the back room. Annoyed with myself for losing my temper more than anything else. Now that stunning woman thought I was a blood-soaked savage. Hadn't she already called me a wild animal? I'd seen the fear creep into those deep green eyes and knew there was no use trying to explain. I'd seen that change before, so many times before. The scar faced man always painted in blood leading bodies into town. They'd gaze at him in fear praying he would leave before killing them. Hoping that he would disappear from their safe little world.

Taking some clean clothes out of my pack before ducking out the back and into the barbers. Thankfully the man didn't blink, just pointed to the tubs. Someone was already back there filling a tub for me. They'd seen the show like everyone else and knew I was coming. It took three tubs of water before it stopped turning red, the last one was barely warm but I didn't care. All I wanted was to get back to the office, lock the door and ignore them all. He knew without looking they had all changed. There would be no kindness or welcoming smiles.

When the barber refused my money I thought it was out of fear until I looked at him. The man didn't look afraid, he looked appreciative. Staring at him for a minute trying to understand why gave me no answers. Finally, he saved me by speaking directly.

"Ain't all of us clueless 'bout what ya done fer this town deputy. Your moneys no good here, I expect it ain't much good in most places."

He would never know how much those words meant to me. They immediately eased the weight on my shoulders and lifted my hope. Even if it was just this one man the knowledge that someone understood changed everything. Maybe it felt different because of the badge? He didn't see someone trading death for money. He saw the law doing its job, defending people like him. For the first time since pinning it on my badge felt like it belonged on my chest.

Sitting behind the desk my mind was slowly thinking about the change. Trying to accept the difference in not only the way they saw me, but in the way I felt. Nothing had prepared me for the change in what people saw. That look of respect rather then fear shook how I saw myself. There would always be those that just saw the blood and guns, but now some would see more.

They would see the promise my badge represented. A simple oath taking in the back of a building. I hadn't thought much about the oath or what it meant then but suddenly it was important. A part of me wished we'd used the longer oath, not that it would make a difference. I was a law man, doing what must be done. My actions would let other people live safely, building a life I might never know.

CHAPTER 21

There was a knock on the door, interrupting my thoughts. I looked through the slit and was surprised to see Bess. The hours had flown by and it was dinner time. Lost in thought, I hadn't registered the time and tried to hide my confusion. She walked in with Miss Gardner right behind her, both women carrying trays. I didn't have time to hide my astonishment.

"What? You think I can carry eight trays of food alone?" Bess laughed, then gave the young schoolteacher a hard look. "Sides, Miss Gardner has something she wants to say."

"Ma'am?" I looked at her apprehensively, preparing myself for another tongue lashing. Despite my uneasiness, her beauty stole my breath away and made it a struggle not to stare.

"I wanted to apologize for my behavior earlier." There was a slight tremor in her voice, as if it was hard for her to say the words.

"Nothing to apologize for, ma'am. I know what I am." I didn't mean for my voice to be so sharp and the fear in her eyes stung. A bloody savage, that's all she saw when she looked at me and it terrified her.

"You!" I watched the fire fill her eyes, consuming the fear. She spun, slamming the trays on the desk and stormed out of the office. She turned left with an almost military crispness then I could hear her trying to break boards again as she stomped off down the boardwalk.

"You young people." Bess sounded exasperated. "Ain't none

of ya have a lick of sense. You know that girl's in love with you?"

"What?" Was she mad? That wasn't possible. Love me? Love a scarred up half wild bloody savage? A woman like that? Not a chance.

"Fools, the both of you! Neither of you can mind your tongues long enough to get at the truth." She shook her head and picked up the empty trays from lunch. Before I could say a word, she was out the door and headed back to her place in a swirl of skirts.

I just stood there, unsure of anything. My mind was running in circles and none of it made sense. There was no way someone like her could love me. Hell, it was obvious to everyone that the woman couldn't stand me. Everything except my foolish heart said this was a trap. My heart was absolutely fine with it though and gleefully told the rest of me to go to hell. People walking by looked at my form, frozen in the open doorway. The men seemed confused but most of the women had soft, knowing smiles. It was as if they knew some secret the rest of us would never understand.

My first response was complete denial. There was no way that brilliant woman could ever love an uneducated savage like me, never mind the way I looked. She was too...well, everything. Too beautiful, too smart, too perfect. It wasn't possible for any woman to actually love me, much less someone like her. That made sense to me. She could see what kind of man I was and had told me so in no uncertain terms. If I gave in to this fantasy and pursued her, she would refuse me and this mad hope would die. The dream would shatter, leaving me to try and pick up whatever pieces were left.

My second reaction was fear, absolute gut wrenching terror. What the hell did I know about women? Nothing, not one damn thing. Literally the longest time I'd ever spent around a woman was with Mad Maggie. The week it took me to drag her to Waco didn't count for much. That crazy half Apache woman either threw scraps of food at me or tried to kill me with anything she could get her hands on.

Aside from that, there were just those brief moments when a vaquero's wife had fed me as a child and those were few and far between. I had some vague memories of my mother but they were hazy, more ghost then memory. I'd never been with a soiled dove. It wasn't that I looked down on them or the men they served, it had just never appealed to me.

The sound of yelling finally broke me out of my reverie. I had a job to do and this skylarking wasn't part of it. I couldn't afford to be distracted, one mistake and those men in the cells would kill me. It was time for me to swap water and slop buckets around and feed my prisoners. I'd also need to figure out how to cut some of them loose. There just wasn't enough space to keep seven men locked up for long.

Leaving two trays on the desk, I took the rest with me and put them on the table in the back. Fresh water and clean slop buckets were my first priority and the ex-sheriff helped me with the job this time. I kept the shotgun trained on him as he opened the cell and swapped buckets. I had to trust the old man a little bit but of the bunch he was my safest bet. I fed all of the prisoners except Carter, who I asked to join me in the office. He sat down at the desk looking uncomfortable.

"Let's chat while we eat." I offered, taking my seat opposite the man.

"Not that I don't appreciate it, but what is there to talk about?" Carter pulled his tray closer and started eating hungrily. Maybe dinner was a bit later than I'd thought.

"I want to bond you out but ain't sure what I can hold to assure your compliance." Admitting the truth couldn't hurt and might actually help me find an answer. The man's response almost made me choke.

"The deed to my land?" He said almost casually between bites of mashed potato.

"That would damn sure cover it." I laughed, after managing to swallow my half chewed piece of steak.

"It's at the land office, doubt they're still open. One more night in there won't kill me."

"It might. Did you know Baxter is Darwin Bennet?" Now it was his turn to choke. Thankfully he managed not to spit coffee across the desk but it was a near thing. "He was planning on killing you then treeing the town. That's were Levar came from, I just left the rest of the gang at the mortician's."

"He's really Bennet?" He was still coughing but managed to croak out the question.

"Yeah, and the kid in there is Stoney Levar. The other three were Big Jack Carlson, Craig Johnson and Patty McCormack. All wanted dead or alive for everything from robbery to murder. Bennet brought them up from the Nations for the job. Figure that's what he was planning for the teacher, had to keep them busy until your cattle money got back from the railhead."

"I..." his voice trailed off. I watched the guilt wash over him. "I really didn't know. They would have destroyed everything."

"Tell me about Dodger. Who shot him? How'd the other deputy get a Dutch ride?" I was still wondering about the missing badge tip but doubted Bennet would ever tell me the truth.

"What? No, he was shot, that's what Baxt...Bennet said. The man picked a fight and lost. Swore it was a fair contest. Even showed me the star with the tip shot off as evidence. What other deputies? I don't know anything about someone getting dragged. I don't even do that to rustlers." The man had paled at the thought. His voice shook from something more visceral then guilt. "I never would an' if you saw my back you'd know why. Got dragged through a canyon when I was young, those rustlers left me for dead. I'd never put another man through that hell."

I let him eat for a few minutes before asking anything else. My mind was still stuck on the star, maybe I'd have to ask Bennet myself and hope he'd want to brag about it. The idea of a Dutch ride had rattled Carter too much for him to have known anything about it. The man wasn't lying, I was certain he hadn't known anything about the other two deputies.

"That makes this easier. You know those two punchers at all?"

"Young and stupid but not gun hands. Probably came to see a show when Blake asked them. They won't give you any trouble."

"I don't mean to sound disrespectful but I have to ask. Will your men still follow your lead?" His head snapped up at the question but after a minute or two he calmed down, understanding why I had asked.

"With the Bennet thing I can't fault you for asking. They will follow me and they'll damn sure follow Red, my ramrod."

"Wouldn't happen to be Red Dempsey, would it?" Something about the way he'd said the man's name begged the question. It earned me another surprised look.

"It would, you know him?"

"Been awhile but he might remember me. I was just a kid back then." Anyway, it didn't matter much whether Red remembered me. "I'll cut those two chuckleheads loose after dinner. Have them tell Red to ride in tomorrow morning. We can arrange your bond then."

"Going to make him the signature?"

"That okay with you?"

"Best man I can think of for it, he's been my ramrod for three years. Never had any call to question the man."

143

He was right. I remembered Red from the Double T. He'd been at the Fort when they found me. The man had a way with numbers and letters and had been one of my more effective teachers. He'd also introduced me to fictional novels, and I still had the copy of Frankenstein he gave me. It was the first book I ever owned.

My assumption had been that he'd died along with all the rest in a raid. Later, I got word that he'd been in San Antonio when the outlaws hit the ranch. It had been just a rumor and I'd never bothered to check if it was true. Part of me couldn't believe the man was still alive while another part hoped he was. He must've thought the same when he found the burnt out ranch and assumed everyone had died in the raid.

"Sorry I can't cut Blake loose. He's going to come at me again as soon as he can. Wasn't my intent but his pride is hurt. He can't let it go or won't. I've seen it before."

"You're not wrong. He's young and trying to build a name. I'll tell the boys to have Red bring his payout and gear with him. I was going to cut him loose anyway, he trouble hunts too much for ranch work."

"Isn't he supposed to be decent with a gun?" I was curious. Every ranch needed a few guards, men who could handle themselves and didn't mind doing it.

"He ain't a bad man, not yet. Worthless with cattle though, ain't ever seen a man so bad 'round animals. Can't even manage nighthawking, something 'bout the dark bothers him."

"Scared of the dark?" I asked, amazed.

"Not exactly, but in a way I guess. He had a horse step in a gopher hole last year, happened right in the middle of the herd at night. Guess it spooked him 'bout riding nighthawk."

"Seen that more than once, if you had longhorns he'd probably be dead." Herefords were fairly calm but falling into a herd of longhorns at night? That could start a stampede depending on how trail broke the herd was. Even without a stampede, those half wild cattle would stomp a man just because they could.

"That's why I've kept him on, I understand why he got spooked. Problem is, it made him more aggressive with the other hands. Sure you know how that goes. They jape him about it and instead of taking it he gets his hackles up an' wants to fight."

"Punchers ain't exactly gentle, I can see why the kid's touchy."

"Especially if you're young and feel like a gun is the answer to every problem."

"Makes sense to cut him loose then. He can find a new ranch and lose the story, at least for a while. He's too young to realize that story will travel. Doubt he'll make it past this town, sadly. Let me get those two out here and send 'em off." I got up to let the two hands out of their cage. Blake looked up expectantly then cursed under his breath when I led them out.

"I'm cutting you two loose. Don't make me regret it." I said, motioning to Carter.

He told them what he wanted and made it clear they had to tell everyone else to follow the rule about guns in town. When they asked about their own weapons, I said Red would get them tomorrow. After that it was up to him and Carter. They didn't seem too happy about it but took it better when I mentioned waiving the fine. Twenty-five dollars is a lot of money to a puncher. They lit out a few minutes later and I went back in to reorganize the cells.

Blake and Carter went in the far cell, Bennet stayed on the opposite end, and the ex-sheriff and Levar took the middle. I really needed to ask the man's name at some point but not tonight. I just wanted some peace and quiet, maybe a few hours of sleep.

CHAPTER 22

For once I got my wish. The peace and quiet held for the night and not one person tried to kill me. I checked both saloons and saw tables set up at the doors with men collecting guns. They were close enough to the edge of town that I called it good enough. After my rounds, I sat in one of the rocking chairs out front to watch the sunset. Bess walked out of her place and joined me in the other chair. To my surprise she didn't treat me to another tongue lashing. As a matter of fact, we barely spoke. I got a good night's sleep with no interruptions.

There was some minor complaining the next morning when I came in to swap out the buckets. Mostly from Blake, who thought he should've been cut loose along with the others. I was going to end up having to kill him, it was written all over his face. The man had mistaken my actions as cowardice, but the bigger problem was he was convinced that I'd made him look foolish. He had his pride wrapped too tight around him and now it was going to get him killed.

The former sheriff looked stunned when I asked for his name. He assumed I must've known it since I'd been sent to remove him from office. Percy Thatcher wasn't a name I recognized but it was a big country, maybe it meant something somewhere. At least he seemed resigned to his fate. We both knew he wouldn't end up being charged with much of anything, that was why he didn't want to give me a hard time. Worst case he might do a year, most likely he'd never see a courtroom.

Bess and a lady I didn't recognize brought breakfast. Bess caught me by surprise when she asked how the sheriff was doing. I wanted to ask her about it but they were running late and had to hurry back. Breakfast this morning was one of my favorites, biscuits and gravy. There was something about that peppery bite that hit the spot.

Not long after I'd collected the trays, I heard a knock at the door. I'd just finished rinsing them at the pump and was drying off my hands. My brain must have been lulled into a false sense of security because I forgot to look through the slit before opening the door. The man standing before me wasn't a ghost but he did go a bit pale when he got a look at me. Memories flooded over me when I saw him. It was the scowling face of a man I hadn't ever thought I'd see again. Someone I thought was long dead among the ashes of an old ranch. The shocked look on his face told me he'd thought the same of me.

"I didn't believe him…" was all he said before grabbing me up in a bear hug.

"Damn it Red, I thought you were dead!" I smiled, hugging the man back. After a second we separated and shook hands like men are supposed to do.

"Too lucky or too damn mean ta die." The big Texan drawled. "How'd you make it out?"

"Was riding the line that winter, remember? Didn't know anything about it until the weather broke an' no one showed up for the gather. What about you?"

"Boss sent me to San Antonio, got held up by that last storm. By the time I made it back everything was done. I'm sorry kid, never thought to check the line shack." He looked a bit ashamed but I understood. I'd had the same shocked reaction to the massacre.

"Red, there's no way you could have known. 'Sides, I settled the score with the bastards." There was ice in my voice as I recalled that time. "Every last one of them."

"Heard someone had, didn't think it was you. Figured it was a bunch of friends or something. When folks said it was just one man I thought ain't no way that could be right. Is it true? You rode into 'at death trap alone?" He was shocked when he realized what I meant.

"True story, but it only worked cause Fisher liked Thad. He pointed me toward the right men and kept the rest out of it."

"Met him once, the man has a sense of honor. Guess that includes folks he liked being killed."

"Stone cold killer, fast too. Still, you never know about a man. He was true to his word."

"Now you're a law dog? If that don't beat all." Then his eyes got serious. "Figure we need to talk 'bout why I'm here."

"Come on, coffee's hot. I'll get Carter." Red stepped inside and I locked the door behind him. He grabbed a tin cup and filled it before taking one of the chairs.

Once we were all seated, I let Carter lay everything out for Red. The more the man talked the bigger Red's smile got. By the time he finished, I thought the man's face might split wide open. Carter looked a bit surprised by his reaction but I wasn't. I knew what kind of man he was. A good ramrod wanted to do nothing but work with punchers and cattle. They had no interest in the rest and hated working for men who cared about such things.

"Boss, I can't tell ya how much I appreciate you saying this. Truth to tell, I been debating pulling up stakes. Never been one for range wars and land barons. Just something about it feels wrong."

"Why didn't you ever say anything, Red?" Carter looked surprised at the revelation.

"Ain't my place to tell a body what to do with his spread."

Red's simple answer didn't surprise me at all. Carter just got a firsthand look at how far he'd strayed away from what he knew.

"Red, once this mess gets settled.... never mind, I'll take care of it today. Have to go to the land office anyway. You're getting a five percent share in the brand. I want you to have a reason to speak up when you see something's wrong. I'll also block out a place to have a proper house built for ya."

"Boss, you ain't..." but Carter cut the man off.

"Red, I know what you've been doing. Keeping the gun hands busy and away from the rest of the punchers." Carter smiled at him. "Besides, I can't afford to lose you and this way you're stuck."

"I ain't sure what to say boss." Red looked a bit lost but happy.

"Just say you'll help keep the ranch and me on the right path."

"Gladly!" The two men smiled at one another and shook hands. Now I had to address another tough subject.

"Eddie Peppers is still at the doc's."

"He's a good man, does what a gun hawk is supposed to." Red was quick to defend him.

"Agreed. Is he in real trouble?" Carter asked.

"No, but I don't want him back at the ranch." I said, managing to keep a straight face.

"Look Chance, I know you have to follow the law but we need men like him out there." Red protested.

"I'll do what you say, Deputy. But I'm with Red, men like him are hard to find."

"Agreed. That's why I want him to pin on the sheriff's badge." Both men were obviously rocked back a bit by the idea. But after a minute or two, Red's face split into a grin again. Carter just stared at me, too gobsmacked to speak.

"Didn't he try an kill you?" He asked, finally breaking the silence.

"He took your money, didn't have a choice. That's something we all understand. You take the money, you do the job. Besides, we've crossed paths before. I honestly believe he'd be the best man for you and the town."

"He's right boss, the man's dead fair." Red agreed. "Hell, the man would arrest me if he'd accepted pay to do the job. You can't buy him off either. Remember that bunch of rustlers last year? The ones he took down?"

"Yeah, four of them wasn't it?" Carter asked, thinking back.

"Yup. You remember him turning over five hundred dollars he found on them? Only reason he knew they had it was 'cause they'd tried to bribe him. Offered him all of it if'n he just walked away."

"That I didn't know. Knew about the money, sure. But I don't remember him ever telling me that part. One of them was married, so I sent her the money. No reason for a woman to suffer for her man's sins." That put points in Carter's box for me. The act was above and beyond fair.

"Sounds like him, honest an' wouldn't bother saying anything about the bribe. It wasn't important an' speaking 'bout it might sound like a brag." I added. "He's going to be on the mend awhile so there's time. Doc says he'll make a full recovery but not anytime soon."

"You think he'll take it?" Carter asked. The idea of a lawman who couldn't be bought sounded like just the thing if he wanted to see some change around here.

"Not without some considerations on my bosses' part, but yeah I think he will. The man's been looking to set down some roots but there's a few things that need changing first." I'd have to get that bounty removed but wasn't sure how to go about making that happen.

"Considerations?" Red was curious about that.

"He's got an old bounty on him. Commissioned by a vindictive relative of a man he killed. I think my boss can get it called off, if not we'll have to find another way around it. Being a U.S. Marshal has to be good for something." I laughed. "If he can call it off, would ya'll agree to it?"

"Long as the mayor does. I'll have a voice in the town but he and the council will be running it." I was glad to hear the man say it, seemed like his perspective was truly changing.

"Now, about Blake." I said, figuring we might as well address the ugly topic head on. "If I let the kid go he's going to challenge me. Don't want to kill him but I won't risk trying to wound someone who's drawing on me. Didn't do it for Ed either, if that's what you're thinking. If you face a man in a gun fight, both of you should expect to die. There's no room for friendship at that moment."

"I have his gear and pay off, but I take your meaning." Red said. "To tell ya the truth, I don't see a way out of it with that one. He's gonna push an' keep pushing until you don't have a choice."

"Sorry Deputy, but Red's right. Doubt you'll have a choice." Carter was sympathetic but didn't have any novel ideas.

"It is what it is then." I had to admit defeat, he would either see reason or he wouldn't. "Might as well get this done."

CHAPTER 23

I rose to my feet and went to get Blake, ignoring the shock on the faces of the two men. It wasn't the idea of killing him that bothered me, it was feeling trapped into it. Situations like this one made it hard not to have a pile of bodies stacked up at my feet by the time Reese got here. Sadly, there didn't seem to be a way around it with this kid. He was too young and his pride was too fragile. Any real gun hand knew that getting caught blindsided by a lawman was just the price of doing business. No self-respecting sheriff went heads up against them, there was just no reason to. Enforcing the law wasn't meant to be personal, the law was the law.

"Boss, what's going on?" Blake asked when he saw Red and Carter.

"I'm cuttin' ya loose, Blake. Things are changing an' I don't need your skill set no more." Carter said. "You'll be paid for the month. You did fine work for me an' there's a letter to that effect in with your gear."

"Cause I let this kid get the drop on me?" He sounded offended but Red stepped in.

"Nope. Ain't got a thing to do with that. Matter of fact, getting caught like that is just part of the job sometimes. Just changing the way we're doing business. Most of the guards are getting cut loose. From now on it'll be just regular work as a hand, even for the guards we do keep." I appreciated Red adding that in but Blake wasn't hearing it.

"That's cause they're all dead." Blake snapped then glared at me. "Just like this backshooter will be once I get my guns."

"Blake, don't make me kill you. Take your pay and pull up stakes." He was trying my patience but if this wasn't personal I had to let it go. "The way I caught you is what lawmen do. A good sheriff never faces a man if it can be avoided, you take every advantage to end it without shooting.

"Meet me in the street like a man 'cause I say you're yella'." He damn near screamed it. It was pointless, there was no way to talk him out of his stupidity.

"That's your choice. Hit the trail." Rage had ignited in me. My anger flared hot then settled into the cold, hard burn I'd used to my advantage so many times before. I took his gun rig out of the lockbox and tossed it on the desk. "You go make a ruckus in the street and leave me no choice, I will bury you. Take your gear and ride, there are other jobs in other places."

He spun on his heel without taking his pay or gear, slinging his gun belt around his waist and stalking out the door. He left the door open and I could hear him yelling while he tied his holsters down. The kid just wasn't going to let it go come hell or high water. Shaking my head, I checked my pistols and threw a glance at the others. Both men knew there was no choice.

"I'm calling out that yella' dog of a man. Deputy, step out here an' face me or crawl outta town like the dog you are. Ya caught me by sneaking up behind me, 'at won't happen again. This time you'll have to face me like a man."

I stepped outside, flipping the thong off my colt. Blake was standing in the middle of the street about twenty feet away, glaring holes in me. His face was bright red, his eyes filled with a burning rage. One look confirmed there was no way out of this. It didn't make a lick of sense to me but that didn't change the situation. He'd demanded this, left me no choice but to walk into the street and kill another man.

"Don't throw your life away on this stupidity, Blake. There's more to a reputation than this nonsense." I had to say it. It didn't matter that it was a waste of air, the people on the street needed to hear it.

"Like being a back shooting coward? Is that how ya gunned down Eddie and Phil?" There was no way out for either of us now. That accusation couldn't be walked back.

"This is your dance kid, call the tune." My voice was calm. The cold flame inside me had seeped into my tone.

I didn't lock gazes with him but I took in every inch of his body, waiting for the twitch or tell. His youth and inexperience gave everything away. First his left eye squinted slightly then his right shoulder shifted. Even his stance telegraphed how green he was, how consumed by foolish pride.

His hand swept up, full of death. My Colt roared before he made it halfway to level. Flame chased hot lead out of the barrel, sending it spinning across twenty-five feet in an instant. The impact snapped Blake's head back and he was dead before the breath left his body. His gun fired harmlessly into the air, every muscle in his body seizing up as his brain stopped functioning. He fell backward stiffly, the dust billowing up around him as he hit the ground.

I heard one last harsh exhale, but that was caused by the impact of his corpse hitting the ground. He was dead the instant my bullet punched through his skull. His hat fell to the ground after floating on the breeze for a second or two. It rolled in a lazy circle before finally coming to rest near his body, brim down. Guess the old adage was true, his luck had run out. A piercing scream to my left pulled me out of my thoughts. I turned and found Miss Gardner, paralyzed by shock and holding her hands over her mouth.

The look of horror and fear on her face spoke volumes, she didn't need to say a word. Even if Bess had been right, any warm feeling she had for me died the moment Blake did. She looked at me through the smoke of my Colt with terror-filled eyes then turned on her heel and ran. My heart stuttered and for a second I thought I felt the cold hand of death wrapped around it. I'd seen that look before but somehow seeing it on that beautiful face broke a piece of me. Hearing Red's voice next to my ear startled my heart into beating again.

"You tried, Chance. I know you did." He rested his big hand on my shoulder for a second before continuing. "I'll go get the undertaker. The boss is ready to head over to the land office once this is done."

"Thanks, Red." The words were automatic, all I could focus on was the burning pain in my chest. As I turned to walk with Carter to the land office, my brain kept replaying the look of horror on her face.

"Red will see he's buried proper. He knows all his particulars. Doesn't have any family so he'll go in my graveyard. I'll see it every day and know that his death is on my shoulders."

"Far too many men are buried in unmarked graves, good to know he won't be one of them. Blake's death isn't on you, the man had every opportunity to walk away. We both did all we could to avoid this."

"It ain't the death that's bothering me, it's my part in it. That kid came here on my money, feel like I owe a debt for that."

"Didn't know you were in the war." I appreciated what the man was doing, he was trying to help me but he didn't understand. Blake's death didn't bother me, it was the look on Ms. Gardner's face that haunted me. "If ya owe a debt, you can pay it by building this town. Make it something worthwhile, neither of us need any more ghosts."

"Supply, I wasn't in the battles. But I saw enough of the aftermath to last a lifetime. So many wasted lives." There was a heaviness to his tone that said maybe we needed to change the subject.

"You know this bond will mean you can't leave the area? Leastwise, not until all this is cleared up."

"I'm not going anywhere. That woman struck a nerve." He nodded toward Bess who was standing in her doorway watching us. "I want to prove her wrong, show that I can help this town grow. Even if the best way to do that is getting out of the way."

It cost me two dollars to put a lien on his property. Red met us in front of the office and did his part. If Carter didn't show up, it gave me the legal right to seize his assets. He paid another two dollars to give Red five percent of the brand then marked off half a section for his house. When we left, the undertaker was taking Blake's body away. I unlocked the door and Red set Blake's pistols and rig down on the desk. They were a matched pair of nickel plated Smith and Wesson model 3's.

"Fine pistols, even if they are in a stupid rig." Red said, admiring the guns. Most men thought trying to shoot with both hands was a poor decision. "He had a fine gelding and some pretty tack too. His Winchester should be with the tack at the livery."

Miss Gardner....

She'd fled the horrific scene in the street, seeking shelter in the boarding house. Locked in the safety of her room, she let her mind replay all she had seen. The damned fool could have been killed! Didn't he know what that would do to her? Of course he didn't you silly girl! You still haven't told him how you feel. How could he possibly know any of that?

There hadn't been a trace of fear on his face and there was a calmness about him she'd never seen before. She was terrified he'd be hurt or killed, the other man was incidental. A man could die so fast in this place, one second they stood there alive and well and the next they were gone. His face hadn't changed in the slightest, it was like he was carved out of granite. How could someone remain so calm knowing the man across from him might end his life?

She'd heard the horrible things Blake had shouted, the same young man who'd tried so hard to impress her. She'd intended to give that fool a piece of her mind but then Chance had walked out of the sheriff's office. Her breath had caught when she saw him and her body refused to move.

His tall, lean frame moved with a feline grace. Just watching him walk had made her cheeks flush with thoughts she'd need to confess on Sunday. Lust wasn't something she really understood, aside from a few racy passages in novels she'd read. But there was no doubt in her mind it was lust that made her knees quiver when she saw him. Even now her face reddened at the thought, shame making her cheeks burn.

There was something about the man that just called to her. His lack of formal education meant nothing to her. His mind was razor sharp and his vocabulary demonstrated how well read he was. There was an aura of strength that rolled off him in waves. Even that day when she'd been shocked to find him covered in blood, she'd still felt perfectly safe standing near him. It must feel like heaven being held in those muscular arms. At least that's what her heart and other unmentionable parts were telling her.

He was the opposite of what she or her parents had ever considered attractive or suitable. He was rough, dangerous and lacking the proper pedigree. Her parents would despise him. Then there was his lack of financial security. But none of that mattered to her, it never had. She was drawn to him, helpless as a moth to the flame.

CHAPTER 24

It wasn't long before Carter and Red left for the Circle T. I was cleaning my pistol when Bess brought in lunch, alone this time. I was back down to just three prisoners and she could manage the trays on her own. As I stood to help her, my mind contemplated what she might think about the killing. Would she disapprove and condemn me like so many others had? Like Ms. Gardner had?

"Anymore dying today?" She asked casually but I knew she was checking on me. She wasn't judging me, she truly wanted to be sure I was all right. A weight seemed to lift just knowing she saw me the same way she always had. She'd been a constant since I arrived, and even though I hadn't been here long part of me had come to rely on her.

"Hope not, though you might want to kill me for asking my next question." I laughed. Earlier today something had struck me and I needed to know the answer.

"I ain't armed so you're safe enough for now."

"Tell me about Percy." The look on her face went from wariness to amusement.

"Why you ask'n boy?"

"You asked about him and it sounded like more than curiosity."

"That old coot's been trying to get the courage up to ask me out for almost a year." She smirked. "Old fool knows less 'bout women than you do. It's getting ta where I'm gonna have to do the ask'n."

"Maybe you can help me out then. I'd like to bond him out but I need someone to be his signature. They'd have to be responsible for making sure he stays in the area until everything is settled."

"What the hell am I going to do with a man running around underfoot?" The way her eyes lit up told me he might be under more than just her feet.

"I could use him around here. Maybe as jailer for a bit, least until this all gets squared up."

"You want the old sheriff to act as jailer?" She laughed but I could see she was interested.

"You tell me. Can I trust him?"

"He ain't worth a plug nickel as a lawman. That being said, I don't think he had any hand in what was going on 'round here. Turned a blind eye and took the money for certain, but he ain't the type for violence."

"That's my impression. Just not sure about accommodations."

"There's a room I let out above the eatery. He can have it for now an' I'll sign for the fool."

"Guess we should ask him?" I smirked, and was shocked to see the woman's cheeks turn a bit pink.

I opened his cell and Percy followed me out to the office without saying a word. He looked shaky and smelled of sweat. Drying out was never a pleasant experience and it had to be worse in a cell. When he saw Bess sitting at the desk, the man ducked his head and almost ripped his hat off.

Percy seemed like a decent enough man, not right for wearing a badge but not a bad man. One look and even I could see the way he felt about her. I could also see that she returned it despite her protests to the contrary. They could figure all that mess out, I just wanted to empty another cell.

"Percy, the deputy is offering to bond you out with me as your signature. He'd have you work as a jailer some and you can stay in the guest room." Bess's voice was crisp but there was a softness underneath I'd never heard before. "You know how I feel about the drinking?"

"I umm, that'd be umm, fine by me Miss Bess." The man finally stammered out. "Yes ma'am, I do know how you feel about it. But I don't think I'll need it like I did before. Taking that deputy back and knowing I was keeping the truth from folks kinda ate at me. Saw his face every time I closed my eyes to sleep."

"You think you can handle being the jailer and not let those two snakes bother you?" I asked.

It was good to know the man wasn't a long-term drunk. Maybe Bess could get him back on track and help him with the shame. Looking at her, I had to amend that thought. She would get him back on the right path even if it killed him. That woman had a spine of pure steel.

"Ain't worth a spit as a sheriff. Not much better as a man but I can manage that. Kinda how I got the job, helped 'round here for the old sheriff."

He met my gaze and I could see the shame in his eyes. I didn't know how he had ended up here but the idea of a second chance seemed to give him strength. Especially if that chance let him spend time with Bess. My decision was made. Besides, if he messed up she'd probably shoot him long before I had to get involved.

"I can't pay you more than meals and the room she's offering." I admitted.

"If it ain't in a cell with them two snakes I'll take it. You know they're talking 'bout some friends coming for them. Also talked up that kid before ya let him go, kinda egg'n him on.

Baxter cursed me for trying to calm him down. Sorry 'bout that, wasn't nothing you could'a done."

"Blake made his own choice, I hold no one else responsible for it. We'll give this a try. You come in with the breakfast trays, work the day an' I'll spell you at dinner time for the night." My smile changed before I continued. "Guess Levar thinks I missed them. Their friends are getting buried on Boot Hill later today. Appreciate you telling me, helps me trust you."

"Marshal, for what it's worth I didn't know nothing about what happened ta them two deputies 'till yesterday. Baxter was talking about it quiet like to that other one. He said they never made it to town, caught them on the way in." The little man gulped uncomfortably. "Figure he had a spy or some look out who spotted 'em. One he shot to rags but the man managed to ride off. The other tried to run with him but his horse broke a leg in a gopher hole. That's the one he took for a Dutch ride. Just ain't human doing that to a man."

"Can you write that out in a statement?" I asked, curious if the man would go that far.

"Yes sir, that an' more. That fiend needs to be buried, folks ain't safe with him above ground. Rattlers got more soul than that one." Percy shook his head in disgust. "Wished I'da seen it afore take'n Carter's money."

"Did Carter know anything about it?" I was sure he didn't but had to ask.

"Not a word. Baxter kept his voice low so's Mr. Carter couldn't hear it."

"Alright, get your stuff moved today and clean up. I'll see ya at breakfast tomorrow morning." I pulled a double eagle out of my vest pocket and flipped it to him. "That's likely all the pay you're gonna get but a man should have some pocket money."

"Thank ya, Deputy. I really mean it, ain't often someone'll let ya have another go 'round." Percy stuck out his hand and I could see the genuine appreciation in his eyes.

"I'll keep him straight and on time, Deputy." Bess said.

I noticed she took his hand when they walked out of the office and it made me smile. Maybe I was overstepping and Reese would chew me out when he got here, but until then I was going to do what I thought was right. Currently, that meant cleaning slop buckets and getting those two snakes some fresh water. That task would be a lot easier with a jailer helping out but it couldn't wait until tomorrow.

After lunch I took another loop around town. It was mostly just to keep a badge in people's minds, but I also stopped by the doc's to check on Ed. He was recovering and hadn't spiked a fever which was a good sign. Infection killed more people than a lead ball ever could. The doc thought he'd be able to see me in a few more days but right now he was still in and out of consciousness.

My next stop was the livery to check on my growing herd of horses. The livery man was an old cuss named Billy. He said not to worry, he'd take care of them as long as need be and we could settle up whenever I was ready. I smiled as my eyes took in Blake's gelding. The man may have been young but he knew horse flesh. The horse was solid black except for a lone white star on his chest. The confirmation was nearly perfect. He was every bit Mia's equal.

Carter had given me the keys to his house and asked me to clear out Bennet's stuff. I checked through the house and was surprised to find the man's clothing neatly folded and ready to be packed. A bit of searching revealed just short of two thousand dollars stashed in the mattress he'd been sleeping on. I added it to the money belt with the rest. It was now packed with a bit over six thousand dollars and the damn thing was getting uncomfortable. It was no longer smooth and bulged out in odd places. Tomorrow I'd go by the bank and deposit it in a new account until Reese showed up.

I was just turning onto Main Street when a boy ran up waving an envelope. I dug out a nickel and tipped him before he could run off again. The telegram was from Reese.

To Deputy Marshal

Cartersville

Arriving in three days with wagon stop

Clean the office stop.

US Marshal Reese

Denver

The last thing I did for the day was to get the paperwork done for the reward vouchers. Including Bennet and Phil Bunker, it came to a little over $6,500 in bounties. All told, it took six telegrams followed by six letters containing my statements and the undertaker's proof to get the job done. Percy showed up with the dinner trays just as I was walking back toward the office. With only two prisoners, things were much easier to deal with. I got a decent night's sleep after my rounds and woke up bright and early the next day.

CHAPTER 25

Percy arrived just after dawn the next morning and brought breakfast with him. Once we got the buckets changed and breakfast served, we sat down at the desk to work out the details of his employment. I told him what I expected from him and mostly it was simple, keep it clean and don't open the cells. There was one more thing that still needed to be dealt with and it would require me leaving town. I trusted the man but didn't want him to get jumped trying to do things by himself. My plan was to leave the keys with Bess, which meant Percy would have backup if he had to open the cells.

Miz needed some exercise and I had to go free that poor soul I'd left in the care of Black Owl. Baxter had already let it slip that the man was just some saddle tramp he'd hired. The last man had left when he found out about the dead deputy marshal. Percy had overheard Baxter cussing about not getting a warning prior to my arrival and that's what reminded me to fetch the man. I'd take him his horse and rig then politely suggest he find friendlier country. After his time with Black Owl, he'd most likely be ready to go anywhere that was away from the crazy medicine man.

I was right. As soon as I'd made my suggestion, the man took off for the tall and uncut. He lit out despite the descending darkness, leaving without so much as a backward glance. The only thing he said as he left was something about Oregon and farming. I wondered if Reese would let me hire Black Owl as a jailer. Might encourage more folks to change their ways. The old Indian's effect on people was like wizardry, a few days with him and they transformed from outlaw to farmer. Maybe the old medicine man really was magical.

My eyes followed his disappearing shape, then I paid Black Owl for his trouble and turned Miz toward town. I'd be back well before dinner tomorrow, in plenty of time to take over for Percy. I'd just have to ride out the next couple of days until Reese made it with the jail wagon, then he'd probably send me on to the next job. He might keep me in Denver or send me to a station somewhere else in Colorado, I didn't have a preference. Denver was a bit crowded for my taste but I'd figure it out if need be. Dealing with crowded cities was just another thing I'd have to learn to do.

The ride back to town gave me time to think, mostly about Miss Gardner. That day in the street had killed whatever dreams I'd harbored about her loving me. Her terror-filled eyes had told me everything, now my heart just needed to accept it. She'd seen the monster hiding behind the badge and that couldn't be undone. Now all she would see was a bloody savage stalking the streets like a beast in search of prey. Her loving me had never made any sense. Any man loving her, myself included, made perfect sense.

How the hell had I fallen for her? Every time we exchanged two sentences she was lambasting me for something. Damn it, I didn't even know the woman's Christian name yet but none of that made any difference. No matter what I did, something just drew me to her and even now she filled my thoughts. It wasn't just her beauty, there was something compelling about her presence. Another mystery of the world that didn't make a bit of sense to me. The more I thought about it, the more ignorant I felt.

Back in Cartersville...

Ms. Gardner locked herself in her room at the boarding house, needing time and quiet to process her thoughts. Every time she closed her eyes that damned man filled her mind. It wasn't fear that made her pulse race whenever she thought of him. She'd accepted that he'd captured her heart, there was no denying it. But that changed nothing and she still had no idea what to do. Why couldn't she mange to just talk to the man? Speaking to him without snapping his head off would certainly be a start.

She remembered that awful day when she saw him in the street covered in blood. Her cheeks burned as she recalled the scene she'd made. He'd tried so hard to avoid telling her it was blood, tried to get around her to bathe without explaining what had happened. And she'd questioned the poor man in the middle of town as if he'd owed her an explanation. She'd made him stand there, covered in blood, just so she could satisfy her curiosity and he'd tried so hard to spare her the unpleasant details. Shame filled her when she thought about that day. Why on earth had she done that?

Then there was that terrible shoot-out in the street. She shuddered, remembering that she had screamed like some pathetic child. She recalled staring at him for a moment as the smoke cleared then she had run away like a frightened little girl. She'd behaved the way she did because she was afraid but there was no way he could know what it was that scared her. It wasn't the young man lying dead in the street, it was the idea that it could just as easily have been him. That he might have been killed right there in front of her, dead without ever knowing she loved him. She'd behaved like such a fool, but how could she tell him what she really felt?

She buried her face in a pillow and screamed in frustration. She'd been warned time and time again about her sharp tongue. That it would drive any man away and she'd be left a spinster, alone for the rest of her days. Tears of exasperation streamed down her face, causing further problems. Now her eyes would be puffy, yet another thing on her long list of failures.

She could hear her mother's voice clearly in her mind, rattling off the many times she'd run off this suitor or that gentleman in her shrill, disparaging tone. The voice went on to list the numerous people her tongue had cut so deeply they wouldn't even be in the same room with her again. According to her mother, her temper had been the talk of Chicago. Her abrasive disposition easily outweighed her beauty in the eyes of eligible bachelors. She knew she came by it honestly, but her mother had somehow learned to redirect her own temper more effectively. That woman's harsh tongue had sent her running to hide her tears often enough to know that much.

She was such a fool. Here was finally a man with the strength she'd so admired in the heroes of her beloved books. A man whose mind was sharp and agile enough to keep up with hers. This man had ridden into a mess of a town and in a short order had straightened it out. He'd done it through cunning, backed up with violence only when there was no other choice.

He'd done his best not to take lives. He'd tried everything with that vile little Blake. She'd felt his eyes on her before and something in his gaze had made her skin crawl. He would have come for her someday, she knew that much about men. First he would've tried to charm her, but when that was rebuked he would have caught her alone and taken what he wanted. Just like him, the thought made her skin crawl.

She could still feel his hands on her, smell the whiskey on his breath when the nightmares came. She'd woken up in a cold sweat so many times, biting back a scream. If her father hadn't come into the office when he did... she couldn't bear to think about how close that beast had come to taking her against her will. She didn't want that fear to have a grip on her anymore. That was the fuel her temper fed on, it was the reason she pushed man after man away.

It wasn't just that night, her family was also part of that fuel. Her father had yelled at her, blaming her for leading the man on. He had apologized to the monster, he'd even invited him to dinner. Then he'd forced her to apologize and made her say it was all her fault.

The look of triumph in his eyes had made her sick. He'd hungrily watched her grovel under her parents' approving gaze, licking his lips and relishing her shame. That was when she'd fled, boarding a train the next afternoon with nothing more than a valise.

She made it to Saint Louis, leaving her last name in the crowded streets and selling her fancy dresses, jewelry, and luggage. She'd used some of that money to purchase a wardrobe that didn't call attention to herself. That left just enough money to move on and gave her a chance to start again. People disappeared into the West every day. From Saint Louis to Dodge city, she made another name change and caught a train to Denver. Two thousand four hundred and thirty-six dollars remained in her Denver bank account.

It was there she'd seen the advertisement for a teacher. It had been hanging in the bank when she went in to check her account. It had been simple to get the job. She sent a telegram to the mayor and he responded back almost immediately. She'd walked a block to catch the stagecoach and she was on her way. That ride had almost broken her. Being crammed between people on that bouncing dust-filled thing had been one of the worst experiences of her life. If she never rode in one again it would be too soon.

Despite Mayor Kelso's lie about the school being up and running, she'd grown to love this small town and the people in it. There was something about the place and it's inhabitants that drew her in. Maybe now that things were changing the school would actually be built. Kelso knew having a school house made a town feel established, and it would draw more families in.

None of it would matter if she couldn't get past this, if there was no one to share her life with. And not just any someone. Him. Her mind wandered into a tentative future where he came home blood soaked and she helped him to bathe. Her cheeks felt hot and her breath came a little faster. The images that played in her mind would have made a soiled dove blush. It had to be him, and that meant she needed help. Bess would know what to do.

She wasn't surprised to find Bess holding a shotgun on the prisoners while Percy swapped buckets in the cells. She didn't interrupt, instead she waited quietly in the office. When Bess came in, she'd told her that Chance had left but would be back in a day or so. Her heart ached. The marshal would arrive any day now and then the man she loved would leave. She'd almost let her one chance at happiness slip away but Bess promised her it wasn't too late and said she had a plan.

CHAPTER 26

The ride back left me far too much time to think. Now that I'd gotten to know the people here, I wanted this town to grow and succeed and I wanted to be part of it. Admittedly, Miss Gardner was at the root of that desire and there was no denying it. But it was more than that, some part of me wanted help in my own way. Maybe Reese would let me stay until Ed recovered, at least until he could take on the job. It would give the marshal time to shut down his bounty, if that was possible.

As I settled down to sleep under the stars that night, I began laying out my arguments to stay. The town was close enough to the Nations that outlaws were always around. A deputy close by would be on hand if there was a problem and could help out along the border. It was a sound argument and I was suited to the area. Learning to work in towns wouldn't be hard but it was a new skill while the wild lands were already part of me. I spoke enough native dialects to deal with those who crossed the line, which would also be a help. I even had a decent reputation among most of the tribes I'd encountered.

The next day when the town rose up out of the horizon ahead of me, it nearly took me by surprise. My mind had been so wrapped up in my thoughts the miles had just vanished under Miz's hooves. If someone had been set to ambush me it wouldn't have taken much effort, and the realization made the hair on my arms stand up. I never let my guard down like that and I knew why it had happened. She was why my mind had been so far away. That's why I'd been thinking of reasons to stay, everything else was just a bonus. Even the slightest chance of a life with her was enough to tempt me.

As I turned up Main Street at the edge of town, a small dust cloud at the far end caught my attention. Moving just ahead of the cloud was the jail wagon with Marshal Reese riding beside it. I gave Miz a slight nudge with my heels and he picked up his pace. We met in front of the jail, the small cloud of dust announcing our arrival.

"Marshal Reese, welcome to Cartersville." I smiled.

"Why do you look as trail worn as I do?" He asked, looking me up and down.

"Caught a tail out of Denver, had to go cut him loose once everything calmed down here." I didn't bother with any further explanation and it made him frown.

"Thought you had prisoners?"

"Yup, down to two as long as we see things the same way. They'll be worth the trip, it's Bennet and Levar." That got his attention but didn't answer his unasked questions.

"Who's been watching them while you were out traipsing 'round the countryside?"

"Percy and Bess."

"And who are they?"

"Percy was the sheriff an' Bess owns the eatery." I grinned, stepping down from Miz. This was getting to him and it made me chucklc.

"You know what? There's gonna need to be coffee an a chair for this story, 'specially the way you're tell'n it. Where can Charlie park that wagon? Charlie meet Chance, my current regret. Chance that's Charlie, the best jail wagon driver an' cook I got."

"Pleasure, Charlie." I tipped my hat to the man in greeting. "There's an empty spot down by the livery, he's expecting you."

"Same, Chance. Glad to see someone making him as miserable as he makes me."

"Hey now…"

"Get up there." Charlie ignored whatever Reese was trying to say, snapping the reins. The wagon moved off toward the livery, leaving both of us standing in the dusty street.

"Come on Boss, coffee should be on." I laughed, turning towards the office. "I'll explain everything."

"Kinda got my curiosity up, I'm looking forward to this story."

Percy must not have heard us coming because jumped up from the desk in surprise when the door opened. He looked from me to the marshal then back again. Realization seemed to dawn on him and his shoulders slumped. I glanced around the office then let out a low whistle. The man had kept himself busy cleaning the place from top to bottom while I was gone.

"You can go for now, Percy. Ask Bess to add two more meals for dinner, will ya?"

"No problem, Deputy." He closed the door behind him and I heard him step off the boardwalk, headed to see Bess.

"That was the old sheriff?"

"Yeah, now you know why I let him bond out. He was never a threat, just a pawn Bennet was using at Carter's expense."

"Yeah, not much point in charging him." Reese agreed while I filled two coffee cups. "How the hell is Bennet mixed up in this mess?"

"Bennet is Baxter." I let that fact sink in first. "He had Big Jack, Levar, Patty and Craig lined up and ready to take the town. They were just waiting for money from a drive."

"Whhoowee! That woulda been a real mess. How'd you figure it out?"

"Luck. I caught Levar sneaking around town, didn't take him long to tell me where to find the others. Tried to take them alive but it didn't work out." I waited for him to get mad but it never happened.

"You'da never took them alive, not those three. Craig said he'd never go back to prison and Patty was worser. On a guess, I'd say Big Jack just got caught up in the mix." Reese cut me off before I could explain. I'd still been chastising myself about their deaths and his words helped.

"Appreciate you saying that. Been reading myself from the scripture about it." I admitted before continuing. "Once that got revealed I started questioning folks. Carter was first, Bennet had told him Dodger died in a fight with a gambler. Used the star as evidence that he'd been shot in a fair fight."

"You believe him?" Reese was angry but still willing to listen.

"I do, an' Percy corroborated his story. The other two he never knew about. Bennet jumped them outside of town. Percy didn't know about that until a few days ago when he heard him talking in the cell. Had seven folks locked up in the three cells for a bit." Reese's eyebrows rose at that.

"That musta been tricky."

"Percy said even then Bennet kept it quiet so Carter couldn't hear him talking. Reason being, Carter's got strong feelings 'bout folks catching a Dutch ride. He got left for dead after being dragged when he was young. Nobody could fake the look on his face when I told him." That took Reese's anger down a few notches. "Carter was also the one who told Percy to deliver Dodge's body. Wasn't any disrespect, he wanted him buried properly if he had kin."

"That does change things." Dragging his thumb across his stubbly chin in thought. "What's his excuse for the rest?"

"Same as everyone else who rode out here first before other folks came. Change and loss of power. Wasn't me who changed his thinking on that. Bess, the owner of the eatery, dressed him down real good. But she did it in such a way as to make him really think rather than just shaming him." I smiled at the memory of that particular tongue lashing. "Think he's a changed man, not from that but because he recognized the need to change."

"I wasn't looking forward to arresting him if I'm being honest. Take out one of the big landowners and it creates a land grab. Always ends in gun play with innocent folks dead."

"Same opinion I had, and it would destroy the town these folks are trying to build. I bonded him out with his property up for security. His ramrod's an old hand I know, he signed for him. Red's a good man, I'll vouch for him."

"Alright, you've sold me so far." He said, sipping his coffee. Charlie walked in and grabbed himself a cup then settled in to listen to the rest.

"They fired the one gun hawk they had that was still standing. Young kid whose ego got bruised when I arrested him. He forced my hand in public and got buried yesterday. Wasn't wanted as far as I know, just a stupid kid with too much pride."

"You'll have that. You said still standing?"

"Yeah, Phil Bunker pushed me the first night then Edmund Vayo took his shot. Phil's in the ground, already sent his paperwork off with Bennet's and the rest of them."

"What about Pepper?" He cocked an eyebrow, catching my omission.

"Healing over at the doc's, I put a round through his arm. He'll be good as new in a few weeks. That's where I need your help."

"Do tell?" The smirk on Reese's face showed his amusement.

"I want him to take the sheriff's job when he heals up.

Known him for a few years, he's a good man. The bounty on him is personal rather than legal, and therein lies the rub. He'd make a good law man and wants to stop runnin'." I could tell by the look on his face it probably wasn't going to happen.

"I ever tell ya 'bout when I met him, boss?" Charlie asked out of the blue.

"You?" Reese asked. Charlie had both of our attention now.

"I ain't telling ya what to do but if it was me, I'd back him." Charlie's eyes seemed to drift back in time as he spoke. "Ya know I was a deputy for a while, but what ya don't know is why I quit."

"Your predecessor sent me up to the far western corner, wanted me to bring back the Tavor brothers." I didn't know Charlie at all but I could tell this tale was important to him. "This was when they first got started, something 'bout a cow pony. Nothing serious. Found 'em, or rather they found me. Parker dry gulched me, a clean hit through my shoulder. I'm why he got hung, well I was one of the reasons."

"That don't matter for this story, just a side note. I was still breathing but the hit knocked me out of the saddle. I could hear their horses head'n my way. When they got about ten feet from me, I could hear them laughing like coyotes. Then from off ta the right I heard a Winchester chamber a round an' this voice follows it out." Charlie sipped his coffee before starting again.

" 'Don't know what y'all are about but I can't let ya kill an injured man. So turn tail or pull steel.' Didn't know it then but that voice was Edmund Vayo. He'd heard the shot and had come up to see what was going on. Reckon he's got a reason for it but I don't know it. Fact is, he hates a backshooter an' considers dry gultch'n worser."

"The brothers turned tail an' headed out at a gallop. Ed got my horse an' pack mule, managed to get me in the saddle then took me to his camp. He played nursemaid for two weeks until I could sit a horse again. Traveled with me into Beacon, it was a little flash in the pan town that died out when the copper dried up. Ain't even timbers left up there now, not after that fire a year or so ago." Charlie sat back, trying to recall the details.

"Don't matter none." He gave up the memory and continued with his story. "At the outskirts he headed the other way. I know'd who he was but the man had done right by me. Wasn't no way I'd go after him, not after that. The wife figured after that fracas I'd be better off on a jail wagon an' here we sit. Don't change the fact that I owe the man my life."

"You never told me that story." Reese said, rocking back in his chair.

"What, that I'd been shot?"

"Naw, that you were so henpecked." Reese laughed and rose to refill our cups.

"An' ya wonder why I don't talk much." Charlie retorted, but I could see both men were smiling.

"I'll see what I can do about the bounty. Problem is, the personal ones are harder 'cause the law can't control them. Think he'll be a good sheriff? What about the town, they agree to it?" The boss had turned his eyes back to me.

"I do. Haven't talked to the townsfolk yet but most have a pretty good opinion of him. He'd stepped in to back off a few rowdies when they cut loose in town." I nodded my appreciation for him topping off my cup.

"Sounds like a good choice then. We either get the bounty taken care of or do it the slightly less legal way by collecting the bounty after making a fake grave. He wouldn't be the first law man with no past." Reese chuckled knowingly before dropping back into his chair.

"One more problem with it." I grinned at him over the desk.

"He's gonna be laid up for a while healing and you want ta stay here?" Reese had already figured it out of course. "That's fine, I was going to assign you down here anyway. I need someone to cover the area and help out in the Nations when needed. Let's talk to the mayor 'bout it after breakfast."

"Well hell, that was easier than I figured. Wasted a whole lotta time working out an argument for nothing." He just smirked at me. "Last thing is bounties and found."

"One day you'll learn, son. Ain't nothing you can think up that I ain't heard before."

"Cause he's old." Charlie added. His timing was perfect, he nearly made me choke on my coffee.

"You're a damn sight older than me!" Reese shot back but Charlie didn't miss a beat.

"True, an' that's why I know what you're up to afore ya do it." He was getting payback for the henpecked comment.

"Truce, old man. Let me get through with this crazy youngster before I have to tangle with you." Reese turned back to me. "If you get the town to agree to it, I don't have a problem with Peppers. Still want to talk to Carter though. Not that I don't trust you, but I've had this particular burr in my boot for a while."

"That's fair."

"Far as bounties go, it's a split with the marshals and the deputy who collects 'em. The money is used to keep the service going." He reached into his wallet and pulled out some familiar papers. "This is half the vouchers for Bennet and the rest, totaled $7,600 so $3,800 each."

"Better than I expected." I admitted. "Half figured we wouldn't get any of it."

"Might change, but for now that's how it is. Figure that's 'bout the only thing that helps some keep the badge on. Ain't like the pay is that good." He laughed. "As far as found, horses, guns and cash that don't connect to a crime are yours. 'Course we can always use the guns and horses but that's up to you."

"Take your pick of the horses from the livery, same with the tack. Should be six good horses and two mules, all with tack. Take any supplies from the packs too, I can't use but so much bacon. I got their guns locked up here, six Winchesters, a yellow boy, couple of Colts, a fancy two gun rig with pretty Smith and Wesson Model 3's. All are in good working order, outlaws always have decent guns and good horses." I mentioned the fancy rig because Reese wore two guns, but unlike most men he could actually use them.

"Might want those Model 3's." He admitted. "Split the rest and ammo if you're willing?"

"Works." I agreed easily.

CHAPTER 27

Percy opened the door and let Bess in before I could continue. She looked the three of us over then made her decision, locking eyes with Reese. I did the only thing possible and leaned back in my chair to watch the show. Reese looked lost for a minute then realized the woman's eyes were focused on him. He'd just started to open his mouth when she beat him to it.

"Why'd it take so long to send someone who could handle this mess?" She didn't even give him a chance to answer. "Cause ya needed someone as capable as that young fella I'm guessing?"

"Yes ma'am." It was really all he could say, anything else would sound like an excuse.

"Good. Name's Bess not ma'am. You plannin' on taking my man?" Percy's eyes about popped out of his head at that.

"No ma'… Bess, my deputy seems to think it wouldn't serve a purpose." It was funny watching him deal with her. It vaguely reminded me of the stories I'd heard about bull fighters in Mexico.

"Good, then ya can eat." She put down the three trays before picking up the shotgun.

Reese was about to intervene but I waved him off. She still had the keys so I wasn't surprised when she turned to unlock the door. We all watched through the doorway as she and Percy dealt with the prisoners. Bess kept them covered while he changed out the buckets. After that was done, they locked the cells up and handed each man a tray through the bars. Bess filled two cups with coffee for the prisoners before locking the door. It looked like they got the dregs, but no one was bothered by that misfortune aside from the two men. She started another pot before leaving the keys on the desk.

"Same for breakfast?" She asked from the doorway.

"Sounds good, Bess. You got a bill for everything figured yet?"

"Gave it to the mayor today, he didn't complain too much." She laughed. "He paid for these but after breakfast you'll have to come across the street like everyone else."

"Thanks for everything, Bess. Percy, when I've got a prisoner I might need you to pitch in. Looks like I'll be around for a while yet."

"He'll be around when ya need him." Bess answered for him. "An' Deputy, you have plans for lunch tomorrow."

"I do?" This was news to me but it was presented as a statement rather than a question. I turned to Percy before I forgot. "Percy, can you ask the mayor to come by after breakfast then ride out and ask Carter the same? If it's not too late tonight."

"No problem, Deputy. I can make it there and back before dark." The little man nodded.

After Percy answered, Bess resumed her instructions for me."You do. Be over to the eatery round noon, don't be late."

"Yes ma'am." That earned me a glare but it gave me back a little of my own. She closed the door but didn't slam it so she'd probably let me live.

"Powerful woman, reminds me of my wife." Charlie smiled while taking a tray of food. "Smells like she's a helluva good cook too."

"Better than I been eatin'." Reese said, watching Charlie for a reaction.

"Gonna be worser going home after that comment. Ever had mule cooked on a stick? Just gotta roll it in some charcoal to make it eatable."

"Don't know how that can happen." Reese shot back, then grasped what the man had said. "You ain't killing one of those mules. Spent too much time of your time 'round them Apache."

That was how we spent most of the evening, swapping stories and drinking coffee. They both camped with the wagon and I spent another night on the cot. They were back at the jail by the time the first light of dawn broke the horizon. I already had coffee on and was waiting for them on the boardwalk.

I hadn't bothered with the prisoners, they'd be gone not long after breakfast. After that I'd have to clean the cells. Percy probably knew where to send the laundry, I needed to remember to ask the man about it. Bess and Percy brought breakfast over not long after we all sat down. They fed the prisoners again and took care of the buckets, which I much appreciated. Percy spoke up before I had a chance to ask.

"Want me to come later an' clean out the cells?"

"Appreciate it, we can talk about paying you then. Don't know how regular the work will be but you'll be paid for what you do."

"Just trying to pay back the folks I let down, I ain't worried about money."

"It's a job, that means you get paid."

"I'll get it done while your at lunch then."

"And don't you forget about lunch." Bess cut in, not so subtly reminding me of my mysterious appointment.

"I'll be there." I assured her quickly. That got some laughs from Reese and Charlie. "Leave the door open will you? Saves time when folks show up.

She did as I asked then headed back across the street. People would be showing up at her place soon and would be expecting their breakfast. Bess was only closed on Sunday. She'd already told me that was because of the churchgoing folks. They claimed working on Sunday was a sin and promised to shame anyone who opened for business. If they had asked me, I'd have told them good luck and stayed in my office. Anyone who willingly confronted that woman was going to have a very bad day. Their plan had backfired at least once that I knew of. They'd asked her to cook for a church social and her reply wasn't repeatable in good company.

After breakfast, I used the bottom of my boot to strike a match then slowly puffed my cheroot to life. It was a quiet reminder that I needed to find some more today. There was something about a good smoke after a meal that just suited me. The mayor walked in through the open doorway with Carter on his heels, the former looking puffed up and the latter looking chagrined. The facial expression did nothing to detract from the danger that hung on Carter like a suit of clothes. It was something men like him could never shake, a byproduct of too many years living in wild country.

"Gentlemen." The mayor greeted everyone. Carter just nodded. He was a man waiting on a sentence so it wasn't surprising.

"Grab them chairs off the porch, will ya Charlie?" Reese asked, and for once there was no backtalk. When he only brought in one, Reese raised an eyebrow in question.

"Figure this is grown folks' talk. I'll sit outside, always like watching a place wake up more then this mess anyhow." Charlie answered before walking outside and closing the door behind him.

"Damned old man." Reese grumbled before getting down to business. "Have a seat gentlemen, this shouldn't take long.

Let's get the most pressing business out of the way first. Carter, like Percy you're not being charged. You can thank the deputy here for speaking up on your behalf. I will say this, there need to be some changes around here or we will revisit the issue again."

"Appreciate that, an' we already got started on some of it." Carter nodded his thanks to me as he spoke.

"He's made some significant changes already. We spent a couple of days working out the best way for the town to move forward. We blocked off the map, defining the town limits and the boundaries of his ranch. We're putting several farms up for sale with competitive financing. Mr. Carter signed paperwork giving me the power to sell lots within the defined town limits. Folks who already have structures built will get a sizable discount on their lots, it's our way of thanking them for helping found the town." The mayor looked happy with the changes. "The land office will be handling the sale of the sections outside of the town, along with the mortgage options."

"I'd recommend a change to that." Reese interrupted. "One man can't ever have all of the power, Mayor. Don't mean any disrespect but it should be a council of three for the businesses. Home lots can be assigned to one person, but for businesses make it a council of three. That way no one can say you stopped or allowed a new business for personal reasons."

"I take no offense." The mayor assured. "You're right, hadn't thought about that. Carter, I'd suggest myself, Lonigan the smith, and Pearson. He owns the saddlery."

"Your choice, mayor. Just make sure it's an even slate." Carter agreed.

"Ya'll can work that out later. Right now I need something for the marshals. I'm going to station a deputy here permanently. That means I need to have an office built and I need the land it will stand on."

"The lot next door is open, we can just add on to this building." The mayor offered.

"That would work, never hurts to have the law all in one place. But it needs to be built like this place, tough enough to withstand a siege. Marshals service will buy the lot and have it built. Already contracted a crew and had it designed in Denver. They'll be here in a week to get started, shouldn't take them more than a month to get it done." Reese had clearly caught the mayor by surprise with his plan.

"Don't suppose anyone refuses."

"No, mayor. The only ones who refuse are outlaw towns and I don't ask them."

"Makes sense and we welcome it." The mayor smiled, thinking about it. "It's another thing that will encourage people to move here."

"It does draw in newcomers, least it has in every other town where I've posted a deputy." Reese grinned. "Now about your sheriff. Chance had an interesting suggestion about that."

"Reese, you mind if I modify the building plans a bit? We oughta join the two buildings and share the cells between the two." I suggested, picturing the idea in my mind. "Means the cost of a jailer can be shared."

"Don't see a problem with it, just watch the expense. I don't want some pissed off paper pusher calling me when they get the bill. I'll leave you authorization."

"Who would you recommend for the sheriff?" The mayor asked. I noticed Carter sharpen his attention too.

"He reckons Edmund Vayo would make a good lawman and after hearing his reasoning I'm liable to agree. That being said, it's your choice."

CHAPTER 28

"I don't know the man personally. He's helped folks from what I've been told. Broke up a brawl or two and stepped in when Percy couldn't stop some trouble or another." The mayor admitted.

"I know the man and he's never been anything but upfront in my experience. Stopped more than one of my hands from acting the fool. Even made me ease off a few times when we've had problems with squatters." Carter admitted.

"Isn't he shot right now?" The mayor asked after thinking about it for a minute.

"Doc says he's on the mend but it'll be a while." I explained, thinking that at some point Ed should be asked his thoughts about the idea. "I can cover for him until he's back on his feet."

"I already agreed to it." Reese shrugged, stretching for his cup then realizing it was empty. He got up to refill it and top off everyone else.

"Job's his if he wants it then. That's if he wants it. Pay's thirty-five dollars a month and found. Room and board have always been at the jail." The mayor gave his approval. "Course that pay won't start until I can swear him in and that won't happen until he recovers."

"I'll keep paying him while he recovers, he did catch that bullet while working for me." Carter evidently took care of his hands and that didn't seem to come as a surprise to anyone. "I also want to be sure something else I have planned is acceptable to the marshal."

"Mr. Carter?" Reese eyed the man, waiting for his explanation.

"Please, just Carter. It's two things really. First, I'll donate the land for the marshal's office free and clear." Reese nodded his agreement. It wasn't unexpected, most towns did that to ensure there was a law enforcement office there. "I have two people to thank for helping me see the error of my ways. The first is Bess, she now owns her place and the land it sits on free and clear. Chance is the second. Not only did he speak to you on my behalf, he also spoke to me about correcting things around here. I want to give him my house here in town as my way of thanking him."

"I don't see a problem with it." Reese nodded then thumbed over his shoulder at the cot. "Sounds like your housing is sorted."

"Still going to add a proper room for the Sheriff on the new construction." I said, glaring at the cot.

"There's one stipulation that comes with the house." Carter spoke up again before we got sidetracked. "You have to keep Miss Angie on payroll. She makes twenty dollars a month, which I'll keep paying. The small house to the left of the main house is part of her pay. She cooks and maintains the house, has done since it was built. Before you say that's not enough, I want you to know I pay her a monthly stipend on top of that."

"Why?" I had to ask. That was a lot of compensation for someone to maintain a house. There had to be more to the story.

"Her husband died while working for me when I first started building out here. She wouldn't stay out here with me for free, won't take more than a small stipend either. Built that house to give her a job, that way I could be sure she lived comfortably." That said a lot about the man. Building a house to give a widow a job and some security? He might be a hard man but you couldn't question his loyalty.

"Seems like a good idea to me, especially since you're paying for it." I grinned but Reese stepped in and stole my joy.

"She works for you not him. You pay her if you want the house."

"Figured you'd say that." I laughed. "But I understand it."

"Good, that's my only concern." Reese agreed to the rest without any hesitation. "Mayor, the rest of this is town business. I just wanted to be sure you didn't feel wronged by us not charging Carter."

"Not at all, at least not after the conversations we've had recently. I think we share the same goals and I understand him better now. He'll have a voice in the business that concerns him or his ranch. The house and the land it sits on will be transferred to Chance but Carter is retaining the mineral rights to all the land. I never considered how building a town might affect his ranch, let alone the impact mining might have."

"It was fear driving me, Marshal." Carter swallowed as he said it and I knew it had to be hard admitting that out loud. "Fear of change and of losing what I'd built."

"You're not unique in that, seen it more than once. You had the strength and drive to come out here when it was wild. Paid dearly for every inch you carved out of the wild." Reese met the man's gaze as he talked. "Then a bunch of folks show up once it's comfortable and start calling it theirs. Tends to make a man disagreeable. Keeping the mineral rights is smart too, lets you control something that might destroy your range."

"I'd never considered how things looked to him." The mayor admitted. "Now that I have and he understands my vision, we shouldn't have any more problems."

"Well, I appreciate the time gentlemen. Now I have to get my prisoners loaded up and head back to Denver." Reese said, effectively putting an end to the meeting.

Before they left, Carter handed me the keys and the signed deed for the house. He'd moved his few things out the day before and explained the changes to Miss Angie, so I was free to move in that night. The best part of the whole thing to me was the large stables and corral out back. I'd need to find someone to tend the horses when I was out, but it would still save me on livery fees. Reese had worked that deal out last night, but only for the marshal's service. It covered two horses and a mule so I'd have to deal with the rest.

I wasn't sure how many horses I owned at that point but I'd prefer they were all in my stables. What a strange thought that was. My land, my stables. Part of it didn't feel right, not after traveling with everything I owned fitting in my saddlebags for so many years. Having a place that was mine? A place to maybe call home? It felt strange, like suddenly I had roots somewhere. I owned land, had a real job. It was all new to me. Part of me was looking forward to exploring the large house that night while another part felt separated from the reality of it all.

Charlie pulled the wagon up while I was having my personal crisis. He walked in with two sets of leg irons and hand cuffs. The leg irons would stay on the prisoners until Denver and the cuffs were put on anytime the men were let out of the wagon. That much I'd learned in school along with a few other procedures for transporting prisoners. Reese and Charlie worked like a well-oiled machine and I made it my job to stay out of their way.

The guns and ammo went into a locked box under the seat. Reese liked the Smith and Wessons and he planned on wearing them himself after he got some practice with them. They'd picked up the horses before coming to the jail and Reese eyed me curiously when I said I was keeping the Morgan. He took Blake's gelding which bothered me until he clarified the animal was intended for him. This man had opened a door for me and he could have anything he wanted.

The supplies had been loaded the night before, and thankfully they'd decided to take the majority. They'd left me mostly canned goods and basic supplies that didn't go bad. The prisoners were last to get loaded. Since they were shacked, they shuffled their way out and into the back of the wagon. Both men looked around like they still expected some kind of rescue to come charging in at the eleventh hour. Unfortunately for them, the redemption they were hoping for was already dead and buried. I was amazed Levar hadn't figured that out since one of the horses Reese took was Big Jake's.

They were done and gone in thirty minutes. Reese promised to try and keep me around town until Ed was healed up. He planned to verify what I'd told him about Vayo then submit the paperwork to collect the bounty. We'd decided faking his death was easier than trying to get the bounty pulled. The undertaker was already carving poor Edmund Vayo's tombstone.

He'd have to pick out a new name before he could be sworn in but he'd get his bounty as seed money. Reese and I had joked about keeping it but there was something poetic about giving it to Ed. Luckily, the town was small and most people didn't know him. Getting those that did on board with the plan was easy, turned out most people liked him. The words gruff and cantankerous were used a few times but he'd never been a bully.

I had just enough time for a smoke before going to the eatery for my mysterious lunch engagement. Sitting outside the sheriff's office watching the small town go about its day gave me a good feeling. It was unfamiliar to me, having spent so much time just passing through places. I was starting to feel a connection to this one. This place felt like home. That little feeling growing inside me was like the soft warmth of a hearth growing in my chest.

I dropped the butt of my cheroot into the spittoon, the soft hiss sounding my finale call. I slowly unfolded from my seat and walked across the dusty road. The smells wafting on the breeze woke up my hunger and my mouth started watering. Soon my stomach chimed in with a loud growl telling me it was time to eat, meeting or no meeting.

Earlier in the eatery....

As Bess watched Mary worry over the meal she was preparing, she contemplated how long it had been since she'd fussed over a man that way. She found it cute but also rather nerve racking. She'd lost count of how many times she'd told the younger woman to keep the oven door closed. No, the roast wasn't done yet. Teaching her how to use the stove was another exercise in patience. Whoever raised this poor girl had failed her miserably.

For her part, Mary buzzed around the kitchen in such a nervous flurry she couldn't have stood still if she tried. The last time she'd reached to check the roast, Bess had threatened to beat her with a wooden spoon. The potatoes seemed to be done and a nice pie was cooling on the windowsill, mostly thanks to Bess. She did feel confident about the green beans though, and they were all her doing.

Thankfully Bess had made the biscuits, insisting that it wasn't something you learned in a day. Biscuits and coffee, if nothing else was edible that would be lunch. Maybe that would be better, she could add some preserves and not risk exposing her lack of knowledge. No, she'd already tried that and Bess had made it clear it wasn't going to happen.

Why was she so damn nervous? Aside from trying to show him she wasn't just a screaming shrew, she'd only cooked a few times in her life. It had been long ago in her parents' house, she'd been five at the most and trying to help the staff in the kitchen. Maybe that didn't count? Bess had assured her this was the best way to get a man's attention. According to the older woman, a man could be conquered with nothing more than a good meat and potatoes meal.

She laughed at the thought. It was ridiculous of course, she was certain it took more than that. She knew from experience most men were caught by a smile, but that wasn't the right kind of attention. Maybe that's what Bess meant, this was how you captured their interest past wearing a corset and a smile. Bess wasn't just trying to help her get noticed, she was teaching her how to demonstrate that she could be a potential wife. Wife? Where had that thought come from?

Was that what she wanted? Did she really want to marry him? He made something in her sing but was that love? She'd already acknowledged that he lit a fire in her and made her feel safe. But it was definitely something more, something deeper than desire alone. Based on the novels she'd read, she was certain it was. Not the ones on the bookcase, the ones tucked in the bottom of her dresser. Her firsthand knowledge of the feeling was more vague. Why was she thinking about that? Was the roast done yet? Her hand started moving toward the stove again but one look from Bess made it freeze in mid-air.

"Girl, leave it be for another five minutes, it'll be done then."

She stepped back, leaning on the counter and studying her trembling hands. This was the old fear coming back to haunt her at the worst possible time. She'd be alone with this man, isolated and vulnerable. She knew it was safe, knew he wasn't anything like that man. He'd never behave like that, it just wasn't in him to be that vile. Yet none of those rational thoughts stopped her racing heart or the fear surging through her. What made it worse was that part of her wanted him to touch her, hoped he would take her in his powerful arms and pull her to him. The idea terrified and thrilled her in equal measure.

"Can't you be there, Bess?" She asked for what felt like the hundredth time.

"No girl, you two youngsters need to find your way through this on your own." She found Bess's smile somewhat reassuring. "He's a good man, Mary. You'll be fine. And the roast should be done."

Action took the place of further questions. She managed to get the roast out of the oven without burning herself and was grateful when Bess helped her slice it. As badly as she was shaking it might have cost her a finger. Percy knocked twice on the kitchen door, making her jump. Chance had arrived and her pulse started galloping again. God, he was here and it was time. Her heart was trying to jump out of her throat as she helped Bess plate the meal. She could do this, it was possible to just sit and have a pleasant meal with him. It was so forward of her though! She was being shameless, tricking him into this meal. No, that wasn't right. Bess had said it was okay and was so sure that it made her want to believe it was true.

"Bess..." She wanted more reassurance but the older woman cut her off.

"It's fine, leastwise it's the only way for you two to stop this silliness. Ain't no other way, given how y'all behave 'round one another." Her tone wasn't unkind but it was final.

"Okay." Mary looked at the floor, gathering her courage. Finally she gave up the fight, took a deep breath and waited for Percy to knock again. When he did she startled so badly she nearly dropped the coffee pot.

Bess held the door open and Mary took the pot and two cups out into the dining area. Her heart stopped when she saw him sitting at a small table in the corner. Just then, he glanced up and saw her watching him. What was that look? She couldn't read what he was thinking. Was he pleased or annoyed to see her?

CHAPTER 29

I turned to look up as the kitchen door opened, expecting to see Bess or maybe Percy. The last person I anticipated seeing in the doorway was her. What was Miss Gardner doing working at the eatery? She must be working, why else would she be carrying the coffee pot? She seemed to be frozen in the doorway, as if she were debating his existence. The door swung back on its hinges, launching her toward me. She managed not to fall and quickly recovered her balance. The red that stained her cheeks didn't explain why she was there but it did tell me where the door had likely made contact.

Her hair was mussed, as if she'd run her hands through it too many times. I tried to hide my smile when she blew a stray piece out of her eyes. Flour was streaked down one side of her face, lining up with a darker smudge on the opposite cheek. Some other ingredient looked like it had been absently wiped down the front of her dress, trailing off onto her apron. She was a masterpiece of stains, some kind of fruit juice, grease, and various powders blended into the off-white color almost obscuring the light floral pattern of her dress.

Sun streaked in through a nearby window, making the sheen of sweat on her pale skin seem to shimmer. A single bead trailed through the flour running down her neck to... My eyes snapped back up to meet hers. They were the same stunning emerald green but still held the fear I'd seen before. It was the same look wild mustangs got when they were roped, a flashing panic that telegraphed the desire to run. None of that changed the effect those eyes had on me, though. They drew me in, giving me glimpses of something below the fear, something deeper.

Suddenly, she half lurched and stumbled forward. Bess's hand had shot out of the door and forced her into forward motion. When she got near the table, I popped up from my chair like there was a spring under me. My attempt at politeness only succeeded in launching my hat which had been perched on my knee across the room. Her eyes tracked it's flight, a hint of amusement creeping into them and erasing some of the fear. She set a coffee cup in front of me with a trembling hand. That's when I noticed Bess smirking behind her. A few awkward moments of silence hung in the air between us before Bess broke the spell. She was obviously done waiting for us to do something.

"Both of you sit down." She put two plates in front of us and took the coffee pot while Mary managed to sit down across from me. My eyes looked from my hat to Bess and back again. Recognizing my continued survival depended on making the right choice, I sat myself down. The hat was fine where it was. "Chance this is Mary, Mary meet Chance. Don't think anyone ever introduced you two properly."

"It'd be a pleasure to call you Mary if you'll allowed it, ma'am." I asked stiffly, reaching to take her hand.

"Please do, Chance." I felt her struggle not to yank her hand away. Did she find me so repulsive? And if so, why was she joining me at the table? I heard Bess click her tongue in frustration.

"Look, I ain't got time for this. You two love each other or have a shot at it anyway. Everyone can see that, everyone but you two evidently. Hell, ya can't even manage a conversation that doesn't end in screaming."

We both snapped our eyes to Bess as she spoke, some survival instinct telling us to not interrupt the woman. I was lost as to why she was doing this. Did she want to shame me for something? There was no way this stunning woman had any interest in me. It just couldn't be, not all scarred up and broken like I was. What did I have to offer her? Sure, I had money and a house now but I was still more savage then civilized. I was like a green broke horse, half wild and likely to buck the saddle. Just the thought of having a home had sent my mind spiraling the night before.

From the look on Mary's face, she was as surprised as I was. It looked to me like Bess had just sprung this whole thing on her too. If I read that look right, she'd be running out the door in the next minute or two. Hell, she might have already bolted if Bess hadn't been blocking her path. Fear flashed through her eyes mixed with something else I couldn't identify, most likely revulsion. That made sense in my head, what else could it be?

"Chance, Mary's spent all morning cooking you a good lunch. Roast beef with all the trimmings, even made an apple pie for dessert." Bess's last statement made even less sense.

The whole idea stunned me, I didn't believe it until my eyes flicked back to Mary. She met my gaze for just a second then her eyes shot back down to stare at the tablecloth. That didn't stop me from noticing the red creep up her neck, slowly coloring her cheeks. Why was she embarrassed? I was flattered by the idea of anyone, much less someone like her, cooking me a meal. I didn't know what to say. No one, as far as I could remember, had ever cooked a meal just for me. Finally my brain stuttered back to life and my mouth managed to form words.

"Mary, that's probably the most thoughtful thing anyone's ever done for me." It just came tumbling out. All I'd meant to say was a simple thank you.

"You don't need to poke fun." She snapped, her eyes shooting daggers when I met her gaze.

"I'm not." I gulped before continuing. "Don't think anyone's made something just for me since my mom died when I was nine. Leastwise, not without me paying them."

She rocked back in her chair like I had slapped her. There was no heat in my voice, nothing but honest sincerity. Even Bess looked taken aback by my words. Mary just stared at me for a long moment, unsure of what to say. When she finally collected herself, she spoke so carefully it was almost as if she were afraid to open her mouth.

"So your father raised you?"

"No, he died with my mother." This got stunned stares and silence from both women again, neither of them sure what to say. It's not that orphans were a rarity but most didn't end up where I was.

"You grew up in an orphanage?" Bess asked. She was caught up in the story now.

"No, when I left the farm the Apache got on my trail. They caught up with me after about a week." Not wanting to go into all the details, I simplified the story. My finger absently traced the scar on my face as I spoke. "They dragged me around with them for three years. Not as a slave, kinda more like a pet."

"How did you escape?" Mary asked. All traces of fear were gone now and her beautiful eyes watched me with a fascination that unsettled me.

"Got a chance to run one night and took it. Three weeks later, a cavalry patrol found me and took me back to the fort with them. Not long after we made it back, a rancher came to the fort selling horses and he took me in to work on his ranch." It was a short version but the main points were there.

"At eleven you escaped from the Apache an' made it three weeks in wild country?" Bess asked the question this time, it made me wonder if they were taking turns.

"I did learn from them during those three years. How to track, find water, run for days on end. How to stay hidden, take game and make fire. They didn't mean to teach me but I learned everything I could from watching them. Even learned to speak Crow, Shoshone, Cherokee, and some Sioux from the squaws they'd caught during raids."

"Did you learn to read and write?" Mary asked. I tried not to sound defensive when I replied, it was a reasonable question.

"My mom started me reading and doing numbers before she died. Thad, that's the rancher, made sure I learned higher math and let me read anything he had." I smiled at the memory of his library. "The man had an addiction to books and shared it with me."

"Higher math?" Bess didn't know what I meant by that.

"Yes ma'am, things like geometry, algebra and such. He'd gotten a copy of Pierce's Linear Associative Algebra somewhere and we worked through it together. The man had a keen mind for learning."

"And you?" Mary was just watching me with a faraway look while Bess kept the questions coming.

"I can do the math but prefer reading. Literature always anticipates life. It doesn't copy, it moulds it to its purpose." I stole the words of Oscar Wilde, I'd always liked the saying. That broke Mary out of her silence with a jolt.

"You just quoted Wilde?"

"I like him, not the most exciting writer but still a good read. Right now I'm re-reading Edgar Allen Poe for the third time." That reminded me to find a new book. I doubted there'd much to read out here but maybe I could find some books back in Denver.

"Who else do you enjoy reading?" Her eyes were locked on mine now and I fell into them, losing myself again.

All concept of time fell away from the table after that. To this day, I couldn't tell you how long we sat there or if the meal was any good. We were barely aware of Bess leaving to go about her business. Both of us were so lost in our conversation and one another's company that everything else seemed to disappear. It felt like all the reality around us just took a step back, letting us exist in our own world. She had an amazing mind, a quick wit, and was more well-read than I was. Every aspect of her captivated me, it was like being caught in a vortex of comfort.

Bess had been right of course. I was so completely in love with this woman. There was no denying it now, it just resonated throughout my being. The initial sense of home I had felt in this town solidified, only now it centered around her. She was my home, not this place. This amazing woman sitting across the table from me, who seemed to be enjoying my company. It was like each of us let our guard down and realized what happiness was for the first time. We sat talking long after the last bite of apple pie was gone. My words tumbled out before I could stop them.

"Marry me?" It came out that simply. No pretext and no warning.

When my mind realized what I'd said it froze in terror. I pictured her storming away from the table, never speaking to me again. Any moment now she would walk out of my life forever. The look on her face was a mixture of stunned shock and complete terror.

I had ruined the perfect day we were sharing with some blundered proposal. I held my breath, waiting for her to bolt for the door.

Why the hell had I said that?

CHAPTER 30

"Yes." The word slipped from her mouth, stealing my breath.

She looked shocked but a soft smile had crept onto her beautiful face. She had said yes? Was this real? Then she spoke again, her voice shaking.

"I must tell you some things first. Not things like we've been talking about but deeply private things. Things that will make you change your mind." Her eyes dropped, a look of shame coming over her.

"Never. I'm yours Mary, nothing will ever change that."

There was nothing she could say that would change my mind, that much I was certain of. She scanned the room, panic filling her eyes. It was empty save for us, the lunch crowd had gone and the dinner rush hadn't started yet.

"I'm from Chicago." She began, her voice trembling. "My parents are wealthy, members of the affluent society there. I fled because they were trying to marry me off to enhance their social standing."

Mary.....

She stared at him as she spoke, this man who had so completely stolen her heart. In one afternoon, she'd skipped all courtship and propriety and had agreed to marry him. Her heart which had sung in her chest a moment before now froze in fear. She was terrified that he wouldn't understand or worse that he'd reject her. It would destroy her if he turned away but she had to tell him. She wasn't worthy but still she hoped that maybe this man could look past her failings. Maybe he could love her in spite of everything.

"That's not what I need to say to you, it just explains how it all happened. There was a man my father did business with. He cornered me one day in my father's office." She could feel her eyes filling with tears as she spoke. No man would want her knowing that she couldn't bear to be touched, not since that day. Looking into his eyes as she spoke, she found safety in those bright blue pools. They were so full of love and patience it gave her the courage she needed to continue.

"My father came in before he could do what he wanted. He claimed that I had led him on and my father believed him. He called me a harlot and a tease, blaming me for tempting an innocent man." She choked back a sob but managed to keep speaking. "At a formal dinner, he made me apologize to the man for trying to seduce him. Right there in a public place, my parents told me if I wasn't so wanton it wouldn't have happened. I knew then they would use it as a tool to manipulate me, to force me into a marriage that suited them."

She watched his face as she told her story, seeing the storm clouds of anger gathering in his eyes. Streaks of light grey shot through the blue of his irises like lightning, and the more she spoke the more they flashed. She could feel the heat of his anger like a burning pyre radiating across the space between them. It didn't frighten her, it felt like a warm protective blanket that sheltered her from the wild storm raging around her. It was an unspoken promise that no one would ever hurt her again. The fury in those lightning eyes promised vengeance while the flame offered safety and protection.

"I don't know if I'll ever be able to bear a man's touch after what happened. What if I can never be a real wife?" She'd finally admitted her greatest fear to him and he didn't look away. He didn't reject her and all the complications that came along with her. A gentle smile graced his lips before he spoke and when he did his voice was full of care and love.

"Mary, I'll never touch you against your will. Wife or not, I'd never do it."

"But..."

"Please trust me on this. I would marry you knowing that you may never let me touch you and I'd still live a happy life. You've stolen my heart, don't you see that?" His eyes were brimming with tears but the lightning was still flashing through them.

"What if I want you to touch me but then I'm afraid?" She knew her voice was shaking but she had to know. She had to know for sure he was patient and loving enough to try and work through her fears.

His hand slowly reached across the table and hung in the air next to her cheek. It stopped there, just short of touching her face. Close enough that she could feel the warmth radiating from his skin and smell his scent. It was rich and complex, like leather mixed with harsh soap and something more. Like the plains smelled after a rain, like sage and wildflowers. He held it there, not forcing contact with her bare skin. It didn't shake, it never wavered just like the man himself. It waited for her, allowing her to choose.

"You decide. You can lean into my hand or not. Nothing will happen if you don't want it to, my love. I promise you that." She knew in her heart he meant every word with an unshakable conviction.

It was a demonstration of his patience and willingness to let her control the physical part. That he was prepared to give her that power took her breath away. How could any man tolerate that? Her head tilted slowly as she tucked her cheek into his callused hand. The sensation of his touch didn't erase those horrible memories but it showed her the difference between beast and man. Instead of repulsing her, his touch ignited a fire inside her. It felt like heaven on earth sitting there with her face cradled in his gentle hand. Silent tears streamed down her face as she basked in his love.

As I waited with my hand beside her porcelain cheek, I was lost in those eyes brimming with tears. When she slowly leaned into my hand it was like being born again. That simple contact changed my life forever. This woman was my other half. I didn't care about her family, her past or anything else.

That wasn't completely true. I cared a great deal but not in the way she was so afraid of. If any of them had been standing in front of me, Boot Hill would need a few more tombstones. But that was for later and my mind quickly pushed the thoughts down. Right now, all that mattered was this moment. My thumb gently wiped a tear away, smearing the flour on her cheek. There was nothing but her in that moment, nothing else mattered. That was until Bess coughed from the kitchen doorway.

"I'm glad y'all figured it out but dinner's coming soon. Didn't think you'd want folks traipsing in unannounced but I can't keep the door locked much longer."

"He asked me to marry him, Bess." Mary said, gently pulling her face away from my hand and standing up. Bess cleared the space between them in two steps. Laughing happily, she scooped up the smaller woman in a bear hug.

"Oh, honey I am so happy for you! He'll be a fine man, with some training of course." She released Mary when I stood and gave me a hug as well. I wasn't sure what to do but just went along with it.

"Thanks, Bess." I managed to gasp out. The woman hugged like grizzly. She let go and stepped back, grinning at both of us.

Without warning, Mary pressed herself against me and

wrapped her arms around my neck. When her lips met mine, explosions went off behind my eyes. Once my brain grasped what was going on, I wrapped my arms around her waist and returned the embrace. I lifted her off the floor without thinking and the feel of her body against mine stoked the flames, turning them from a warm campfire to a raging bonfire. I closed my eyes, memorizing the feel of her in my arms.

Her delicate scent made me dizzy. There were faint traces of lavender with just a touch of apple and cinnamon from the pie. But there was something else beneath, something that was entirely her. She was a spring breeze, full of promise. A gift that could dispel the cold dead winter, pushing it to move on and birth a fresh new world. It was the most intoxicating thing I'd ever smelled, especially combined with her body pressed against me. She suddenly stepped back and my legs gave out. I fell back into my chair with a blissful smile on my face that made both of them laugh.

"I think ya broke him." Bess laughed. She turned to look at Mary who was flushed pink and trying to catch her breath. "Might have done yourself in as well."

I recovered after a minute and started to find my feet, albeit carefully since my legs were still shaky and my mind wouldn't stop spinning. The smile that split my face wouldn't budge and my cheeks were starting to hurt. Those unused muscles were getting a workout, my normal smirks and half grins were nothing by comparison. A true smile felt very different but I'd happily adjust, especially if it meant more kisses like that.

"Did ya want to come see our house?" I tried to sound casual but couldn't hide my mischievous grin.

"Our house?" Her surprised response was perfect. Bess eyed me warily, trying to figure out what I was talking about.

"A kiss is okay, but.." I cut her off before she finished that thought.

"Nothing like that. Carter gave me his house in town and I still need to explore it."

"The man gave me the deed to my place the other day. I was shocked when he thanked me for helping him see things the right way." Bess said with a smile. She was clearly delighted with the security of owning her eatery outright.

"Aren't we going to have to move?" Mary asked. She must have already accepted that I'd be assigned elsewhere.

"I forgot to tell ya'll, Marshal Reese assigned me to this district in the territory. For the next month I'm acting as sheriff." I didn't want to mention Ed taking the position until I'd talked it over with him first.

Once again, my arms filled with this incredible woman who kissed me deeply. This time I managed to keep on my feet when she broke the kiss, though I'll admit I did stumble a bit. She seemed to be making some miraculous progress with her fear, and the glint of passion in her eyes sent chills down my spine. I had a strong suspicion that our marriage wouldn't be a celibate one. Her passion evidently matched her temper.

"I would have followed you anywhere but I didn't want to leave. I can't explain it but I feel at home here." She admitted.

"I'm glad you're staying but I can't let you two wander around that house alone. The sun's setting an' Angie's likely gone for the day. It wouldn't be proper without a chaperone." Bess laid down the law and her tone left no room for debate.

"She's right." Mary blushed at the thought. "Can we do it tomorrow?"

"That suits me fine, gives me a chance to move my stuff in and make sure anything unwanted is gone." I didn't think anything of Bennet's remained but it was better to be sure.

"Then it'll be a guided tour." She said. Her cheeks were still pink but she smiled at the idea.

"And Miss Angie will be there." Bess added, a hint of warning in her tone.

"Yes ma'am." Bess glared at me but I ignored her look and turned to Mary with feigned formality. "Breakfast in the morning, Miss Gardner?"

"It would be my pleasure, sir." She curtsied elegantly. Her response made Bess snort with laughter at our shenanigans.

"Get you two!" She shooed us out the door, still smiling as we left.

I held the door for Mary and we shared a smile before parting. She headed to her boarding house and I turned toward the large house at the end of the street. It was time to explore my new home, maybe sleep in a real bed for the first time in a long while.

CHAPTER 31

The house was a pleasant surprise, not just owning a home but in what it held. Carter hadn't spared any money building this place, that much was easy to see. Every board fit tightly to its neighbor, joints fit tight. Even better he'd left all the furniture, all of it masterfully crafted. I had no idea how much money most of these things cost but knew enough to recognize quality. He must have had everything brought in from Denver. None of it looked like it was made locally unless there was a craftsmen somewhere in town I hadn't met.

The front parlor was nicely appointed with two couches facing each other and beautifully carved table in between. Two chairs sat at the back of the room facing the fireplace. Obviously meant for more intimate conversations. They had a shared game table between them, currently set up for chess. Each chair also had their own small table beside them.

The room across the hall was a less formal living room, more of a gathering place. There was another fireplace, this one used more often from the look of it. There was a lone comfortable looking couch flanked by two high back chairs. Paintings decorated the walls, mostly forest scenes but a few featured horses or cattle. There was a larger painting over the fireplace that depicted some sort of hunting scene. Men in red coats mounted on horses seemed to be following dogs through a field. It was all nice but felt impersonal. Like it had been picked out of a catalog but not personalized.

The next room took my breath away, it was a fully stocked

library. Every wall was bookshelves, every space filled with books. Walking down the wall gently running my fingers over the bindings, my eyes read some of the titles. There was fiction, history, technical books on medicine and ranching. Various works on building or governing, more books than I'd ever seen in one place before. It was even larger than Thad's collection. There were two comfortable chairs with side tables in the center of the room. They sat opposite a large desk with a leather covered chair behind it.

The wall directly behind the desk held various reference books on business and blank ledgers. There was a few gaps where some had been removed, probably Carters business ledgers. There were still thirty or forty empty ones I could make use of. One day soon I'd have to sit down and record account balances and such. I knew about how much money I had in various banks but it would be good to have it reordered somewhere. The desk felt like it had just been delivered and set up as a package. Complete with everything you'd need. An ink well sat flanked by two quills in the center. There was even a stack of blank paper in one of the drawers. It lacked anything personal but was ready for use.

The room across the hall made me wonder if I'd ever judged Carter right. It was a gun room, complete with worktable and gunsmith tools. The small drawers I checked had various cleaning supplies, brushes, and more tools. There were holders for every type of weapon, long rifles down to pistols. One wall was filled with brackets to mount pistols, the other wall for rifles. The back wall was a mixture, a place to display the more decorative weapons maybe. It looked more like a trophy case then the others.

Below all the racks were drawers full of ammo. I was shocked to find them full, boxes of almost every type filling them. Every caliber was stocked with only a few of the 44 boxes missing. I was amazed by the wealth on display. My fingers traced over the swirling carved wood that framed the racks. Leaves and scroll work were intricately carved in them. Each slowly climbing up to join the trim around the ceiling.

The stairs were next to the gun room but I wanted to see the rest of the first floor before going up. Next to that was a water closet, it was a surprise to see one here. It beat dashing to the outhouse in the dead of winter but was still unexpected. Finding such a luxury this far from a big city really displayed the money Carter had spent on this place.

The tub looked large enough for two people which brought back memories of Mary's passion. I did my best to quash those thoughts and continue through the house. Still, I couldn't wait to use the bath, whether she was with me or not. It was another unexpected luxury.

The dining room could be seen across the hall. Fully stocked with delicate China displayed in a cabinet behind glass doors. A decorative buffet with serving silver held pride of place under a window. When I checked the drawers they were full of silverware that matched the china. The table would seat eight easily and was as decoratively carved. Each foot was an eagle talon gripping a ball and the feathers transitioned into leaves as the legs rose. The chairs matched with three to either side and one at each end of the table.

Beside the water closet was the solitary bedroom on the first floor. It was a master suite, with two large closets. A dresser fit nicely between them, again hand tooled designs made it as much art as furniture. Faint hints of cedar in the room told me both closets and the dresser were lined with the insect repelling wood. The largest bed I'd ever seen sat with its headboard centered on the opposite wall. It was easily twice the size of any bed I'd slept in before. The headboard displayed a carving that reminded me of my mother's tales of the fey folk. This would be considered a winter master, close to the kitchen but with its own small heating stove.

Upstairs was another master, larger than the rest with an

attached lounge. The furniture was slightly different but just as grand. There were four other bedrooms, all nicely appointed with the accompanying scent of cedar. Except one, it had been completely emptied. Bennet's old room was my guess, Carter had gotten rid of everything the man touched evidently. I thought it was a waste but could understand the man's reasoning. Mary would have likely insisted on it so it saved me time.

The steps that lead to the crow's nest on the roof were at the back of the hall. I already knew what was there. Carter had probably disposed of everything up there already. I'd need to add a new chair or two if we wanted to use it. Just because it was built for one purpose didn't mean I wouldn't use it for another. The view from up there would be breathtaking on a clear night. The area was large enough to sleep on if the urge to be under the stars took me.

For now, I'd use the room downstairs. The bed looked comfortable and to be honest going up and down stairs seemed a waste. Once we were married Mary might change my thinking but it was just me right now. I meant what I said earlier, it was up to her. If need be there would be separate bedrooms for each of us. I'd stick to that but every fiber of my being prayed it wouldn't be the case and after that kiss part of me knew it wouldn't be a problem.

Wandering into the kitchen I just admired everything around me. The pantry was fully stocked and I was making myself a sandwich using some of the ham from the cold room. Someone must have told Angie I was coming because the stove still had embers in the box making it easy to get it going again for coffee. Everything I'd heard about the woman was good. Bess seemed to hold her in high regard which spoke well of her.

After my dinner I went out to look at the stables before the sun completely set. It was a surprise to find so much space. There was a small carriage pull through on the side, a new looking buckboard sat in the space now. It was designed for a two-horse rig and the tack was in a room off to the side. Having access to the wagon would be nice and I'd have to make sure Carter meant to leave it.

The barn itself had eight horse stalls and a good-sized tack room. There was plenty of room in the center to tack up or brush down as needed. The hay loft was fully stocked just like the rest of the place. What there was would easily see me through this coming winter. The small heating stove at the back insured the animals wouldn't have any problems in the winter. The pump was close enough that it should keep it from freezing. Either way Miz and Meat would be comfortable in here. The Morgan and three other animals were still at the livery. Maybe two of them would be good for the wagon if Carter left it.

The corral out back was as well built as the rest. Open and clean with enough room for grazing. It made me wonder how big this lot was. I took out the deed to study the map in the fading light. My mind spun when I read the footnote, it was an entire section. The back of the corral was surrounded by deeply wooded hills. I couldn't believe I owned all of it. According to the deed I owned the lot to the left as well, that would be Angie's house. There was an attached lifetime rental agreement with zeroed out rent amounts. From our two building lots the rest of the section rolled out into the foothills as far as I could see.

While I was looking around in amazement something behind the corral caught my eye. I walked back there and in the fading light looked over a well-built target range. The rifle part went from 50 yards out far enough that I couldn't see it in the fading light. I'd guess it was four or five hundred yards at least. To the side of that was the pistol range. It had fixed stands at different ranges and a special set up of swinging targets. I'd make good use of this, maybe teach Mary to shoot if she wanted.

Walking back to the house a small building coming off the side of the stables caught my eye. A grin spread across my face when I recognized the chicken coop. It was empty right now but that was a problem I'd easily solve. Having fresh eggs and a ready meat source was just too good to pass up.

My mind was still trying to take it all in. In the span of a day, I'd gone from just starting out as a deputy marshal to engaged. Owning one of the nicest homes in town with an attached six hundred acres of land was just one more impossibility. It was one hell of a swing in fortunes. It'd take more than a day or two for it to really sink in. So much was happening so fast but in the end this is why I had agreed to the badge. I just hadn't expected it to happen so fast.

Unsurprisingly sleep didn't come easily that night. When it did find me the dreams were of bright futures and happy times in this home. The background music was the patter of little feet echoing through the house. Something I'd never considered before, more then a home or wife. Being a father had never even crossed my mind but here it was. A true possibility for my future.

The next morning doesn't start peacefully unfortunately. It started with me scaring the hell out of a middle-aged woman. Not intentionally, but my mad dash to the water closet in my long handles had that effect. A short time later, once we both calmed down and I was dressed, we met properly.

CHAPTER 32

"Not my best first impression ma'am." I apologized walking into the kitchen.

"My fault, forgot Carter said he was giving you the house yesterday." She was short, thin and had a pleasant smile. There was a sadness in her eyes that she tried her best to hide.

"Miss Angie I presume, please call me Chance."

"No need for the Miss, just call me Angie. Carter started using that an never managed to break the habit." I watched her study me. Her eyes slowly tracing the scar down my face. To my relief there was no pity or fear in her eyes. She was a frontier wife and knew the hardships people faced out here often left their mark.

"Well, I'll be happy to have someone keep up the house for me. I'll be around for a bit but after that I could be gone for long stretches."

"No wife?" I heard the apprehension in the question.

"Aside from getting this yesterday I got engaged last night. I'm sure she'll want to keep you on." I hoped my smile was reassuring. "Again, with my job taking me away she won't want to be alone."

"Who'd you ask to marry you?" She wasn't relaxing yet. Her curiosity about what kind of woman I'd be marrying was plain to see.

"Miss Gardner." I answered simply and was relieved when

she smiled.

"She's a good woman, only met her a few times. Though if memory serves she has a bit of a temper." A sly smile lifted the corners of her mouth. Evidently she'd heard about our previous encounters.

"Yes ma'am, she does that. Already experienced it a few times, not something I recommend. She'll be by today to tour the house." I chuckled admitting my familiarity with her temper.

"You sure you'll want to keep me on?" She asked. I could see the uncertainty on her face. She wasn't ready to sit at home and do nothing, this was someone who wanted a purpose.

"Absolutely Angie, I'm sure she'll feel the same. Besides I have a hunch she's kinda used to having help."

"Good to hear. Want some coffee?"

"Normally yes, but right now I'm almost late meeting her for breakfast." She laughed at my hurried look.

"One thing a woman learns quick is that men folk are very rarely on time."

"Probably true." I grinned. Waving over my shoulder as I headed for the door. "Good to meet you Miss Angie."

I didn't run but moved faster than walking on my way to Bess's. Slowing my pace when I saw her coming down the boardwalk, glad it wasn't just me running late. The sun seemed to dance through her hair. Creating an almost perfect halo of light around her. Guiltily my eyes traced her figure, my cheeks burning from it but I couldn't help myself. The smile that spread across her face when she saw me waiting on her nearly stopped my breathing. Then my heart froze in my chest.

I recognized the two men coming up behind her, not them personally but their ilk. Pinkertons, the dark suits and bowler hats weren't the only give away. It was their singular focus on the target, my betrothed. At their current pace they wouldn't catch her before she reached me. That didn't mean there wasn't a threat. My eyes scanned the area not finding any other men who stood out. That didn't stop my hand from casually flipping the thong off my Colt.

When she reached me instead of sweeping her into my arms as she expected, I stepped past her squaring up in front of the two men. She hadn't noticed them until I'd moved, then she recognized the threat. I heard a heavy sigh escape her lips, it wasn't shock or fear. It was sadness, she knew something about this. My mind caught up quickly, she'd told me about her family and about running away from them. The wealthy used the Pinkertons to find lost people. Usually to bring them back whether they wanted to or not.

"Gentlemen why are you following my fiancé?" I spoke calmly but it had a tone of authority backing it. The sun glinting off my badge add to its strength.

"Marshal we're here on a private matter and.." his partner cut him off since he'd caught my full question.

"Fiancé? Marshal her family's made other promises." He was a little smaller than his partner but aside from that they were a matched pair. Each one had a fighters build, broad shoulders tapered to their waist. Knuckles that showed scars from years of brawling. Their faces had that toughened leather look fighters got over time. Not gun hands then, probably strike breakers or bully boys.

"She's an adult and not beholding to whatever promises her family made. This isn't a fight you can win, not legally. Tell them you found her too late and the law stepped in."

"You can't stop us marshal, the man she's promised too can strip that badge in one telegram." His partner was obviously the smart one because the glare he gave the speaker could have killed flowers.

"Those bulges wouldn't happen to be firearms under your coats?" I smiled calmly.

"So, what if they are law dog?" The dumber of the two took the bait before the smarter but evidently slower of the two could stop him.

"Then you're under arrest." My colt filled my hand before either man could register what I said. "There's an ordinance still in effect about carrying guns in town limits."

"You're a deputy marshal not the local sheriff." The smarter one got there first this time. It wasn't a bad legal argument, had to give him that much. Sadly it wouldn't work this time but not a bad try.

"First, that doesn't matter. I'm free to enforce local ordinance as I see fit. Second I'm also acting sheriff." I grinned at his surprised look. "Now very slowly use your left hands and reach in there to pull out those pistols. One at a time, you first."

I used my colt to indicate the dumber one. He hesitated but the hammer of my colt locking back helped him decide. I made a hand motion for him to continue and watched the sweat bead on his forehead. When he was holding his weapon by the barrel in front of him I had his partner do the same. I was just starting to wonder how to take their guns when Bess spoke up from the doorway.

"Go ahead Marshal. I'll keep 'em covered."

She punctuated the idea with the sound of both hammers on her shotgun locking back. If they had been sweating from just me, the idea of a woman behind them made it pour out from under their Bowlers. I smiled holstering my colt and easily stepping forward to disarm the two.

"Bess I'm gonna have to make you a deputy if you keep this up." I laughed covering the two men with their own guns.

"That'd be a thing, a female deputy! Ain't got time for all that anyway, folks count on me to feed 'em." She cackled easing the hammers down then walking back into the alley. She must have seen the confrontation through the window and come the back door.

"Mary go find us a table. I'll be back after these two are locked up."

"Yes dear." Her voice didn't tremble. She stood on her toes to give me a quick kiss. Then her soft steps moved inside letting me relax a little.

"Come on gentlemen, it's only three days in jail and a Twenty-five dollar fine. Should be able to write it off on your expense reports." I grinned trying not to blush too much.

"You know this won't end here." The smart one spoke, turning to walk toward the office. "Three days ain't going to change a thing."

"I think it will, especially as we'll be married in two." I wasn't sure if Mary would go for that but they didn't need to know that.

"Won't matter to them that hired us." The dumb one spoke before his partner could stop him.

"So, they'll just have you kill me and take her?"

"Not us and not the agency." The smart one answered. "We don't do that work, least wise not against law men. It's bad for business."

"Is missing this really going to cost you two that much?" I figured he was being honest.

"Bit of a bonus but we get paid for finding her. If we had managed to bring her back there would have been a bit more but not enough to fight you over." The smarter one said.

After that we walked in silence and my mind went to work on the problem. I'd have to send a telegraph to Reese, letting him know someone might come after my badge. They could make problems for him and I owed him the warning. He might be able to do something to stop them but I didn't know if he had any contacts with enough political clout for that. Either way he'd be prepared for whatever came.

The two grumbled but were mostly decent about the process. Each man had a blackjack and a knife on them. Nether man argued when asked for them. They were almost standard issue for Pinkertons so it wasn't a surprise to see them. They asked to be in different cells and I agreed. They hadn't been difficult so there wasn't any reason to be rude. I finally got their names and even offered them a checkerboard that was tucked in a desk drawer. Both were from Chicago, the smarter one's name was Ben Wilson and his partner was Mike Loniker. I left them with the ever-present buckets and bonus checkerboard to send a telegraph to my boss.

Marshal Reese

Denver

Two Pinkertons arrested stop

Trying to take Mary-now fiancé for family stop

Family has influence threatened badge stop

Fair warning of politics stop

 Deputy McElroy

Cartersville

CHAPTER 33

Mary was almost chewing on her coffee cup when I walked into the eatery. She shot to her feet and dove into my arms, leaving the cup rocking on the table. Everyone in place glanced at us but turned away, public displays weren't common but no one seemed upset by it. When she'd calmed down enough we took our seats. She began talking almost as soon as we sat down, her voice filled with nervous energy.

"What are we going to do? I can leave, you don't have to deal with this. Three days is a head start if I got through Denver I might lose them..."

"Mary stop." I gently put my hand on hers, breaking her stream of words. "We'll find a way, there will be no more running."

"But Chance you don't know these people." She protested nearly in tears. "They'll never stop."

"If they pull my marshals badge I'd wager even money the mayor would slap the sheriff's badge on me. If you want to leave we can, I know places no white man has ever seen but running has never solved a problem. There really is just one immediate question we need to answer." My voice was calm and soothing but there was a hint of amusement mixed in too.

"What's that?" She'd caught it and I'd piqued her curiosity.

"Well, I can hold those two for three days. Do we want them to send a telegram that they found you single or already married?"

"They'll send a telegram?" Then she realized what I'd said.

I had guessed that her reaction would be big but I hadn't been ready for her to launch herself across the table at me. The chair fell backward when she hit me and we went down in a heap. The impact knocked the wind out of me. The impact stunned me for a minute leaving me unable to move. She looked down at me with joy and desire sparkling in her eyes. When I started gasping for air she realized what she'd done and started to panic.

"Oh my god! I'm so sorry are you okay I didn't mean to do that but you said..."

She started her constant stream of words while she was still laying awkwardly on top of me. I wasn't used to town life but was pretty sure this wasn't appropriate behavior for a young lady. Bess saved me for the second time that day by lifting Mary off me. Just over Mary's shoulder I could see her laughing as she did. The grin on my face was probably twisted since I was still trying to breath.

"Mary I don't think the man can breathe an I'm pretty sure you're not helping." She laughed.

"Oh." It was all Mary said but her face turned bright red when she looked around at the shocked people. "Please umm forgive me."

"Missy if a man makes you that happy don't never apologize." One old man said from the corner. By the look on his wife's face, she agreed with him.

I looked around the room from the floor and smiled at the grinning faces. They were all folks I'd seen around town but hadn't met most of them yet. For the most part they were all smiling at our antics. The single people had a hint of envy and the couples smiled knowingly. The lone exception was an older lady. She looked like someone who'd sucked on a lemon, it announced her disapproval clearly. I didn't care one bit, the smile on my face wasn't going anywhere. Finally my breath was coming back now that Mary wasn't laying on my chest. As soon as it did I started laughing.

"Chance!" Mary's sharp voice barked at me but when she looked down at me her giggles started. She managed to gasp out a few words in between them. "Let's get married today or they might run us out of town for such indecent behavior."

"I wasn't the one tackling people to the floor my dear." I chuckled back.

"Always carry my book, we can do it right now." The old man who'd spoken earlier announced holding a bible up. "Got my notary book too."

"We will take them to the church." His wife said firmly then scolded the man with an impish grin on her face. "For a minister you have some heathen ways."

"Blame the wagon train." He smiled at her. "Folks got married every which way on the trail. Most of 'em still happily married I'll remind you, including us my love."

"And now you have a town and congregation, old fool." But I saw her lips twitch up when she looked at him.

"Fine then, the church it is." He gave in knowing he'd lose the argument anyway. Then with a smile at us he added. "Maybe after breakfast."

"This afternoon will be soon enough you reprobate. That young lady needs a dress and flowers." His wife had turned her eyes toward Mary, joy filling them. "And a broom."

Things happened fast after that and I never did get my breakfast. The women descended on Mary and they were gone in a flurry of giggles and skirts, including Bess. Percy was standing in the kitchen door looking as confused as I was. The men solved that almost as quickly. The old minister reached a hand down to help me up.

"Time ta get off the floor deputy, ya got some things to get done as well." I didn't know when the mayor had arrived but he was standing in the crowd now. "We're off to my store, you'll need a suit and a ring."

"I got a pair of them fancy shoes ought to fit him." A man I hadn't met yet chimed in. I think he was the blacksmith.

"He already has a house thankfully, Carter gave him his, ought to be suitable for a young couple." The little man I'd met in the land office added.

"I'll get to prep'n, Bess will be back quick enough to start cooking." Percy piped in before turning back to the kitchen.

The mayor was dragging me toward his store as the rest followed along loudly planning everything out. With no clue what was going on I figured trying to fight this would be a waste of effort. Truthfully it didn't matter, the whole town seemed to have decided how this was going to work. I couldn't hide my happiness, both about marrying her and the town joining in the lake it an event. Life was hard out here, most your days were filled with just surviving. Anything that broke that cycle had to be taken advantage of.

It was still strange to me, these people I hardly knew going through all of this for me. That feeling of belonging struck me again. For a second my eyes just looked at the people around me, the sense of belonging to something more was almost overwhelming. Word was spreading like wildfire through the small town. One hand from Carters was riding out of town at a full gallop, hell bent for the ranch. It looked like Carter would be at the wedding, probably with most of the hands from the ranch. If he brought Red with him I'd ask him to stand as my best man.

When we reached the mayors store he unlocked the door and the small crowd pushed in with us. In only took a few seconds for him to recognize the problem. Smiling in that way all politicians had he whistled getting everyones attention. He quickly took charge of the chaos and start directing people.

"Okay everyone out but Chance, I need space to work. The rest of you go help where you can to get everything ready. Vick go fetch those shoes, I'll need to make sure they work." He bellowed over the din.

"Come on boys, let's get the church done up for the ladies." I thought it was the minister but couldn't be sure in the crowd.

"Wait, there's a carriage over to the livery." It was the livery man. "Carl, Pete come with me. We'll get it cleaned up an ready for the bride, got them matched greys for it."

The men cleared out moving in different directions with a purpose. Small groups breaking off to get various tasks done. It just left me and the mayor. He pulled me toward the rack of broad cloth suits in the back of the store. I was still reeling from the floor but felt that sense of belonging again. The whole town was getting everything ready for my wedding. Doing it because it made them happy, that much had been obvious. No one mentioned pay, they just set to work with zeal.

"Come along son, let's find you some proper attire." The mayor walked back toward the suits.

"I have a suit in my bags." I tried to protest but he wouldn't hear of it.

"Not enough time to get it cleaned properly. I'd bet you're like everyone else who lives on a horse. Got it rolled up in the bottom of a saddlebag." He sounded amused.

"It might be." It was and the look he gave me said he knew it.

"If the shoes don't work we might need them. Likely Vick's aren't what he remembers them being. The man probably hasn't seen them himself in a decade." He was already sorting through the rack after looking me up and down.

"Why's the town doing this? It can't be just a wedding." I finally got a chance to ask the question that had been on my mind.

"What?" He turned to study me before he continued. "You don't see it truly?"

"No."

"You saved this town son, we all know that. Not only did you save it, but did it in a way that'll almost certainly help it grow." He reached up to put his hand on my shoulder while meeting my eyes. "Young man the people who are here came to build a town. Just a few days ago, we all believed that dream was dead. Your clash with Carter had to happen but there were so many ways it could have killed this town."

"But it didn't, that's not down to me. Hell if anything Bess did that, at least started it."

"It is and we all know it. You think she would have spoken like that if you had been a different man? She did it because of you. When I saw this young man ride in wearing his badge I never would have thought this would be the outcome. For someone so young to have the foresight to see the right path through everything, well that's astonishing."

"Lucky." Was my only response. That was my honest belief too. I'd done what I could but assumed it was what anyone would have done.

"No, it wasn't. You moved carefully from the start. Did everything you could not to kill people, even when they tried to kill you."

"That's because of Marshal Reese, well him taking the risk in hiring me. He had to see me do the job legally."

"That don't matter to me or the rest of town. You saved our town twice over. Once by being careful and smart, working to educate instead of crush a stubborn man. The second time by uncovering a plan none of us even knew about. Even now you're putting off your marshal duties to fill in as sheriff. Yes, before you ask, I've already agreed to hire Mr. Vayo for the job."

He turned back to searching through the suits, finally grabbing the one he wanted.

"I'm no hero." The idea that these people saw me as one made me uncomfortable.

"Here try this on." He thrust a charcoal grey suit toward me and pointed at the changing room in the back. "It's not about being a hero, we don't see it that way. Unlike many folks you thought about the situation you saw, didn't rush in guns blazing. This is just our gratitude for you taking the time to find the right solution. Just let us do this for you."

Taking the suit uncomfortably before walking into the small room to change. It didn't feel like I deserved any of this, I'd just done my job the best way possible. The sentiment they had toward me seemed disproportionate compared to what I had done. Admittedly I'd tried to make the right decisions to preserve the town. Doing my best to work something out with Carter just made sense. Bess had made the man think and in turn he spoke to me. The man's own beliefs had done the rest, all I did was give him a few hints. None of this was me doing anything exceptional, it was just the best way to do the job.

The suit coat was a soft grey paired with a black vest and white shirt. I was surprised at how well it fit considering Kelso had just eyeballed my measurements. The pants were a little long but my boots would hold them off the ground. The jacket was loose at the waist, which would keep my guns out of sight, but fit my shoulders nicely. The curtain opened and a hand thrust in a pair of dress boots, my dress boots.

"Had to get yours. Vicks shoes would have been too big." Kelso's voice came through the curtain. Taking the boots from him, I sat on a stool to put them on. Looking in the mirror I had to admit the suit made an impression.

"Nice fit Mayor." I said stepping out to find he and Vick chatting at the counter.

"Practice, that and it's the only one I had that might fit your shoulders." He laughed and examined me more critically. "Have to admit though, it does fit you well."

"Look'n all churched up Deputy." Vick grinned at me.

"Thanks an I don't think we've really met."

"True." The man stepped forward and shook my hand. Like every blacksmith I'd ever met he was big, his hands calloused and strong. Pleasant brown eyes peek out from under heavy black brows. They almost joined the beard that started not far below them. "Pleasures mine."

"Enough, time to change back and get to the barbers, he's expecting you." The mayor cut us off before we started chatting. Quickly shooing me back into the room.

CHAPTER 34

The rest of the day was a blur, I only remember arguing with barber about my hair again. The man felt strongly about how long I wore it and wanted to cut it to a 'decent white man's' length. Everything else was lost in a blur of motion as I was shuffled from one place to another. Red showed up on a lathered horse while I was in the bath. When he agreed to stand as my best man the mayor dragged him off to get properly dressed.

All I know for sure is that somehow by midafternoon I was standing at the alter with Red beside me. Both of us freshly scrubbed and dressed in new clothes, nether of us looking comfortable. He allegedly had the rings, rings that I had yet to see, but that was more of a hope then from any certainty. Someone had 'helped' me find those when I admitted my ignorance regarding jewelry.

It seemed like the whole town had turned up for this event. The small church was crowded to standing room only. Not only where the people who lived in town here but I spotted more then one family that looked like farmers. Every hand on Carters ranch had come in with him and Red. For a second I worried about rustlers or the ranch being raided while they were all here. The man himself sat in the front row next to the mayor and his wife, chatting quietly.

The organ started playing, bringing everyone to their feet. All eyes looked toward the doors at the back of the church. My heart started racing in my chest, trying to climb out of my mouth. Was this really happening? The answer to that question filled the door a moment later. Mary, wearing an amazing white dress started walking toward me. Bess proudly walking with her, she wore a beautiful cream dress a few shades darker than Mary's.

My body went numb, it all seemed like an impossible dream. Mary seemed to float down the aisle toward me, the perfect vision of beauty and grace. A veil hid her face but I could see her green eyes sparkling at me through it. A mix of joy and nerves seemed to radiate from her as she walked. Sweat started tickling my back when the nerves really kicked in. Doing my best to control my breathing I waited.

Everything seemed unreal, it stayed that way until her hand touched my arm. Finally, I could breathe again. Her simple touch making it all real. Hints of lavender and rose floated on the air, tantalizing my senses. This stunning woman was here to marry me. Everything that came after that didn't matter. With her by my side anything was possible.

The first part of the ceremony just required me to stand there, which I managed well enough. It felt like Mary was swaying in time with me while the minister read from the scripture. Silence hung over the crowd but the feeling of joy filling the small chapel. Finally, the little man took a breath then looked at each of us before he started the vows. Thankfully they were short and simple.

"I Chance McElroy take Mary Gardner to be my lawful wife. To have and to hold in sickness and in health. To be hers through good times and bad. This I swear before God." I spoke in a firm voice despite my trembling hand holding hers. Slipping the simple gold band slipped onto her finger felt like attaching myself to her.

"I Mary Gardner take Chance McElroy to be my lawful husband. To have and to hold in sickness and in health. To be his through good times and bad. This I swear before God." Her voice sounded like music to my ears. When she slipped the cool gold band on my finger it felt unreal. Something I'd never thought possible had happened.

"By the power granted me by God I pronounce you husband and wife. Chance, please kiss your wife." The ministers voice carried over the crowd, gathering all their attention.

Gently lifting her veil revealed the most amazing woman I would ever know smiling up at me. I leaned down to kiss her but paused just before touching her. For a second she hesitated, her breath gently caressing my cheek. Then finally she realized what I was doing, waiting for her to decide. She leaned into me, our lips meeting in that one perfect moment. Everything around us disappeared, there was just her in my arms.

The church, people, even the ground we stood on. It all just went away, there was nothing but her and I standing in each other's arms. No worries or concerns intruded on us, no fears about the future existed in that moment. It seemed to stretch out, filling my heart and soul with a nourishment I never knew I needed. Feeling her filling up my arms, her warm body pressed into me. I didn't want it to end, this one moment could be the rest of my life and I die happy.

When our kiss broke the thunderous applause from our town washed over us. We were back in the world, she was now my wife. Everyone was celebrating, smiling faces filled the church as we stood in front of them. She took my hand, gently pulling me off to the side. I didn't understand until Bess step forward where Mary had been. Two men carried Percy toward the front, the poor man looked confused until he saw Bess.

When their eyes met he stopped fighting and almost ran up the isle on his bowed legs. Mary stood beside Bess and Kelso appeared beside Percy. This time I got to see the whole ceremony. The culmination was watching Percy take Bess in his arms and kiss her. It held the same love and joy that ours had. When their kiss broke I lent my voice to the crowd whooping for them.

This was a day to remember for the whole town, almost like it washed away the past. There was a bond that was renewed that day among them all, this time it included Carter. He was smiling as broadly as the rest, feeling the acceptance that filled the church around him. It was a tangible thing, one everyone would carry with them long after this day.

"Alright ya'll there's going to be food at the eatery and everyone's invited." Bess broke through the noise. Her voice easily getting everyone attention. "Buzzards been barbecuing a steer all day that Mr. Carter donated. Percy and me added plenty of fix'ns to go with it. The Drapers brought plenty from the bakery, including a cake that appeared like magic. The Lazy Ace and Trails End saloons donated the beer. Half the tables and chairs from the town are strung out on Main Street so let's get ta celebrating."

I hadn't taken the time to study the crowd but now I took it all in. At the back of the room stood several soiled doves, waitresses and bartenders. Some gamblers were mixed in and more than one drifter was hanging around the outskirts of the crowd. It made me smile to see them all mixed in together. If only for this one day all the social barriers were forgotten. I wondered if it would survive past sunset but decided not to let the worries take hold. There were better things to focus on tonight.

That thought made me look at the woman beside me, knowing our night might not go the way of most newlyweds. Even that worry didn't bring my spirits down. It just didn't matter in the long run. She was mine, I was hers that was all I cared about.

Everyone spent the afternoon and into the evening celebrating. I'd taken a plate for my prisoners, even brought them a couple mugs of beer. They appreciated the gesture and even congratulated me on my nuptials. This wasn't personal to them, it was a job and being arrested wasn't a new experience. They'd admitted to never having a better stay in jail. They understood why I was keeping them locked up for the three days, assuring me there was no hard feelings.

It was nice seeing the town like this and I realized that part of their joy was our wedding. The majority of it was celebrating the return of their dreams. I could admit that and didn't begrudge them that. With everything getting back to normal word had spread quickly about the newly formed town council. Already news was spreading about the vacant farmland and business spaces up for sale. These people had feared for their future last week, today was a rebirth of sorts for them. Everyone could feel it in the air, hope was filling them again. With it came the drive they'd lost.

Mary and I snuck out while everyone was still mostly sober. I'd noticed Percy and Bess disappear a few minutes ago and guessed we'd fulfilled our social obligation. The house was lit softly, the warmth from the fireplace carrying through the house on the breeze. Angie must have left minutes before we arrived, somehow knowing when we'd be there. At the door I swept Mary into my arms, carrying her across the threshold. Her giggling laughter echoed down the hallway ahead of us.

"What would you like to see first my wife?" I asked remembering she hadn't seen the house yet.

"Sorry dear husband but I've had the tour. Angie showed me the house when I moved my things in earlier." The mischievous grin on her face made me smile even more.

"And does my humble abode meet your high standards?"

"What do you.." she cut off her sharp tone before finishing with a gentle smile. "Sorry, I know you didn't mean it like that."

"Nothing to apologize my love." I said encircling her with my arms. "I know you're nervous but nothing will happen you don't want."

"You mean it?" She seemed apprehensive but there was a heat buried under the fear.

"I do." I set her down. Steping back letting her take the lead.

"You'll get tired of my sharp tongue." She hung her head fearing my response. "Everyone does."

"I fell in love with you when every other word you spoke to me was sharp." I laughed thinking back to just a few days ago when I'd first met her.

"Oh, our long history of a week?" She snorted. Before I could respond she took my hand quietly leading me to the bedroom. Her voice carried a heat I hadn't expected. "Come we have things to test husband."

She sat me on the bed then stepped back slowly removing the layers of fabric that hid her shapely form. My eyes never left her, I was mesmerized by every move. With each falling layer more of her pale skin was exposed, the alabaster white dotted with small patches of freckles around her shoulders. They slowly faded, falling in a cascade toward her cleavage. Soon she stood in front of me clothed in nothing, flushed and breathing heavily.

There was no fear in her eyes anymore, now they were filled with a fiery passion that threatened my control. With another moment's hesitation she stepped to me, undressing me far faster then she had. I heard two buttons bounce off the walls when they slowed her too much. I stood, slowly letting her remove my the rest. When she reached for my guns she hesitated and I took them off for her. Hanging the belt over a hook near the bed.

Soon she was stepping into my arms, our bodies feeling skin for the first time. She pulled me to the bed with her, laying me on my back still giving her control. After a long deep kiss, she pulled me on top of her. I took it as permission and started slowly kissing down her neck. Her breath caught as I moved but she never stopped me. Soon whatever fear she had was washed away in pleasure and passion. I worked to please her, exploring her smooth skin my lips and hands. Teasing out every bit of her passion. There was no rush and I wasn't going to hurry with any of this.

When she couldn't take anymore she pulled me up, our lips meeting again. She slowly pulled me to her, our bodies joining together finally. There was nothing but our passion now, it was feverish and fast. Both of us driven far beyond fear or any other thoughts beyond need for one another. Later collapsed together, her sweating body draped half across my naked chest, her breath still coming in panting gasps. My fingers lightly trailing up and down her bare back, gently caressing her as she lay there. I could feel her chest moving against me with every breath.

"I can't believe I ever feared this." She snuggled deeper into my side as she spoke.

"You're okay then?" My voice was soft, filled with concern and love.

"Mmmmm better then okay. That was more than any novel could ever describe." Her fingers trailed across my stomach making mindless patterns.

"Agreed." I could feel my body responding to her touch. With her leg draped across me she knew exactly what effect she was having.

"Truly, you're ready for more?" Her breath was hot washing across my chest when she spoke.There was a hint of desire in her voice.

"That my love is up to you, as always." I said gently kissing the top of her head.

Without another word she shifted on top of me, the sounds of our passion filled the night again. It was an indescribable night, one where we both lost all inhibitions and fears. Hours later I fell asleep with her draped across, her head resting on my chest where she snored softly. My last act was pulling the quilt up to cover both of us.

CHAPTER 35

I woke up to find her still asleep, still draped across my body. The scent of her mixed with lavender filling my nostrils. A soft laugh escaped my lips at her gentle snoring. I would have laid there for days but my body insisted on getting up. When I opened the door to leave the water closet I found her waiting. Still naked as the day she was borne and it stole my breath away.

Cocking her head slightly up to meet my lust filled gaze for an instant. With a smirk she darted past me quickly closing the door. I crawled back under the covers to wait and enjoy the show when she returned. She did not disappoint, slowly sauntering across the room to the bed wearing nothing but a wicked smile. Watching her crawl across the bed toward me had the desired effect. It was another hour before we thought about getting out of bed.

I dressed first, leaving her laying languidly in bed. After starting the stove and coffee I searched through the kitchen looking for a skillet. Finally spotting it waiting on the back burner of the stove it made me laugh. My mind was still back in bed with her, I must have looked past the skillet a dozen times. The bacon went into it, the first step in a simple breakfast of bacon and eggs. The bacon cooked while I cut bread into slices. Mary walked in shakily wearing a dressing gown, drawn by the scent of cooking food. I handed her a cup of tea when she leaned against me.

"Dear husband I may need to beg off my wifely duties for a

few days."

"Are you okay?" I asked concerned. Her smile instantly took away those fears.

"Just a bit sore from inexperience my love, nothing to fear. Bess warned me about being too enthusiastic." The sheepish giggle that escaped her made me laugh. "It was my choice not to listen."

"Umm yes of course." Uncomfortable with the idea of hurting her.

"None of that husband, I was in charge. Remember?"

"Yes ma'am." I said grinning at the memory of last night and this morning.

"Good now serve me my breakfast like a good man." Her grin was infectious and soon enough we were both talking happily across the small kitchen table enjoying our meal.

I'd managed to leave the keys with the mayor last night. He'd promised to feed the prisoners this morning but swore he wouldn't open the cells. I'd have to head there soon to change the buckets. I didn't think they'd mind too much if I was a bit late and if they did it wasn't really my concern. They had come to take Mary by force if necessary. I may recognize it was just business and not hold a grudge. That it didn't mean I was happy about their presence or job.

Kissing my wife goodbye after breakfast, promising I'd be back before too long. The kiss had a bit more desire in it then I meant and we were both still panting when we separated. I walked to the jail with a smile on my face. It was a beautiful day and the town was doing what towns do. Returning to the life they wanted building, shopping, trading and talking. I tipped my hat and waved to them on my walk, smiling at how peaceful it was.

Opening the door to the sheriff's office I was surprised to see the mayor playing checkers with Ben. Mike napped on his bunk with a two week old Denver paper covering his face. Smiling I picked up the keys to empty the buckets. After that was taken care of I went back to the desk. There was an envelope sitting on it waiting for my attention. A weight lifted off my shoulders as I read the telegram.

Deputy McElroy

Cartersville

Contacted head marshal stop

He talked to Pinkertons stop

Then talked to her parents stop

No more problems from them stop

Badge secure stop

Congratulations stop

Marshal Reese

Denver

There was another telegram under it. The envelop read Mary McElroy. Someone had scratched out Gardner and written McElroy below it. Smiling I tucked it in my pocket, I'd drop it off on my rounds in a few minutes. Turned back to the cells I couldn't help but smile. The mayor had trounced Ben and the bigger man was almost sulking. What did he think was going to happen? The mayor spent a fair amount of his day playing checkers with the other men in town.

"I still think you tricked me somehow. Not cheated mind, but I missed something." Ben protested.

"Overt aggression isn't a bad tactic but you must watch for patterns." The mayor smiled at the frustrated man.

I almost wanted to keep them locked up because they looked like the break wasn't bothering them. Sadly it wouldn't be right, no matter how you sliced it. That ordinance wasn't approved by the mayor or anyone else. It needed to be rescinded and that meant releasing them. Hopefully now there was no reason to keep them locked up. Maybe her parents had truly given up on their foolish ideas.

"Gentlemen I sincerely apologize for the interruption. Mayor Kelso would you like to rescind the ban on firearms." It caught them by surprise but the mayor recovered quickly.

"That's your call marshal, I support whatever decision you make."

"Sadly, that would mean I have to release these fine gentlemen and waive the fine." I said unlocking Ben's cell. He didn't seem in a hurry and waited on his partner. Mike grumbled as he woke up almost glaring at me when I opened his cell. "Coffee gentlemen?"

"Sounds good." Mike rubbed his eyes before getting to his feet. Ben shrugged, joining us in the office. The mayor made his exit saying if he didn't get back to the store his wife would be on the warpath.

"Figure once we contact the office they'll call us back to Chicago." Ben said after I handed him a steaming cup.

"Not sure how much I believe it but her family has been warned off. There's a telegram for her that came in. I'm going to bet it's from them but I'll have to wait and see."

"Could be they changed their tune. I'd be surprised but you never know with rich folks." Mike rumbled out over his cup.

"I don't have much experience with them myself. Indians and outlaws sure, rich folks though they are a complete unknown." I admitted.

"My advice? Don't take that telegram as gospel, either of them. You seem like a decent guy an she loves you, any fool can see that much. Her family though, they only respect someone with power or wealth." Ben said thinking as he spoke. "That's why they might have backed off. If the person who contacted them had enough power that is. They'll let it go an figure you're connected. If not, they'll lie, cheat and backstab if they need too."

"Have to see what they do I reckon." Shrugging, it was all I could do. "Stage will be heading out in about an hour for Denver or did y'all want to stay locked up?"

"If my choices are that cell or a coach, I'll stay in the cell." I was beginning to think Mike was also the grumpy one.

"Agreed but that cell don't pay an the wives'll be waiting for us." Ben laughed slapping Mike on the back. His rumbled response was incoherent, making both of us laugh.

"Just waiting on the pay you mean." Despite this he finished his coffee and stuck out his hand to me. "Never been locked up by a nicer law man."

"Well, y'all are the most polite folks I've ever locked up. You're both welcome at my fire anytime."

"Same marshal, you ever need a Pinkerton ask for us." Ben shook my hand and they both turned to leave.

Outside of Carter's Ranch....

He was slowly packing his things. Yesterday Mr.Carter told him to shut down the listening but he was stalling. Not only because it meant he'd have to start doing real work again but partially because he liked listening to the tapping machine. It was something he'd always liked, a magical language only he and a few others across the country knew. His greed had cost him that, taking one bribe and getting caught for sharing information had brought that life to an end.

The machine tapped. A message starting, it wouldn't hurt

to listen to one last message. First came the query, then the authentication. Finally the actual message started.

Director main office 004

Girl married to deputy marshal stop

Advise next stop

Agent 116

He waited knowing there would be a response, then he could finish packing. This was interesting and he had a hunch Mr.Carter would want to know about it. This involved that deputy and that woman, he knew they had changed things. Maybe they'd done enough that he could get the mayor to hire him. Being around machine again would be better then work around the ranch.

Agent 116

Return to Chicago stop

Other team hired by family stop

Leave Denver fastest possible stop

Direct office 004

He smiled thinking this might pay off. If they wanted to know what the agents were up to anyway. Wait that was the office again.

Agent 014

Report to Train station Chicago stop

Meet Client Palmer at station Stop

Travel to Denver retrieve Daughter Stop

Waylay husband only if necessary Stop

Family will bribe stop

Direct Office 004

Mr.Carter would want to know about this. He forgot about packing and left to saddle his horse. There was no time to waste.

I worked around the office the rest of the morning, finally starting to get it straightened up. Ed should be able to talk today so we can figure out what he wants to do. I found a stack of wanted posters hidden in a desk. Likely ones Percy never looked at before stuffing them in there. After studying the new ones, they got posted on the board behind the desk. The old ones that were dead got taking down and set aside. You never wasted paper, it had more than one use until a fire consumed it, or it ended up in the outhouse. The rest of the junk in the desk got thrown out. Between that and cleaning the cells lunch time seemed to come quicker than expected.

Walking through the front door of the house voices carried down the hall from the kitchen. When I started walking that way I recognized them. Mary and Angie were chatting away happily. It sounded like they were getting along just fine. It made me happy to know she wouldn't be alone if I got called away. The assumption proved true when I walked into the kitchen and saw them both smiling. Angie was stirring a pot on the stove while Mary was kneading bread dough on a countertop.

"After noon ladies." The smile on my face told both how happy this all made me.

"Angie made you a sandwich for lunch, there will be stew

for dinner with fresh bread." Then she frowned down at the dough and added. "If I manage to get it made."

"You're doing fine darlin don't you worry none about it." Angie smiled at the younger girl. "Bread is a touchy thing sometimes, I've ruined more than I've made. Sit down and have lunch with your husband, you know where his sandwich is. Coffee should be hot an ain't too old."

"I don't know how you do it all but I'm so glad to have you here Angie." She took a plate out of the cold cellar and set it on the table before pouring me some coffee. She brought over her tea before joining me at the table.

"This came for me and there's one for you too." Placing both telegrams on the table.

"You didn't read mine?"

"Wasn't addressed to me." Reading it would have felt like an invasion to me.

She read mine first, looking up at me in surprise when she finished. Shrugging to indicate I knew as much as she did about it. With a little trepidation she opened hers, her eyes darted back and forth reading the short message. After reading and rereading it she handed it to me.

Miss Mary Gardner

Cartersville

Understand engaged to deputy marshal stop

Would like to meet in Denver in two weeks stop

Please bring him stop

Father

Chicago

Handing it back to her, unsure of what to do about it. From

the look on her face, she didn't know either. We would go because it was the right thing to do but I don't think either of us wanted to. The hard part would be the two-week deadline. I didn't know how Ed was going to be doing by then. There were several things that would have to line up for us to make that timeline. There was also a lot of questions that would have to answered before we went but it could be done. That is if she wanted to, that was the first thing to decide.

CHAPTER 36

"What do you think dear wife?" My teasing tone broke through her thoughts.

"I don't know. My parents haven't ever been good people, I don't believe they've changed. After finding happiness without them, I'm just not sure I'm willing to risk them hurting me again." There was both pain and hope in her voice.

"But you want to believe they've changed?"

"Of course I do, it's my family. I just don't believe they have, not that easily." Gently taking her hand in mine before speaking I made my offer.

"It's up to you my love. We can go and see, prepared for the worst but hoping for the best." I added a reassuring squeeze. "Or we can stay here, ignore them and their games."

"How can we prepare? We have no idea what they're up to."

"We have two weeks, but I already have a few guesses. Admittedly there nothing but assumptions but it's what I have."

"Money." She said the single word like it was the vilest curse she knew.

"Yes, probably the lack of. There's only one reason to hire Pinkertons to find you. They need something and it has to do with you."

"I fear you're right." A lone tear trailed down her cheek, gently I reached to wipe it away. "But I can hope they've changed and just want to see me."

"We'll go and find out. Prepared for the worst but hoping for the best." Even as the words came from my mouth I was planning for every eventuality.

"Thank you. I can help pay I've saved some..." my laughter cut her off and she looked at me in annoyance.

"Dear wife, we haven't had a chance to talk about money. Let me inform you here and now, it isn't a concern. Not in the slightest." I grinned at her shocked face.

"What do you mean?" She asked suspiciously.

"I've collected a fair amount from bounties over the years. Had the good luck to meet some interesting men along the way. Some I invested in and those have paid off in most cases. There's a little over thirty thousand dollars in the Denver Bank, plus a bit more invested around the country. Hell, there's almost seven thousand here in the house." The stunned look on her face was worth it. I watched as it dawned on her. If I had that much in the bank, how much had I invested and with who?

"Who have you invested with?" Her eyes narrowed studying me closely.

"Swift in Chicago, but I let him vote my shares. Fifty percent of a cattle ranch in Dakota territory. Now that I think of it the profits from that are in a bank there. The ranch is forty-five thousand acres, last I heard he was running a few thousand head. Some investments with Colt and Winchester and there's business properties in Denver, Dallas, Dakota and some land in Montana. Oh, and a property in New York that I won from a traveling drummer." If she was stunned before her reality was altered now. The only one she could lay her mind to was Swift, they were based in Chicago.

"You own enough stock in Swift to vote?"

"Ya, met Gus a few years back. He was cash short at the time an I was flush. He sold me five percent of the company. The dividends go into a different account in Chicago. I'm not sure what's in that one, haven't check in a few years."

She just started laughing, it turned into a very cute snort and she cut it off looking embarrassed. Then the giggles started again, she rocked back in her chair trying to catch her breath. It became infectious and soon I was laughing with her. Finally, we managed to get ourselves under control to speak again.

"Gus, as you say, is a man my parents could only hope to meet much less call Gus." She broke out in giggles again and had to recover again before continuing. "You're the man my parents wish they knew, one they only dreamed of me marrying."

I joined her in laughing, now that I could see the humor. Money had never meant much to me. The investments had been in the men who stood before me, not some financial genius move. Those years chasing bounties hadn't been about money to me, I'd just been trying to kill the pain of loss not get rich.

"Sorry you've fulfilled their wishes?" I finally managed to ask.

The entire time Angie had done her best to ignore us but she finally had to stop and look at us. She hadn't heard what we said, only the laughter but it had become loud enough that she worried about us. I waved, assuring her that we were fine. After all the laughter was done we decided to go. I needed to send a few telegrams off and see if my idea would work.

The rest of the afternoon cost a little over five dollars. The mayor claimed I was trying to cripple his fingers with the number of messages being sent. Mostly they were collecting information or requesting it. Some responses came in that evening, others trickled in over the next two days.

The town was quiet and the sun sinking slowly toward the horizon when I finally had time to talk to Ed. He was sitting up in bed, his arm tied in a sling that kept it immobile. His color had returned giving him the appearance of a man instead of the living dead. The first thing he said answered my first question.

"Nice shot kid." He smiled up at me. Using his other hand to wave me to the chair beside his bed.

"Luck, damn sure wasn't intentional. How ya feeling?"

"Not bad for a dead man."

"Yeah when do I get introduced?"

"Pleasure to meet you Chance, names Jake Harrison." He grinned broadly at me.

"Jake huh? Pleasures all mine." I laughed then added. "Suits a good upstanding lawman like yourself."

"Thought it might, sides I used it for a while as a puncher so it's got some history. More importantly I'll answer to it."

"Seems custom made then. Doc say when he's letting you out?"

"Should be part of the walking dead in a few more days. Have to take it easy for a while yet. He says a month before he'll stop fussing about it. Think he's just tired of feeding me."

"Well Jake it'll be good to see you up and about. You can stay up at the house."

"Wouldn't want to impose." I expected this response and cut it off.

"We're heading to Denver soon, besides the construction at the sheriff's office would keep you out of there. Angie will take care of you at the house. Ya won't even have to cook."

"Construction?" He eyed me curiously.

"Guess you're behind on some news. You got the offer as

sheriff?"

"Talked to the Mayor yesterday, swore me in already."

"My boss is stationing me here. I'll be covering the southern part of the state and helping in the nations as needed."

"So, the construction is a marshal's office?"

"Mostly, the mayor and I worked out adding some decent quarters for you with the construction crew. Better then that cot in the corner at least."

"Glad to hear that. Course if I'd have known that I might not have negotiated for room and board so hard." He laughed at the mayor getting one over on him. "How's the end building look?"

"Like a fortress disguised as a law office. We ever need to hole up that'll be the place to do it." I grinned answering his curiosity. "Even going to have a pump inside and stables out back."

"Sounds fancy."

"I mighta added a few things. The offices are joined don't know about you but I hate sitting in an office alone. Combined the cells too. Figure we might need to share them and a jailer."

"I like the idea but you're fooling yourself if you think you'll be there much."

"Probably not, but a man can dream."

The rest of our conversation was mostly catching up. After another five minutes the Doc chased me out. I left with a handshake and told him Angie would expect him soon. Leaving the docs I turned to check in with the mayor. It was quick since he knew everything that was going on already. I picked up a few odds and ends the ladies said we needed before walking back toward the house.

It was another three days before Ed...I mean Jake was well enough to walk easily. The next morning we packed the carriage. I'd bought it after the wedding, knowing we'd prefer it to the buckboard. Nether of us wanted to take the stagecoach and I'd picked up camping supplies that rose above my normal rough camp from Kelso's Mercantile. The carriage gave us an easy way to carry it all while traveling in comfort. Mary swore she was okay with roughing it but I didn't see a reason to if we didn't have to.

Mayor Kelso waved to us as we headed out of town. He was just unlocking the shop to start his day. The sun broke the horizon just as we passed the edge of town. Setting off on our first adventure as a married couple. The road wasn't exactly perfect but it was easy to follow. The construction wagons had just passed this way, their heavy weight smoothing the road a little. I'd packed for five days travel but hoped we'd make Denver in less.

It spoke to the growth of Colorado that we didn't run into any problems along the way. A couple of buckboards passed us and we set up camp with a nice family headed to Texas the second night. They agreed to check out Cartersville and might change their plans after I told them about the town. He was a farmer looking for land and they seemed like a good family. Just the type we want in our growing community. A group of four men rode up on us the next day. When one of them pointed at me, they wheeled around before coming into our camp. He must have caught sight of the badge.

We made Denver midafternoon on the fourth day with no real problems. Both of us happy to be done with the trip but remembering the nights spent together under the stars happily. It was a pleasure getting to know her more. We'd fallen in love without really knowing each other and we took advantage of the time rectifying that. Her mind was as sharp as her tongue and I quickly developed a healthy respect for both rather quickly. When I told her what all I had planned out she added a few things I'd missed, filling in a few gaps.

CHAPTER 37

"Which hotel are we staying at my love?" She asked when we made it into the city proper.

"None." I smiled mischievously at her. "I made other arrangements."

"What did you do?" She knew me well enough to know this was part of my preparations. "I know you made reservations at one, you told me the name, I just forgot.

"I asked a friend if we could use his house. He usually isn't in town but still keeps a small place here."

"Don't think I didn't notice the omission of said friend's name."

"I'm sure you did my love. Please allow me my secrets, the answer will become apparent soon." I guided the carriage off Main Street and down one of the side streets. Houses lined the road after a few blocks, each one a mansion. This was one of the more prominent districts in Denver. Wealthy miners and businessmen owned most of the houses. She gasped beside me when I turned into a house halfway up. The placard on the gate read, Swift house. A guard stepped out of the gate house, waving for us to a stop.

"Can I help ya sir?" He asked politely. He was older but still moved with the grace of someone who could handle whatever you threw at them.

"Yes I'm Chance McElroy. I believe Mr. Swift sent word?"

"Yes sir, got the telegram yesterday. The house is yours and the staff have prepared everything for you. Rodger should meet you at the door." The man was professional and polite. "My names too long, prefer Sarge if you don't mind. I run security for the place, if there's a problem just let me know."

"Thanks Sarge, I'll remember that." Reaching my hand down, he took it in a solid grip and shook. He swung the gate open a minute later letting our carriage move up the twisting driveway.

The house rising in front of us was impressive. Rising to four stories, it was easily twice the size of our house. It fit the Denver motif for this district, most of these places were built by miners who struck gold. Poor men turned wealthy trying to brag about their success. When they left or lost their fortune the houses were sold off. Since Denver has growing the wealthy businessmen from the bigger cities tended to purchase them. Most weren't used often but owned either as investments or in hope of moving here as the country grew.

"The Swift house? You don't mean?" Mary asked in shock. Our carriage moved slowly toward the house, allowing her to look around the grounds.

"I sent him a telegraph cause he told me about this place. He doesn't use it much, business keeps him tied to Chicago most of the time." I shrugged innocently. "Figured it'd be nicer than a hotel, safer too."

"Oh, that's what you figured was it? Nothing to do with my parents?"

"Oh? Why would they be interested in this small thing?"

"They wouldn't, not at all, they'd probably think you're just being cheap."

"Really? Hmmm we shouldn't tell them about it then. Maybe they'll expect us to stay at one of the cheaper hotels in town."

"You mean like the one you made reservations at?"

"I suppose that would make sense. I am planning on keeping those, it's always good to have a backup plan after all."

"Deputy, you sir are a very devious man." She bumped into my shoulder laughing as the carriage eased to a stop.

An older man was striding down the steps to meet us. He moved like someone in control of everything around him. Dressed in a clean, crisply pressed suit the man looked professional. This was the man in charge of this place, there was no doubting his authority. Two younger men flanked him, one looked like a stable hand, maybe 15 years old. The other was a servant of some kind most likely a porter to carry our bags. He had a similar air of danger to Sarge.

"Good afternoon madam." The man stepped to Mary's side of the carriage, offering her a hand down. "I am Rodger, the butler. I will see to your every need while staying at the Swift house."

"A pleasure Rodger. You can leave the camping gear in the carriage. Just bring the two valise inside." Mary spoke like this was normal while I was still bumbling along.

It was accurate, she'd grown up in this world. Smiling to myself at how quickly she shifter back to that role. I'd have carried my own bags in despite the obviousness of the situation. I didn't trip over my pride and just let her deal with it all. Rodger's knowing smile told me he'd already figured all this out. The man was quick, I had to give him that and remember it.

"Sir a Marshal Reese dropped off a horse for you earlier. Would you like to have him brought up?" The stable hand had paused holding the lead of the carriage. He was waiting for my response to Rodger's question.

"Go ahead dear, take care of those things we discussed and see the marshal. I'll get us unpacked and be ready for dinner when you return." Even her speech patterns had changed, it was a bit unnerving.

"Yes thank you." I nodded to Rodger and the stable boy led the team away. Turning to Mary I asked. "Shall we say six?"

"Yes, it's been a long day. I think we will dine in tonight." She informed me before turning to Rodger. "If that's enough time for the kitchen?"

"I believe it should be ma'am but it won't allow them to truly show case their abilities."

"I'm sure whatever they manage will be far better than my cooking." Mary said with a smile before turning toward the door. "Am I right in guessing there is a bath inside?"

"Of course, ma'am I'll have it prepared immediately." Rodger responded dropping in behind her.

Laughing to myself I ignored the rest and perched on the porch railing to wait for the horse. Checking my guns and Winchester out of habit, it had become a reflex years ago and had saved me more then once. A few minutes longer and the clip clop of hooves on stone echoed around the corner. Leading a brown gelding the young man came around the corner. The animal didn't stand out as anything particular unless you knew what to look for.

He was a near perfect example of what a horse should be. Just what I would have picked to stay unnoticed. Nothing distinctive in color or markings but he had one of the best confirmations I'd ever seen. Reese knew me well and sent the right horse for the job. Having the saddle branded US Marshals didn't hurt. That would detour most would be thieves from touching it. My Winchester slid into the scabbard cleanly, my nose caught the smell the fresh oil. Someone, probably the stable hand, had recently cleaned and polished the tack.

Stepping into the saddle felt like a returning home, being back on a horse was comforting. The last couple of weeks I'd spent most of my time in town. It was a hard change I was slowly getting used to. Being on foot and around people after years spent alone except for a decent horse wasn't easy. Luckily it wouldn't last, Ed was up and moving which meant soon my assignments would start again. In the time being I was going to enjoy every second possible with Mary.

Relaxing my grip on the reigns, my heels barely touched the gelding. The animal was well trained, that light touch got him moving toward the gate. It swung open ahead of me and I rode through with a nod to Sarge. It swung closed behind me with the light clang of metal before I turned toward my first stop.

Riding through town toward I watched the people moving around me. My destination was the hotel I'd made reservations at, might as well check-in to start our cover. Taking off my star before looping the reigns over the rail I walked up the short stairs to the front desk. After paying the full amount for our stay I told the front desk I'd be back sometime tomorrow before my wife arrived. He smiled knowingly and told me to have fun.

His assumptions would fill in the blanks regarding my plans, it would be what he sold to whoever asked about us. There was no doubt her family would send someone to gather information. Letting the clerk make some money while leaving false information suited me fine. He'd tell them I came in first and then wandered off probably to a brothel or bar.

The marshal's office was back toward the center of town, stepping back on the horse I turned that way. After a block I put my badge back on and continued moving with the traffic. Slipping a loose knot over the hitching rail out front I turned and looked around me before stepping inside. Something felt off, like someone was standing on my grave. Turning to my left I spotted him, half standing in a shadow.

Across the street and down a few doors was Harvey, glaring daggers at me. It took longer then it should have to recall his name, a laugh escaped my mouth when I did recognize him.

It hadn't been intentional but I couldn't stop myself. With everything going on this was what had my hackles up? To him it must have seemed like I was laughing at his hate filled glare. It might not have been my smartest move. He stepped off the boardwalk with anger flashing in his eyes and started toward me. With more then a little surprise I watched the man cut between wagons and horses.

"Reese! Might have a problem out here." I yelled at the door behind me. My voice wouldn't make it inside but it wouldn't hurt to try.

"Ain't no one here to protect ya now kid." He snapped striding toward me. I had to stifle another laugh at him calling me kid, he wasn't more then a year older then me.

He blatantly flipped the thong off his gun while staring at me. His desire to kill me combined with too much who-hit-john muddling his thoughts. So much so that he didn't notice when his thong dropped back into place. It wouldn't stop a man from drawing but there was no way it was coming out fast. He'd have to either break the thong or take time to flip it off again. The fool was far too drunk for a gun fight. Even if he didn't know that I did and that stayed my hand.

"Harvey don't make me kill you." I sighed in frustration but couldn't help the slight smirk.

"If anyone's dying today it's you. Unless your yellow jus' like I always know'd ya was." The grin that split his face was part anger but mostly alcohol.

"Always known? You met me once." The words slipped out, I hadn't meant to banter with the drunk.

Frustrated with the situation I shook my head. Stalking toward him my eyes never left his. At first he looked happy, I was going to met his challenge. When my forward motion didn't stop at whatever invisible line he thought was right for a duel his look changed. Fear crept into his eyes when my stride never slowed. Suddenly I was too close, everyone knew if you were to close both men would die in a gun fight.

He panicked, trying to snatch his Remington out of the holster when I was fifteen feet away. The fear made his eyes go wide showing the whites when it refused to come out. Instead of checking the thong he gripped it with both hands trying to rip it out. He never got the chance to recognize his mistake. I was too close now and he didn't know what to do.

A quick left snapped out in a hard jab that landed perfectly, rocking his head back. The crunch of bone and spray of blood announced his broken nose. His eyes crossed trying to look at the smashed thing trying to understand the pain. The alcohol was still making him pull on the pistol with both hands. My right cross landed high on his jaw before the pain cut through the haze of whiskey. The lights went out, his eyes rolled into the back of his head and he fell into the muck.

Letting out a heavy sigh I leaned down taking his gun belt off and tossing it across my shoulder. After grabbing an ankle I started moving. It wasn't my intention to drag him through horse shit but I didn't dodge around it. Swinging open the door to the marshal's office a shocked deputy sat behind the desk. He hadn't expected anyone, much less someone dragging an unconscious man behind him.

"Marshal in?" I asked calmly.

"He's two doors down at the sheriff's office."

"Thanks." Turning I dragged my charge behind me toward the other office. The sheriff was probably the one to see anyway, this was a local matter after all.

CHAPTER 38

When I open the door Harvey was starting to make noise behind me. He'd vomited somewhere between the two offices and it had added to the mess. Still not fully conscious, it would be maybe another five minutes. The deputy sheriff behind the desk gawked for a minute before speaking up.

"Can I help ya deputy?"

"Two things, is Marshal Reese here? Second thing can you lock this fool up? He tried to have a shootout with me but was too drunk. Got outsmarted by his thong."

"See that tarpaulin there?" He asked pointing a piece laid out in the floor. "Drag him on that an follow me, keeps the floors clean."

"Nice trick." I made a mental note to remember it and tell Jake about the idea. I was still struggling to use his new name, it was a challenge. "Names Chance, this fool is Harvey don't know his last but the Marshal does."

"We know him, names Elijah by the way." He said opening a cell at the back of the jail. It was the furtherest away from his desk. "Just roll him off and leave him on the floor."

He locked the door after I stepped out. Harvey was starting to wake up. Back up front I put the tarpaulin where it had been before stepping to the desk. I handed him Harvey's gun belt and without a word he put it in the lower drawer.

"They in some secret meeting?"

"Nope, but they been yelling about something for a while.

Want some coffee rather than risk walking into that mess?" He offered. That sounded like a much better option then getting caught between two ornery law men.

"Sounds better than the alternative."

"It's over there, cups hanging on the wall are clean. Mind topping this one off?"

"Nope." I took his cup from the desk and got myself one before folding into a chair by the desk. It must have been for a deputy because it was angled to see the door and the cells. "He might need to see a doc, pretty sure I broke his nose."

"Reckon so, noticed it when we put him in. Too bad I can't leave till the Sheriff comes out. Shame about his nose, too long an the doc'll have to re-break it." His tone wasn't very sympathetic.

The deputy occasionally flipped through various reports breaking the silence. He was older maybe early thirties, wearing a wedding ring. It was comfortable, two men with no interest in filling the silence with small talk. Occasionally a yell broke through the walls letting us know our respective bosses were still at it. Harvey yelled once and Elijah told him to shut up. That went on for another full cup of coffee. Finally, a door at the back opened and my boss walked out laughing.

"You know one day I'll beat you." Reese's voice carried down the hall. I looked at the deputy behind the desk questioningly.

"Cribbage." Was his one word answer and suddenly it all made sense.

"Never happen Reese but keep donating to the cause." The sheriff's voice was deep and full of humor.

"Chance? How long you been waiting?" Reese had come around the corner to see me grinning over my mug.

"Bout two cups worth." I laughed. "Nothing to worry about, it was nice to just sit for a bit. Needed somewhere to lock

Harvey up anyway."

"What did that drunk fool do this time?" The sheriff came around the corner filling the hallway.

The man was almost as wide as he was tall and he was a tall man. The massive mustache seemed to shift with his words, almost dancing in a weird way. His hair was salt and pepper, cut short accenting the curled mustache further.

"Sheriff Dan Dittmer meet one of my more troublesome deputies, Chance McElroy." Reese waved his hand in some weird attempt at a formal introduction.

"Sheriff." I got to my feet and the big man's hand engulfed mine.

"Pleasure Deputy. Reckon you're the one bringing trouble to my town?"

"Guilty as charged, hope you didn't mean Harvey. He tried to draw on me in the middle of the street. Did it when he was too drunk to know how his thong worked."

"Mighta been a kindness to just kill him." Elijah muttered from the desk.

"Boys not beyond hope yet." Dan said but there was a hint of sadness in the words.

"Went ta school with him, he's a born a waste." Elijah evidently had strong opinions on the man. "If we ain't gonna let him die I might as well go fetch the doc since you're done hiding in the back. Looks like his nose got busted in the fracas."

"I know you don't like him. Let's leave it at that and fetch the doc." Dan glared at his deputy for a second then he turned back to me. His deputy slowly got up and pulled his hat on before leaving to find the doc. "Your boss has been telling me about what you're cooking up. I hope it works the way you plan cause I'd rather not have a war in my streets."

"If my wife's right it shouldn't come to that an she ain't been wrong yet." I reassured the big man.

"You'll get used to that." His laughter boomed out. "In ten years mine ain't been wrong once, just ask her."

We all shared some laughter breaking the tension. He wasn't wrong to be worried but nothing I knew said this would turn into gun play. We chatted about the next few days and the plans I already had in place. The sheriff already had his part taken care of and agreed to would do their part. I had to depend on him to take care of his part. Marshals could operate in the city but when a good sheriff was in place, it was far better to work with them when you could.

"I do appreciate the help Dan." Reese smiled rising from the chair he'd been sitting in. "Figure he ought to get back to his wife and I need to check in with my office."

"About right, I know this puts you out an appreciate the help." I said matching my boss's actions.

"Don't mention it. If folks don't do anything stupid it'll be easy. If they do they're breaking the law in my town. That isn't something I tolerate, no matter how much money you got." The man's smile was somehow kind and ferocious at the same time. It was easy to see why Reese liked the man, friendly but dedicated to his town.

With a nod of farewell, we stepped out of the office. I pulled the door closed behind me before following Reese back toward his office. When we got there he waved me off toward the horse.

"Get some sleep. I'm sure dealing with this mess isn't all your wife has planned. Unless I miss my guess tomorrow's plans are shopping." He grinned at me knowingly before adding. "Try and enjoy yourselves, you've got two days before the games begin."

"I do think she has some plans for tomorrow now that you mention it." I grinned knowing she wanted to add her own touches to the house. He was right, tomorrow had already been designated for shopping, so was the day after.

"I bet." He laughed turning into the office.

Stepping into the stirrups laughing myself. I rode back toward the Swift house slowly enjoying the feel of a fine horse under me. I was just in time for dinner, which was served in the massive dining room for some reason. With just the two of us at the table it felt a bit ridiculous to me. My opinion didn't seem to matter, the servants didn't think it was strange at all. Still, it wasn't the most comfortable meal but the food was damn good.

After Dinner we spent some time in the library looking over the selection of book. Mary found one on animal husbandry that caught her eye, I found one on steam engines that looked well written. A few hours later we both agreed that it was past our bedtime and we walked up the stairs. The bedroom that was prepared for us was massive. If I'd known we could have just come here to read.

In the back of the room near a heating stove sat two very comfortable looking chairs. The bed was worth the walk though. It was one of the most comfortable night's sleep I'd ever had. So much so that I made a quick note to get a mattress like this tomorrow while we shopped. I don't care how much it cost, I wanted one.

CHAPTER 39

I asked Rodger about the mattress the next morning, he said we could order one at Kinley's Mercantile but it would have to come from Chicago. That was our first stop anyway and it turned out to be the only one we managed that day. I'm still not sure how she spent almost a thousand dollar in one store, but she did. I admit to contributing a few hundred to the bill aside from the mattress but it still amazed me.

The smile on her face was worth every dime though. A few things would be delivered to the house later today, the ones we could take home on the carriage. Most of it would arrive in Cartersville in a few weeks via local shipping company. They had to be ordered from Chicago or New York. A few items would be even longer since they had to come from overseas, I couldn't remember what those were but she'd wanted them. I'd said it when we walked in and meant it. If she wanted it, she got it.

"Are you sure we can spend that much?" She was still nervous about the large bill.

"Absolutely my love." I smiled at her concern. "I don't ever want you to go without."

"You know I don't need any of it to be happy but admit I'll enjoy having the house the way I want." She blushed slightly before adding with a grin. "Especially the new mattress."

"Let's hope it's durable." I said laughing despite my ears burning.

"You're incorrigible!" She laughed playfully swatting my arm.

"But not wrong." We shared a laugh as we turned up the path to the house. Sarge smiled at our happy conversation while closing the gate behind us.

The next day wasn't nearly as expensive but we spent more time going from place to place. I did manage to drag her into a gun shop and ordered some ammo for the house and office, two greener shotguns and couple of derringers. When I offered one to my wife she laughed before showing me the one already tucked in her sleeve. We'd have to talk about her familiarity with guns when we got home. Something told me she'd downplayed he knowledge when I first asked.

I'd picked up enough clothes to fill the massive dresser and closet. It was more clothes than I'd ever owned before. Just another thing that was changing as I became part of civilization again. We both got heavy winter coats along with other clothes that would be needed. There was also a stack of heavy quilts and blankets, more than enough to bury both of us. In a leather shop, another store I'd dragged her into to order new chaps. We found a heavy buffalo blanket that got added to our purchases.

After a nice lunch at a cafe to refuel halfway through the day, there was more shopping. I did manage to pause long enough to go into the bank and check my accounts. I'd wired the bank in Chicago and had them transfer everything but a thousand to this account. my new balance was a bit over sixty thousand. It wasn't enough in Denver to make me a top depositor but it did make me one they valued.

I got a draft for ten thousand to deposit in Cartersville. In part for our regular use. The deposit would also help the bank in Cartersville with some much need funds. The deposit would let the bank make loans to new families coming into town. Mary tried to tell me there wasn't ten thousand dollars' worth of things to buy in the whole town. That didn't change my mind, if it was my home this was one thing I could do to help it grow. It would also keep Carter from holding all the mortgages. I trusted the man but that didn't mean he needed that kind of power.

This would be our last night of freedom. Her parents would arrive tomorrow, several days ahead of what they told us. Finding that out had been the purpose of a telegram. The police chief in Chicago was someone I'd done a favor for a while back. His son had gotten in some trouble and ended up on a wanted poster. Instead of turning him over to be hung in Texas I'd put him on a train and sent him home. He was one of nine men I'd caught while they were rustling a few hundred head of cattle. Their leader was the only one I cared about. He'd been a dumb kid who'd fallen in with the wrong punchers after running away from home.

His father had no problem finding out when they planned to leave. He swore it didn't clear the debt for saving his sons life and he'd done it gladly. Sending his kid home hadn't really cost me anything. The kid was so knew there wasn't even a description of him on the dodger when I found him. That was part of what helped me believe his story about just getting caught up with the wrong crowd. Last I heard he was about to graduate from a blacksmith apprenticeship and was engaged to be married next year.

Reese had verified their arrival once he found the hotel they were staying at. It hadn't been hard to discover, it was the best one in Denver of course. Between the sheriffs and the marshals, they would be tailed no matter where they went in Denver. That was just one part of what the sheriff was doing for me. Another one was the deputy staying at the same hotel they were. I was paying the bill for the room beside them, his job was to listen and note what they did. They might not want anything other than reconciliation but I wasn't willing to risk Mary on that hope.

Stopping inside the gate to give Mary a kiss before sending her toward the house. It was time to fill Sarge in on what was really going on. I'd noticed the man's careful demeanor and tight security. He'd earned my respect and having him know what was going on would only help our security. There was something about him and Rodger that caught my attention, they were men used to danger. I couldn't put a finger on it but they had some connection and could help keep everything safe.

"Mind sparing me a bit of conversation Sarge?"

"Sir?" He met my eyes without hesitation.

"I want to make you aware of what's going on. It's not as simple as we've let on."

"Does it involve a threat to the lady?"

"It does."

"Let's include Rodger then, he's actually my old commander." He grinned expecting me to look surprised but didn't seem bothered when I wasn't. "The man's a genius at strategy and handles security within the house. He's also the one who hired me."

"As efficient as he runs the house that makes sense. I was wondering what it was about y'all."

We chatted for a few minutes until a younger man arrived to cover the gate while Sarge was gone. It made me wonder how he knew Sarge needed him. For that matter how had the stable hand seemed to know when I got back the other night. There was more to these men and this place then I thought. Rodger was much more subtle and organized than expected. What scared me about it was that I hadn't noticed until now.

"Sarge, how did he know to come down here?"

"Noticed quicker than most. Course most of the guests are rich folks who just expect things to go a certain way." He grinned at my question. "I can't answer though. If Cap wants ya to know, he'll tell ya."

"Fair enough." I noticed the man's speech had changed and took it as a good sign.

Rodger met us at the door with a smile, one that knew far more then he let on. He led us to a small parlor around the side of the house. It was attached to a small office and I guessed the other door was to his bedroom. These were Rodger's quarters, that was my best guess anyway. Once we were all seated Rodger spoke first.

"Decided to clue us in sir?"

"Figured it was about time. Most of it isn't anything you'll need to worry about. I don't expect either of you to get involved outside these walls." I said trying to assure them I wasn't asking for anything above their normal duties.

"Too late." Sarge smiled easily as he spoke. "We already decided to get involved."

"That was your men following us?" I asked curiously. I'd assumed they were sheriffs but kept track of them while we shopped.

"You noticed them?" Rodger sounded surprised.

"Three of them." I admitted and Sarge just laughed.

"You did catch them all." Rodger grinned, admitting the truth. "Sarge bet me you would. He seems to think you have some pretty sharp instincts."

"Live long enough on the frontier an ya start feeling people's eyes on your back." I smiled not at all insulted by Rodger's words.

"Tell me what's going on then. More to the point how can we help." The man who sat back to listen wasn't Rodger the butler anymore. This man was the Captain, his mind already analyzing the situation.

"First thing I need is for you to pull the tails. They might give away the plan." I grinned leaning back myself. I liked the man sitting across from me, more importantly I trusted him.

Both men's respect rose as I laid out the plan, they complimented me on getting it all done so quickly. Smiles spread across their faces the more I explained. These were military men who admired someone who not only faced a problem but did it with planning and forethought. Both men pointed out things I hadn't thought of and helped cover those gaps. After an hour we had hammered out what we hoped were any weak points. They both agreed to help without question. I'd worried that it would get them in trouble with Gus but that made both of them smile.

"That clever old German knew something was up when you telegraphed him." Rodger chuckled as he spoke. "Told me to help you in any way we could. Said he'd cover any legal problems that might come up."

"Shouldn't be any legal issues, both the Sheriff and the US Marshal are in on all of it."

"Don't matter, things were getting boring around here anyway." Sarge interjected with a smile. "Got to have some fun every once in a while."

"How did you two come to work for Gus?" I had to ask, because my curiosity was killing me.

"No mystery there. He pulled me out of the gutter, gave me a job and a purpose. I dragged that reprobate out with me." Rodger made me smile the way he said it. His words were full of respect and loyalty. "It was after the war, when I got released from Elmira I'd crawled into a bottle. Trying to blur the memories of that place and what I'd lost in the war. My side lost that little disagreement, everything I had was destroyed in the process."

"Same." Sarge added and I could feel the heaviness they both felt, but it didn't stop Rodger from continuing.

"Both our families were dead an we were working on joining them. Mr. Swift saw something in me and refused to let me die in the gutter. He paid to have me trained as a butler but always used me for more than that. I served him when he was building his business, sometimes as a butler but most often as security or gathering information for him. Sarge was there for protection when Mr. Swift needed it."

"He's a good man." Was all I said before Sarge picked up the story.

"He had us working in Chicago but the cracks in our table manners were showing a bit. When he bought this place he asked us to staff it."

"We jumped at the chance to get some distance between us and the cultured crowd of Chicago. Not to mention the memories that folks kept bringing up, wealthy people think the war was just an inconvenience." Rodger had picked the story back up now. "Most of the staff we hired are either veterans, their widows or orphans. Every one of them hired and trained by us."

"This whole place really is a fort?" I laughed.

"That and more." Sarge said with a grin but Rodger pointed out the truth.

"It is but it's also a second chance for a lot of folks. Eight of our people have left to go to school or bought their own place. We just helped them get on their feet. There's a fund we created to help pay for an education, if any of the younger folks want it. People can also borrow from it to buy land for businesses, farming or ranching. Our information gathering network has spread every time we help someone. There's so many veterans that fell on hard times after the war it's been pretty easy to do."

I sat back in my chair stunned, just staring at the two of them. These men had started their own charity here and were doing it without anyone knowing. Right alongside that they had built a network to gather information. I had to wonder how far it reached. The idea of it amazed me, not only its originality but also it was done to help others without serving some other purpose. Not only had the managed to help people get back on their feet but they'd turned it into a valuable network giving them a purpose.

"If either of you know someone looking to start over, send'em my way. I'm based out of a town south of here called Cartersville. Things have changed down there an the towns starting to grow. Plenty of farm and ranch land coming on the market, a few businesses too. It's in a good community, already got a school teacher." I laughed at the last bit, Mary had been happy to discover I didn't expect her to quit.

"We might have a few thinking bout it." Sarge admitted.

"Tell 'em to ask for me. I can get them pointed to the right people."

"You're a good man Chance."

Coming from someone like Rodger that was high praise. When I left to have dinner with Mary I had more allies and more of the gaps were covered. They wouldn't tell me how many people they had but assured me it was enough. The longer they stayed here the more the numbers grew. Getting past the old hates and helping all veterans, welcoming any who needed it. I was determined to find a way to help to their cause.

That night with Mary's sweating naked form pressed against me I ran through it all again. The act was more of a challenge then usual because I kept getting distracted every time she moved against me. There was no way I could ignore the feeling of her body against mine, the woman was everything to me. Eventually sleep came for me but even my dreams were filled with scenes of what might happen in the next few days. I trusted the men around me, knew they would do whatever they could but still I feared for her safety.

CHAPTER 40

We stayed at the house the next morning, waiting for news from the train station. Reese had a deputy on board by pure luck. He'd been escorting a prisoner and happen to still be in Chicago when Reese contacted him. He'd report to Reese immediately after the train arrived, letting him know who traveled with the family. He'd hang out just long enough to see who, if anyone, met them at the station before reporting.

I paced the house like a caged panther most of the morning until Mary finally got me to look at the library again. I found a book on constitutional law and started reading it. There was always something that fascinated me about our legal system. It was also out of self-preservation. The country was changing rapidly and someday the law of the gun would disappear. Law would become men in suits, sitting in courtrooms across the country. To protect myself and my family I would have to understand those men and the mysterious language they spoke.

It caught me by surprise when Rodger came in and announced that Marshal Reese had arrived. I'd gotten lost in reading the opinions on Minor v Happersett. The various legal arguments that ruled women did not have the right to vote were fascinating. I had a sneaking suspicion the Suffrage ladies wouldn't let it go that easily. It wouldn't be long before they too would have their voices heard at the ballot box.

"Not the best but not the worst." Reese announced walking into the library. "Nice little place you managed to find here."

"It's barely livable." I shot back grinning. "What did he see on the train?"

"Well," he hesitated looking at Rodger in the doorway, "might be best in private."

"Marshal Reese this is Captain Nathanael Rodger, he and his organization are pitching in on our side for this skirmish."

"A pleasure Marshal." Rodger stepped forward to shake Reese's hand.

"So, you're the one." Reese grinned.

"One what sir?" The grin on Rodger's face said he already knew what he was talking about but wasn't going to admit it.

"The one who's managed to help clean the drunks out of Dan's jail. Just Reese please, at least outside of court."

"Guilty as charged, we do try and help our fallen brothers and their families." Rodger bowed slightly at the compliment.

"Doing a damn fine job of it from what I've seen. Dan would like to shake your hand if you're ever of a mind. We've both admired the way you've handled things." Reese openly admired the man for what he was doing and I had a feeling the sheriff did to.

"Possibly later, but today's business must take precedent." Rodger smoothly got the conversation back on track.

"Right. The family traveled in a private car so we couldn't get much that way. There was a total of five Pinkertons on the train, two are normal for the trip. The other three disembarked here. Luckily they stuck together and are staying at the same hotel you're booked into." He chuckled at the predictability. "They looked none too happy to see you had already registered. Two requested the room next to yours and the third took the room at the stairs. That one went straight to her parents when they found out you were here already."

"They might just be there to gather information." Rodger

offered but Reese shot him down quickly.

"Not these three, well for certain two of them. I took a peak when they left the station and recognized them. Dealt with them a while back, they were fetching someone's son back to Chicago. Kid was underage so I couldn't get involved but one of them talked enough. That's all they do, usually retrieving some rich man's wife or some such. They aren't the nice type, you're going with them and no one is stopping them."

"What's your take on them?" I asked.

"They'll take her if they can, do their best not to kill you but will if they have to." He paused when there was a knock at the door. Rodger stepped out to answer it, there was a hushed conversation then the door closed. Rodger came back into the room with a thoughtful look on his face.

"Bad news?" I asked when he didn't speak.

"Interesting and important I think. When did they say they were going home?"

"A week from the original date." Mary spoke for the first time. "They wanted us to spend the week with them so they could get to know Chance."

"According to a friend at the rail yard their car is scheduled to leave with the morning train tomorrow." Rodger didn't look happy but he didn't look worried either. "They gave the excuse of business but it times with the report from the agent."

"We'd planned to meet them at their hotel for dinner and surprise them."

There wasn't a hint of worry in Mary's voice as she spoke. It made me smile because it demonstrated how much faith she had in us. Reese got a wicked grin on his face, happy this was going to happen fast. He studied Mary and his grin got bigger, without any warning he started laughing. The big man doubled over gasping for air in between laughs. I didn't know what was so funny but had a feeling it was going to be good.

When he finally stopped laughing he spoke to Rodger.

"Do you know Becca Thatcher?" Rodger's eyes went wide and he studied Mary for a second. He started laughing softly and his grin spread.

"Someone want to fill us in?" I asked for both Mary and me.

"Becca is a soiled dove, been working here for five years and wants nothing more than to leave." Reese chuckled as he continued. "She shares enough in appearance that they might not spot it in a dark room."

"She'd take the chance in a heartbeat." Rodger agreed.

"Okay I can see how it might work but why is it so funny?" That was the part I didn't understand.

"Ever run across any hide-peelers?" Reese asked.

"Never met a more foul bunch of men." I admitted.

"Becca was born to a particularly nasty group of hiders. She became a whore to avoid marrying her brother. Bathes and keeps her appearance up but still has the manners of a hide-peeler. Honestly she might have enough mouth to put even them to shame." Rodger filled in the blanks for me.

"You mean..." I couldn't finish speaking through my laughter.

"Would one of you men explain this please?" Mary snapped, her sharp tongue making its first appearance.

"Sorry Miss." Rodger's was the first to be capable of speech. "Railroad policy is tickets cannot be downsized by anyone but the ticket holder. Once they pay for her passage on the private car, they can't remove her legally. What truly makes this perfect is Miss Thatcher knows about that particular policy."

"They won't be able to name who the passenger is or they could be arrested for kidnapping. That means it'll be a general description which should fit her perfectly." Reese picked up the idea. "Ma'am think about your family stuck in their private car..."

Mary's laughter cut him off, the realization finally hitting her. Her parents trapped inside their private car with a foul-mouthed soiled dove was just too much. She fell back into the chair, tears streaming down her face. We all broke down into laughter again, the picture each of us created in our heads left us no choice. It took a few minutes to get the laughter under control again. Finally though we got back on track, discussing the plan. We had a lot to do before dinner if this was going to work. Rodger immediately sent a runner to find Becca and ask her to come to the house. He and his team here would handle that part.

I gave him a hundred dollars to give the girl. I wouldn't just have her dumped in a big city with nothing. Mary gave up one of her dresses, then added two more in a valise with all the trimmings. Another friend of Rodger's would carry it on the train and give them to her in Chicago. It wasn't much but maybe it would be enough for her to have a chance at a new life.

The plan was simple really, when we left to meet her parents they would smuggle her into our room at the hotel. Later after dinner we would return to the hotel. There would be a loud disagreement in our room and I would storm out and leaving alone. That should be enough to tempt them into acting. Especially if one tailed me to a bawdy house. Reese and Rodger both assured me Becca could fake sounding like a lady long enough to pull it off, at least until the Pinkertons drugged her.

I worried about that and Reese had to assure me the men knew what they were doing. This team did this full time as far as he knew and wouldn't ever risk hurting a target. The Pinkertons are not a forgiving company and I had to trust that these men knew their job. The rest of the details I left up to Rodger, he knew the players and understood the board far better than I did. After insisting on any more involvement from me would just put the plan at risk he gave up and took charge. Mary and I did the smart thing and left to room. We had a dinner to prepare for.

That was the first part of our plan, surpassing them at their own game. They hadn't expected to see us for a few days yet. Obviously they knew we were in town, but without giving themselves away they couldn't contact us directly. Our plan was to 'accidentally' run into them at their hotel dining room. We'd use the excuse of celebrating our wedding to explain why we were at such an expensive restaurant. That would start the game of cat and mouse, I could only hope my mousetrap was better.

An hour later freshly bathed and dressed I met my stunning bride at the bottom of the stairs. Floating down them she smiled at me, knowing that I only had eyes for her. Captivated by the light dancing in her eyes I was speechless. When our eyes met, just like that first time, my awareness sank into those pools of welcoming green. I still couldn't believe this woman was my wife, that this beauty had picked me as hers. Standing before me she did a quick spin, grinning wickedly at me.

"Satisfactory my husband?" I could see the slight upturn of her lips. She knew exactly how much she could effect me.

"Perfection my good wife. Ready to play the demure lady you hide under that sharp tongue?"

"Whatever do you mean?" I was impressed at how innocent she looked.

"Come on Trouble, if we keep at this we'll both need to start over again." I laughed offering her my arm.

"Lustful man, for shame." She shot back taking my arm.

"It wasn't me who prolonged our bath wench."

"You didn't complain." She was right I hadn't put up much resistance.

"What chance did I stand against your feminine wiles? What with me being just a lowly man I could never escape your wicked grasp."

"None! Exactly as it should be." She smirked while taking the offered hand.

We were using one of the carriages from the house because it was enclosed. It wasn't uncommon for out of towners to rent carriages if the owners were away. It was even more common for it to happen without the owner's permission. We would swing by the hotel where we were supposedly staying. A couple of Rodger's friends dressed similarly to us would get in.

They would stay in the carriage while we ate, enjoying a diner prepared by the chef for them. Then when we leave they'd take our place going back into the room at the hotel. Becca would get in the room while the Pinkertons were following us. The woman would slip into the room we had prepared on the same floor and the man would be storming out.

All the humor stopped as we passed through the gate. It was time to be serious, everything is in place but we had to play our parts perfectly. The loving newlyweds trying to balance happiness and a lack of money. Me the poor deputy marshal and her the wealthy daughter trying to raise me up from the muck. All while hiding the fake problems we had as a couple. It would be an interesting test of our acting abilities, and those of people we barely knew.

We rode in silence toward the hotel, both of us nervous. After we picked up our doubles we started chatting, in case anyone could hear us we added some tension. She repeatedly checked to see if I had enough money. I snapped back about money not being the concern of a woman. It was all made harder because we couldn't laugh at how ridiculous it all sounded.

When I checked my Colts for the third time in ten minutes

Mary put her hand on mine. I hadn't realized how wound up I was until that moment. She was trying to calm me down, reminding me that everything was in place. All this was done with the simple touch of her hand on mine. It was like a cooling breeze on a hot summer day. My mind slowed and my breathing leveled out by the time we stopped.

Someone from the hotel opened the door, offering their hand to assist Mary out of the carriage. He was another friend of Rodgers, there to ensure no one looked in the carriage. I followed her out pasting a fake smile on my face. The fact that it looked forced would just help sell the story. Offering her my arm stiffly we walked up the stairs to the front door. I felt her tense up when we entered the lobby. Her eyes locked on three people standing ahead of us. The games began there, just as we'd planned.

CHAPTER 41

"Mary?!" The man spoke first, sounding surprised.

"Father? Mother? You arrived early?" Mary played her part perfectly, sounding completely caught off guard.

"Well yes, I had some business to deal with. It made sense to come early to get it taken care off before you arrived." He sounded off, this man wasn't an adept liar. We already knew it was a lie, her family was tottering on the edge of bankruptcy.

"Mary, you're looking well." Her mother cut in before her fathers poorly said lie was noticed. This woman was the controlling factor and it was obvious.

"Mother." Mary curtsied to them before continuing. "Allow me to introduce my husband, Chance McElroy. Chance this is my mother and father, Mr. and Mrs. Palmer."

"Sir," I stepped forward and offered my hand then bowed slightly to her mother. "Ma'am."

"Please your family, call me Jennifer. My Husband's name is Marcus." Her mother still held hints of her youth and resembled her daughter but lacked her presence. I doubted she'd ever had that indefinable thing that made someone beautiful.

Her father looked exactly like I expected. His back was ramrod straight, salt and pepper chops trailed down from a full head of hair. His thin lips were shaped into a smile but it didn't reach his eyes. This man had already painted me as the villain in his story. I had no clue what the two men I'd cut loose reported but knew what this man thought. Moreover, he wasn't nearly as deft at hiding his feelings as his wife was. She was the truly dangerous one of the two.

"Thank you both, please call me Chance."

"I am told this is best food in the entire state." Jennifer took her husband's arm. "Did you plan on dining here this evening?"

"Yes we had heard the same and I convinced Chance that it would be a proper place to celebrate our honeymoon." Mary sounded perfect. Exactly like the cultured woman leading her uneducated husband around by the nose.

"No matter how much it costs." I grumbled just quietly enough to be heard but not like I meant for it to be. It had the desired effect, her mother's lips twitched giving away her satisfaction.

No one introduced the third man, that told me what I needed to know. Mary had said he would likely be there. He was her father's private security and assistant. His name was Drake and he'd been by her father's side as long as Mary could remember. I didn't spend much time on him but spotted the shoulder holster and knife. He wasn't dangerous like a man out here was, this man operated in the shadows. He was a knife in the dark, cold and uninterested in anything but his job. I felt his eyes on me, like a cat studying a rat before it pounced.

"If you'd like to join us then please do." Mary spoke before anyone from the restaurant could ask.

"We wouldn't want to intrude?" Her mother's politeness was an act, she fully intended to join us.

"Of course you're welcome." Mary answered, timing it perfectly to cut off my response. I took the opportunity and scowled adding to our performance.

After a quick conversation with the maître d', we were seated at a table and coffee was served. Our performance was added to when he said that her parent's reservation was enough for our party. Mary glared at me muttering about warning me we needed a reservation and me not listening to her. The waiter appeared with the silver pot and offered it around the table. I motioned toward my cup knowing it would be the watered-down coffee most fancy places served.

"I'll have tea please, Mary will also." Her mother ordered without asking and I felt Mary tense.

"I'd like a scotch please." Her father said. "Join me Chance?"

"Thank you no sir, coffee suits me for now."

"Not a drinker?" He asked like I had somehow offended him by refusing.

"Heard a lot about this place, just want to taste the chow first." I grinned back doing my best impression of an ignorant puncher.

"Ahhh yes it should be fine fare for this area of the world. Nothing like what we have in Chicago of course but it is the frontier." Her mother tried to cover her husband's frustration with mindless speech. "You must be struggling to eat since Mary was never much in the kitchen. Not her fault of course, just a product of living in a wealthy household."

"She's been trying to ma'am, sorry Jennifer." I'd play along, but damn these people were mean. I think Drake even flinched at that one but he never looked away from me.

"If she was provided for properly she wouldn't need to be scullery maid just to serve a man." Her father wasn't playing nice. That meant I could match him barb for barb though.

"Perhaps if she had been taught the skills one needs to survive without being dependent on others it wouldn't be a problem." I locked eyes with the man and saw the hatred flash across his face. Drake's eyes hardened too, the man didn't like the fact that I wouldn't just take the insult.

"Chance, do not embarrass me." Mary snapped, using her

tongue much like she did when we first met.

"Don't worry dear wife I'll keep my poor common upbringing hidden." I snarled.

"Now this has taken a more serious tone then intended. Please let's just have a good meal. We need to get to know one another." Her mother pulled everyone back in, trying to smooth the rough edges. She smiled at me but it was the cold smile of a rattler. "Tell us about your family Chance."

"My folks passed away a few years back, sod busters in Oregon. The family farm wasn't worth the dirty it sat on so I started drifting." We had already talked about my back story. It should be poor and without connections. "Met my boss a few months ago. I have a fair hand with a gun so he hired me as a deputy. Pays better than punching, lot less work too."

"Well, that's a …" Her mother struggled to find the words. She had no idea what to say about my life story. She finally landed on an answer and went with it. "Interesting."

Her father, who already thought I was a low-down dog, looked even further down his nose at me. The man who married his daughter was not only an uncultured fool, he was also lazy. Dangerous maybe, he could admit that much other then that he saw little use for the me and it showed on his face. He was far too easy to read. The thought of getting him at a poker table was tempting, I'd pick his pockets all night.

"As requested the chef has created a menu for you this evening. He had no problem adding the two additional guests." We were all saved from further conversation by the waiter. "It will begin with an appetizer of Rocky Mountain oysters. Followed by table served prime rib with butter cooked potatoes, fresh spinach sautéed with olive oil and garlic. Dessert will be a delicate soufflé served with cream."

The look on her parent's faces was priceless. They had expected something more than prime rib obviously. What they didn't know was that this was more of Rodger's handy work. If convincing them that the best meal here would be less than expected, so much the better. Mary was playing her part perfectly and I tried to match her performance.

"That sounds amazing." I said it with real enthusiasm. It wasn't hard since I really did like prime rib.

That last comment of mine seemed to cement the evening. All other conversations were small talk, no one spoke about anything of substance. I had no idea you could fill so much time with talk of uncomfortable travel and the weather. The one real constant was Drake's glare, I had the distinct impression he wanted me dead.

Drinks were offered after dessert and this time I joined her father but turned down the scotch and ordered whiskey. Partially to help digest the heavy meal but mostly to start my performance as a drunk. In the time he had one I had two and that prompted Mary's next performance.

"Dear please be careful." She had the worn-out tone of any woman married to a drinker had.

"Don't forget your place." I snapped. That was all the motivation her mother needed to wrap up the evening. She had bought our act completely.

"It's been a long day of travel, I'm afraid we must retire." She smiled standing from the table. Not wanting to be part of a scene, even in this backwater. She was ready to put some distance between them and us. She was also convinced that Mary wouldn't fight them any further.

"Of course mother. Maybe I could join you for breakfast tomorrow? We can see the city together." Mary's voice shook when she spoke, glaring at me when I changed her plans.

"Lunch, I plan on sleeping in tomorrow." I growled slurring the last word. I wasn't even feeling the whiskey but it helped the story along.

"Yes dear." Mary's voice dripped with venom.

"You're welcome to join us for breakfast." Her father spoke up but I couldn't let that go.

"No sir, she'll be in bed attending to her wifely duties." That was the final nail.

Her mother and father spluttered for a minute then spun and stalked up the stairs. Drake glared daggers at me before following his master up the stairs. I could hear Mary struggling not to laugh but she was disguising it as angry curses. She took my arm leading me out the door toward our waiting carriage. I moved with her, swaying slightly on my feet. I was doing my best not to laugh at how well that had ended.

We managed to keep it together inside the carriage. Halfway to the hotel the carriage passed by a streetlight that was snuffed out by another of Rodgers associates. In the deeper shadow we ducked to the floor and the other two sat in the seats. They exited at the hotel going up the stairs arguing quietly. The carriage turned around to return to the Swift estate. We stayed on the floor until the driver banged on the roof twice. That meant the people following it had bought our act, staying at the hotel.

Now there wasn't anything we could do but wait. From here on it was up to others. Our involvement could only cause problems if we showed ourselves. Neither of us slept that night, I did my best to read and not pace. Mary switched between laying on the couch in a very interesting pose that kept my attention and trying to relax. Watching her made my brain come to a stuttering stop more than once when I looked over at her. Aside from distracting me in the best of ways she was reading the same book I had on steam engines.

CHAPTER 42

There were snacks and plenty of coffee set out for us thankfully. We both dozed off somewhere in the night, it was the sound of the kitchen staff starting the day that woke us. We were both groggy from lack of sleep but a bath helped clear some of the fog. We ate breakfast in the kitchen with the staff, after finally convincing them we didn't like the formal dining room. Both of us enjoyed the chatter of the three maids and two cooks much more than the echoing silence of the dining room.

Reese arrived halfway through my second cup of coffee. His man had reported Mary's parents checking out and boarding the train. He verified that they planned on kidnapping Mary and taking her back to Chicago. Evidently after dinner they were both so mad at my behavior they didn't keep their voices down. He heard the entire plan through the walls. They firmly believed their status could easily protect them from any retribution I might seek. What was truly funny is they were sure I wouldn't object.

"It's funny they think money could stop a bullet." Reese laughed.

"Rich people think money can fix everything." Mary admitted. The next arrival was the sheriff carrying an envelope. He also wore an amused smile. His man had been at the hotel where we supposedly stayed.

"The Pinks left this in the room when they took Becca." It had my name on the front in neat script. Inside was a letter folded neatly around a bank draft for two thousand dollars, drawn on a Chicago bank.

Dear sir,

We have taken our daughter back to the life she belongs in. Please take this and do not try to contact her or our family in the future. Your marriage will be annulled at our earliest convenience.

We wish you no harm but please know that should you arrive in Chicago we will do all we can to ensure you never leave. We are safe in saying that should you manage to leave you'll certainly not take our daughter with you.

Sincerely,

The Palmers.

I started laughing before passing the letter to Mary. She looked truly offended that they only thought she was worth two thousand dollars. I calmed her down by pointing out that it wasn't what they valued her it, it was what they thought I could be bought for. It seemed to help for a minute, then she got mad because they thought so little of me. We were still debating that when Rodger came in. The last piece fell into place with his arrival.

"They have left the station, the Pinkertons delivered the bound package to the private car. I doubt with the hood they had over her head anyone noticed it wasn't Mary before they left." With a chuckle he changed it slightly. "Well, the Pinkertons are on the train. Being of common stock they aren't welcome in the private car of course."

"Oh, I would pay anything to know how that goes when they let Becca loose." Dans deep laughter rolled out.

"We'll get that story in a day or so, their porter is one of our friends." Rodger grinned.

"Can't wait for that report." Reese admitted smiling at the thought.

"Say two days for lunch gentlemen, we'll all hear the story then?" I said standing up from where I sat. "For now, between the sleepless night and stress I am exhausted. Today we're just going to relax."

It was enough to break up the party, everyone was exhausted from the long night. The rest of the day was spent relaxing, eating and napping now that the pressure was off. It lasted until the next morning when Sarge came into the room gasping for breath. Rodger stood immediately and helped the man sit down to catch his breath.

"Drake...got off...the train. Sent to ...kill you." Sarge eventually managed.

"Kinda thought they might try that." I said noncommittally. Everyone looked at me in surprise.

"You didn't mention that." Mary had that tone in her voice. The one that informed me I should choose my next words very carefully.

"I wasn't sure, it was the way he looked at me. That man wanted to kill me that night. I didn't know if your father would let him off the leash."

"I'll accept that," She said but then added with a warning, "for now."

"Yes dear loving wife. He'll be coming on horseback, I'm going to meet him on the road." I had to cut off the protests before they got started. I had my reasons and they understood them once I explained them. "The man's a back shooter, he won't meet me straight on unless I force him. He's also not used to traveling by horseback, catching him tired and off guard is to my advantage. I'd rather catch him on tired from the road where he can't avoid me then let him stalk me at his leisure. It also has less risk of innocent folks getting caught in the crossfire."

"I may not like it but you're right." Mary admitted after a few minutes of silence. "The man has done things for my father over the years. I don't know how many he's killed but I don't doubt he has."

"Y'all have taken most of this fight in your shoulders for us. I appreciate everything but this part has to be mine. I don't trust the man to not kill her if that meant he could get to me. There's something dead in him. I've seen it before in men, you know the ones I mean."

All the men around me did. They'd all met folks like that in some way. Either on a battlefield or ones they arrested or killed. It was like some connection inside them was broken and all their humanity was drained away. It only left something cold and dead that only existed to kill or harm others. Most of the time that meant killing or torturing people, it gave them whatever feeling they needed.

"Then let us come with you." Sarge implored, but he already knew my answer.

"I need you and Rodger here. If you're here I don't have to worry about her. Dan can't, I'll be outside of his jurisdiction and he's already pushed it helping me with a private matter. Reese?"

"I know better, some snakes you have to stomp personally. If ya don't they can haunt ya." Reese acknowledged my reasoning. "Just remember you're wearing a badge."

"I'll remember, if I can charge him I will but unless he breaks a law." I let that hang in the air and Reese nodded his understanding.

"Likely the only law he'll break is drawing on you." He finally admitted. "That won't give you a choice an I ain't asking you to risk it."

"I gave ya my word. If he doesn't draw I won't force the man. He'll have every chance to walk away." I knew Reese wasn't really worried about me committing murder, he just wanted to remind me. "I'm keeping my badge Marshal."

That seemed to satisfy him and he nodded his understanding. Rodger whistled out the back door, sending a boy to saddle my horse. They all knew I wasn't going to wait, even as I turned to go. Upstairs I put on the same trail clothes I'd worn on the trip here. The staff had cleaned them but you couldn't wash out the comfort that came from well-worn clothes. Making sure my colts were loaded and ready to go, I carried my Stetson down the stairs to meet the worried look of my wife.

"Everyone's gone back to work my love." She smiled up at me when I stepped into her arms.

"I'll be back as soon as it settled." I promised

"I know you will, remember you're not allowed to get shot." She smiled up at me with those beautiful green eyes. I got lost in them for a moment, cherishing the love that surrounded me.

"Yes my beautiful wife. I hear and obey." Then I kissed her. It held all of the love we felt for one another. Each of us trying to express our feelings in that one physical act. When it finally broke her hand gently traced the scar across my face. Almost like she was memorizing it.

"I love you deputy."

"I love you to school marm."

She walked me out to the saddled horse, waiting patiently while I checked the cinch. She laughed when I checked my Winchester before stepping into the saddle. Our eyes met one more time than I turned slowly riding toward the gate.

It didn't take long to weave through the early morning traffic. Reaching the outskirts of Denver faster then planned. I stopped there just to breath in the open air for a few minutes. It was sharp, hints of the altitude and biting cold on the wind. The warmth of a horse under me while I looked across the land filled me with familiarity. Some part of me reached out, connecting with the land around me. A feeling of being home again resonated through me.

The road followed the tracks northeast as they moved through the mountains. It would easily be a few hours before he'd be in the area but I wanted to find the right location to met him. Not for an ambush but one that would force him to face me head on. I found it before lunch. Cliffs rose on either side of the road and it narrowed beside the tracks. Unless you went days out of your way you'd have to come this way. The sharp cliffs of this canyon wouldn't let him sneak around me.

Backtracking to the furthest edge of the cliffs I looked back at the road. There was at least three hundred yards where it all narrowed down. Half that was filled with railroad tracks making the area even smaller. It was the perfect spot to force a coward face you. Coward wasn't the right word and I knew it, the man wasn't from this world. His behavior in the big cities skulking in the shadows was a way of life. It wouldn't be fair to hold him to the standards of the west.

I set up a small camp there. Gathering enough wood for the fire meant having to backtrack a ways but I had time. After getting it started I put on some coffee after stripping the saddle. I pulled a stump back with me for a chair, and sat down with my cup. Now I just had to wait.

CHAPTER 43

Sitting beside the campfire gave me some time to think. Suddenly it hit me that less than a month ago I'd ridden out of Denver heading to Cartersville. So much of what I thought my life would be had changed in such a short period of time. I'd found a wife, owned a home and felt a sense of community with the people there. Things I'd never considered having in my life were now important to me. I had friends, people to care for and that was something I'd lost years back when the ranch got raided. That had been the closest thing to a family I had known since my folks died. As the afternoon passed I thought about who I was and what I really wanted now.

The work as a deputy would keep me away but it also would help keep me level. I couldn't fool myself, there was a part of me that still very much needed the tall and uncut. The freedom to wander across the land, seeing what was over the next mountain. Maybe a part of me would always be half wild, claimed by the land as her tax. Once that had been all there was, me and the open land.

Now there was a growing part of me that loved the life I was building in Cartersville. I was looking forward to getting back to my small town and the friendships that were growing there. This was all uncharted territory to me, an adventure I'd never expected to have. There were no regrets, nothing held back but that didn't mean my drive to be out in the wild would go away, not yet anyway.

The soft clop of horse hooves broke my reverie. Lookin

through my field glasses I saw him. Slowly riding in to the canyon on a small paint. The poor horse looked as miserable as he did. The man looked about as uncomfortable as one could on horseback. Every motion of his body contradicted the horses. It almost looked like he was fighting the horse for every step it took. This wasn't a man used to long hours in the saddle, probably no more than a jaunt in the city park. Part of me smiled at the grimace on his face. I didn't usually revel in someone's misery but in this case I made an exception.

"Looks like that's a new experience for ya." I'd let him get well within rifle range before I spoke. He froze in the saddle staring toward my voice.

"Deputy, that you." His voice sounded dry. It made me wonder if he had brought any water with him.

"Got it in one Drake."

"That was one hell of a trick you pulled. Don't know where you found that hellcat but nicely done. Have to give you credit for that, don't think I've ever seen the Palmers at such a loss. Especially not when they found out they couldn't kick her off the train, or even out of their car."

"That why he sent ya to kill me?"

"Mostly, course I wanted to kill ya last night." He smirked painfully at me. "Pretty sure you knew that though."

"Noticed that, you should work on that stare it's a bit obvious."

"Don't suppose you'd do this with a knife?"

"Don't think that's going to work out any better for ya." I laughed thinking about how many Apache's I'd killed with a blade.

"Now that I think about that scar you might be right. That's a might though. I couldn't match you with a pistol, there is no might there."

"If ya want the truth you're probably gonna die no matter how we do this. Want to know why?"

"Sure, give it a shot."

"You want to kill me just so you feel something for a second. I want to live for reasons you'll never be able to understand. There's no part of me that wants to kill you, I'd prefer never seeing you again. Just get back to my life and be happy, but that's not an option for you."

Silence met me and I knew I'd hit the mark. The man's life was one long blank spot with brief moments of feeling. Those feelings were hollow and short lived but it was all the man had. That brief moment of pleasure he felt from killing never lasted long enough to fill the void. Most of his life was just one day after another of nothing, that was all he'd ever known.

The one exception had been working for Mr. Palmer. He had felt something when the man gave him a job. That was the only thing that could have created the loyalty he had to the man. It was unshakable because of that feeling. You couldn't buy him off or beg out of it, nothing would change his course. He'd been sent on a mission and that was all he needed to know. Now the man he had been sent to kill had just thrown that truth in his face.

"How?" It was the only thing he didn't understand. The answer stripped away some of his power. More than he could have ever expected. How did he know?

"You're not unique, I've known others like you. Some wore a badge but it didn't change anything. That's who taught me about it, an old sheriff down in Texas. Spent his whole life on the side of good but had never once felt what that meant, not really."

"What happened to him?"

"He got tired and quit." Sam had got out of bed one morning and killed himself after a cup of coffee. No note or any other hint as to why, but I knew. Almost expected it after the last visit. He couldn't find a reason to keep walking around. That was it, no other reason.

I could see the understanding flicker in the man. His whole posture changed, his shoulders just lost their strength and he slumped in the saddle. The realization that if he wasn't killed by someone else someday he would kill himself. There would never be anger or hatred, never be love or joy. His entire future would be a hollow empty void.

"What choice do I have?" His words sounded as empty as the man felt.

"I don't have a clue." I felt for the man but really didn't have any idea how to help him. Or even if there was an answer, it seemed to me he'd been born this way. Maybe if it had happened in war or some other event it could have been fixed. Born that way? I doubted there was any answer to the question.

Just then a bullet whistled by my ear close enough to burn. My eyes whipped up expecting to see Drake at a full gallop charging me, rifle in hand. That wasn't what I saw, he looked just as surprised by the sound. His eyes locked on something down the trail behind me. Whatever it was made him jerk into action. The man kicked his heels into the paint and leaned low in the saddle.

The sound of a lever jacking another round in made me break out of my daze. Diving forward in a roll trying to get behind a small boulder for cover just as the booming crack of a rifle sounded again. The sharp impact of hot lead on the bottom of my boot spun me wildly off course. By luck it knocked me behind a larger rock just in time to watch the ground erupted where I had been kneeling. When I looked around what I saw had me stumped. How in the hell was Bennet shooting at me?

The bark of a rifle drew my attention back to Drake and my heart leapt into my throat. If I was caught in a crossfire between them I was a dead man. There was no way to avoid both. My hand worked on autopilot, levering a round into the chamber of my Winchester. Before I could draw a bead on Drake my brain stopped. He wasn't aiming at me. His eyes where focused on Bennet or the man with him. My brain finally noticing it was Levar. Somehow the two had gotten free, that was bad news for someone.

I drew a bead on Bennet and fired, with a curse I jacked another round in. His horse had just saved his life with that stumble. Drake's rifle barked behind me again and I watched Levars horse buckle. The front legs collapsed at a full gallop and sent both rider and mount into a roll that nether would survive. My eyes snapped back to Bennet and I lined up the crosshairs.

His rifle fired, flames obscuring him for a split second, just as my finger slowly tightened on the trigger. The stock bucked into my shoulder but I didn't notice. A second before the smoke filled my vision a bright red spot appeared on his chest. Then it was gone along with the man, hidden behind acrid gun smoke. I had to shift my attention because I felt more than heard Drake's horse coming close. It wasn't galloping anymore which I thought was odd, it had slowed to a walk.

When I turned to look the man was slumped in the saddle. One hand on his chest, the other hung limply at his side. Ten feet behind him his Winchester lay on the road. Slowly his weight shifted in the saddle, his body slid gracelessly to the ground. I picked the man who'd saved my life to check first. For whatever reason he'd sided with me and paid the price. It might have been that he didn't want to be denied the pleasure of killing me himself but I preferred to think it was something more.

"Drake." I said stepping to the right side of his horse and gathering up her reins. The poor paint was blowing hard trying to catch her breath. I led her over beside my brown gelding and let her walk a bit after loosing the chinch.

"That wasn't expected." He groaned when I rolled him to his back.

"Why?" It was all I could think to say. He was dying, nothing would change that but maybe sharing his story would be something at least.

"Wish I'd have known," his speech was interrupted when he coughed, blood flecked his smile when he spoke again, "before that helping gave me something."

Before I could respond the man took one more deep wheezing breath and died in my arms. Easing his head down to the ground with a soft smile on my face. In the end he'd found something new, for a man like him that was the best he could hope for. All I could do for him now was to make sure he was buried properly.

I left him where he lay and went to check on Bennet. Levar was probably dead. One look at the mangled mass of horse and man was all it took. From here it was hard to see which parts went where and I had now desire to take a closer look. Bennet on the other hand was still living, even now I could see him trying to move.

His shaking hand was slowly reaching for the Remington at his side. I didn't bother to rush, the way his hand shook there was no way he'd even get the thong off. I could take all day and doubted he'd get that gun out in time. Especially not with that broken wrist, he was so far gone he didn't notice the lack of control.

"Don't bother dead man." My boot pinned his arm to the ground making a weak scream escape his lips.

While his foggy mind tried to process what was going on I studied the man's situation. He was gut shot and it looked like his leg was twisted at a bad angle where it hung in the stirrups. I gathered his horse reins in my left hand and crouched beside him.

"Damn kid, just die already." He rasped through gritted teeth.

"How'd you get here Bennet?"

"Ain't telling you nothing." His eyes pinched in pain but the man's anger still burned in his eyes. He hated me, hated me more then he wanted to live.

"Bennet your gut shot, you got a busted leg hung in a stirrup. I can't imagine the pain of getting a Dutch ride in your situation. Ya might want to answer me if you don't want to find out." I'd never do it but he didn't need to know that.

"Can't do that deputy." He laughed but it mostly came out as foamy blood. "Gotta take me back an patch me up so's ya can hang me."

"You're forgetting who I am." My smile wasn't a pleasant one. He was right I wouldn't break my word to Reese but I needed him to think otherwise right now. "You dying being dragged behind a horse sounds 'bout like justice to me."

"Some fool kid at the jail messed up." He confessed with a look of fear at what I might do. "Left him in a cell, knocked him over the head. Don't think he's dead."

"Ya bought a reprieve for now." I rocked up to my feet and turned to untangle his leg.

Suddenly a bullet sped by me from the mess that had been Levar. I looked just in time to see his hand fall to the ground, his pistol spinning out of his grip. Then I was slammed in the chest by something heavy, it felt like I'd been hit with a cannon ball. The breath whooshed out of my lungs as I hit the ground rolling across the ground. Laying there face down in the dust it took a few tries to get my lungs working again. Then a few more to check for whatever bullet had hit me. Slowly rolling onto my back trying to figure out why I wasn't dead or even bleeding.

What I had thought was my heart pounding in my ears at first started to fade slowly. Maybe I was dying? That didn't feel right, dying shouldn't hurt this much. Finally the fog started to clear as my breath came back. It made me realize the sound wasn't my heart. The accompanying screams that filled my ears as the world came back into focus confirmed the guess.

That impact had been Bennet's horse taking off, scared by Levar's last shot. Thinking about it that wasn't right, the angle where he was laying meant that round had have grazed the horse. That sudden pain spooked the animal because it took off, ramming right through me. That's what had knocked me rolling and it made more sense then being shot.

Turning my head to look down the road I could just barely make out a flash of red across the horse's hindquarters. Staggering to my feet, I jumped shakily into Drakes empty saddle. After a mile Bennet's limp body finally bounced loose of the stirrup, the horse slowed not far from there. The lathered animal stood with its head hanging, exhausted and spent. It'd be hours before it would be half ready to travel and might never recover enough to ride again. The shock from the graze then fear from Bennet bouncing in the stirrup had made the poor animal run until it couldn't anymore.

Sighing I grabbed the lead of the panting animal. Taking the rope hanging from the saddle I walked back to tie one end around Bennet's ankles. Turning back toward my camp I led the other horse behind me with his body a good ways further back. My little camp had some graze and fresh water, they would help the horse recover somewhat. Hopefully it would come back enough to make it to Denver.

An hour later I was sipping another cup of coffee when I heard horses coming from Denver. Using Drakes horse and mine I'd managed to drag Levar's horse off the trail far enough that scavengers wouldn't cause problems for travelers. There was a shallow gorge a quarter back that I'd dumped it in. That was a bit closer then I liked but it was the best there was. The last thirty minutes had been spent trying to figure out how I was going to get them all back with only two horses.

None of the answers I'd come up with made me happy. Most of them involved me walking. With one boot heel shot off that wouldn't be any fun. I'd laid Levar and Bennet off to the side a ways from my little camp, Drakes body was a little closer. They were all rolled in their own bedrolls and the three horses left alive were picketed on some grass near the stream. When Reese and two deputies I didn't know rode up they studied the scene with confused looks before dismounting.

CHAPTER 44

"Coffee?" I offered from where I sat on my stump.

"Have a feeling this story's gonna need something more but it's what we got." Reese smiled as he walked over. He introduced the other two men with a wave. "Deputies Sackett and Cassidy."

"Pleasure, help yourselves." I motioned to the coffee pot before pointing at one of the saddlebags. "There's a decent bottle of who-hit-jon in the bag if ya want, even has a label on it."

"We'll stick to coffee." Reese's tone brook no debate. "Spill it Deputy."

"Strange thing to have the man sent to kill you save your life." That was how I started the story. It only took a few minutes to fill them in on what had happened. Reese took it all in without interrupting me.

"You're serious?" Cassidy laughed. "That's some luck you got. He ever needs a pard send me with him boss. Any man that lucky I'll ride with."

"I ain't told y'all about his first job, this ain't nothing." Reese laughed. "A just remember the man who saved him is laying over there before you go jumping up to partner with him."

"Now that just ain't fair Reese. It's not like I asked for his help." I protested. "I want Drake to be buried right, I'll pay for it if need be."

"I'll see to the burying. You need to get back to Cartersville."

Reese knew how to get it done and I trusted him. "Jake's a good man but he's still wounded."

After tossing the dregs out of my cup I stood. While I poured water on the last of the fire the others tied the corpses onto the two horses. Bennet's horse had recovered enough to carry Drake but it would be a slow ride back. There wasn't another choice unless one of us carried a body and no one had volunteered for that.

"Ya'll ride ahead we can bring these three in." Sackett's southern twang filled the air as we stepped into the saddles. "Hear ya got a lady threatening folks 'bout your safety."

"Sounds like her." I laughed. "I'm sure she'll appreciate y'all letting us ride ahead."

Reese set out at a trot that both our horses could keep for hours. We rode in silence to the outskirts of town where we slowed to a walk. I finally broke the stalemate and asked the question that had been bothering me.

"You believe me about what happened to Bennet?"

"Never once thought otherwise. If ya had wanted the man to die that way, you woulda told me." He stopped his horse and turned to face me when I pulled up beside him. "Chance I may have questioned your willingness to change the way you did things as a bounty hunter but you gave me your word. You can stop thinking I question that, if I had any doubts you'd have never been hired."

"I know you took a risk hiring me. Just want to make sure that doesn't come back on you."

"I don't feel that way. I hired a man who'd served justice his own way for years and discovered it didn't work anymore. I could see that in your eyes when we met. You were looking for a better answer, I just happened to have on handy."

"It was more than that." I wanted to explain, to tell him what he had really given me but couldn't find the words.

"I know it was, we aren't meant to be alone in this world." His smile said there was no further explanation needed. He understood, probably saw it and knew I was at a crossroads when he met me back then.

"Thanks." I needed to say it even if he didn't want to hear it.

"Come by and file a report before you leave." He said turning down Main Street toward the office. I turned the other way toward the Swift house. Shortly after that Sarge was stepping out to open the gate for me.

"Welcome back Deputy. Guessing everything worked out."

"In the oddest way Sarge." I smiled reaching down the shake the man's hand. "Thanks for everything."

"Been nice feeling like more than a gate opener for a bit." He laughed.

"If you're ever bored I know a sheriff who needs a deputy." I offered riding past the man with a wave. "He's working on his second chance too."

"Never know." His voice followed me up the road toward the house. As usual the stable boy rounded the corner as if notified of my arrival, the mystery still made me smile.

Mary was waiting at the door with Rodger. Her smile brightening the day with its radiance. She was in my arms before my feet had fully touched the ground, ignoring the blood stains. I filled myself with the scent of her in a deep breath, calm settling over me like a warm blanket on a cold night. This is what I wanted to come home to. Knowing she was there made the idea of having a home that much better.

"It's done then?" She asked peering up at me.

"It is."

I'd tell her the whole story soon but right now she just needed to know it was over. We stood there holding each other for what felt like hours but in truth it was only a few seconds.

Slowly we turned and I handed the reigns to the waiting stable boy. Meeting Rodger's gaze as I stepped forward to shake his hand.

"Words can't express how much I appreciate everything you and yours did."

"No need Chance, it's been fun using the network for something other than business."

"Still I can't thank you enough."

"You can by remembering us, help those like us when you can."

"You have our word on that." Mary said breaking into the conversation. "More than that you have our support. Should you ever need anything just ask."

"I'm sure there's food ready." He changed the subject switching smoothly back into his role as a butler. Leading us into the kitchen where plates were already set for us.

The next few days passed normally, hell for us they might be considered downright boring. We had lunch and heard to story of my parents arrival in Chicago. Becca had made an impression and the way we heard it my parents had run from the car. Fleeing the woman who stepped down with a bottle in one hand and a chicken leg in the other. The picture it painted in my mind was almost worth what we'd gone through.

The next day I filled out a report for Reese, detailing the events on the road. He recommended a blacksmith who checked out the horses and carriage before we left. Once it was given the all clear we prepared to leave. Packages were loaded the night before and there was a goodbye dinner the last night at the house.

We met more of Rodger's friends, Reese and his wife joined us. Sheriff Dittmer and his wife came with their two kids, both of whom enjoyed running around the large mansion. It was a good evening full of laughter and new friends. Again that feeling of belonging almost overwhelmed me. Not nearly as bad as it had when I first came to Denver, but I was beginning to feel crowded.

At first light we pulled the carriage out of the gate for the final time. We took the full five days going home, slowed by the added weight in the carriage. It didn't bother either of us, we enjoyed taking our time admiring the leaves changing colors in the early fall. The nights were cool but not cold and the days were pleasantly warm. We both sighed in relief when we turned into Cartersville. Waving at people as we drove down main street, finally turning down the short side street to our house. Mary grabbed my arm in surprise turning to face me.

"Dear husband what have you done?" She asked staring at the house.

"You mentioned wishing we had a porch my good wife."

I smiled at the brand-new wrap around porch that had been added to our house, it was perfect. One end had a chain swing bench seat but it was the two rocking chairs that held pride of place on the front. Along the side where it wrapped around there was a small table with four chairs. Angie was sitting at one as we pulled up sipping a cup of tea. For the first time in more years than I could remember the thought of being home held meaning again.

"Glad to be home my love?" Mary was beaming with happiness from beside me on the seat.

"I am." Was my simple answer but it meant so much more than I ever thought it would.

Epilogue

Over the next few years Cartersville underwent many changes. More people came in as word spread about the town with its available land. Farmers and small ranchers were followed by merchants each bringing their families with them. The discovery of a copper mine twenty miles south of town brought in miners and the other industries that supported them. All of it added to the wealth of the town which was reinvested in developing it. The mayor stuck to his plan and slowly his dream became a reality.

Jake managed the job of sheriff alone until the mine opened. By luck or fate Sarge showed up at just when he started looking for a deputy. He was the first, three more followed in short order as the population grew, all of them brought in by Sarge. None of them were gun hands and most of the time the only one not carrying a shotgun was Jake. He picked up the habit when on patrol but other than that he stuck to his pistols.

There was some violence from the miners at first but the town quickly got a reputation for handling troublemakers. The reputation was solidified when fifteen men rode into town to rob the bank. Thirteen died in the attempt the last two were hung after being arrested. It wasn't just the deputies who'd faced them, Rodger and Sarge had spread the word about the town. Some of the new residents where vets who didn't take kindly to the disturbance.

The new combined office of US marshal and sheriff was expanded to add more cells after the mine add a smelting facility. The mayor didn't hesitate to invest the money and it paid off. Miners knew the town and its laws were fair but unforgiving and learned to act accordingly. Fines for drunk in public paid for the additions inside of a year.

The next big project was a Town Hall. It was put in the center of town, according to the mayor's plan. Again, the money paid off when a year later the law came to stay. The circuit court assigned a judge to the county. Cartersville was assigned as the county seat for the judge and other organizations that came with it.

Mary and I we made our contributions. Our first child was born ten months after returning from Denver. Gertrude Bess filled my life with joy from the first night she came into my life. She was never that awkward child, as soon as she could walk she did it with grace. More than that she did it like the world should move around her because she wasn't giving an inch, just like her mother.

Her brother Thaddeus Reese joined us a year later and completed the family. He was every bit the spawn of his father, according to his mother that is. If asked I would have said he obviously took after her. The boy was hell on wheels from the moment he could walk. If he could walk why not run, if he could run why not sprint. Despite enthusiastic effort throughout our marriage no more children joined the ranks. It never stopped us from trying and in truth we were both happy with just two.

I worked as a deputy marshal for another five years. It kept me away, sometimes for weeks at a time. After one stint where I was gone for a month we both decided it was enough. I'd missed too much time with the children and that wasn't a price I was willing to pay anymore. To my surprise a month after I left the circuit court offered me the newly created county sheriffs' job. It created some confusion until Jake and the mayor correctly renamed his office to town marshal. That kept me doing what I loved but home more nights than not.

We sold the big house after I left the marshals service but only sold the house and an acre around it. We built a small horse ranch outside of town on the rest of the land. I say horse ranch but it wasn't really a working ranch. The small spread was only most of a section but it had good water. Most of it was wooded creating an ideal world for the kids to explore and hunt.

We did have horses and Mary's fascination with breeding helped us raise a herd that sold well. We only sold a few horses a year, most of them went to law men. We didn't raise them for a particular look, we raise them for use. If we bred a mare it was because of her confrimation, the stallions we had were for the same reason. Mary did it because she loved the animals. I did it because she wanted it and I discovered a love for breaking and training horses.

Rodger showed up the same year we moved and bought a small spread next to ours. He had married a widow with three kids about the same age as ours. The two families quickly became friends and there was never a fence between our homes. Rodger and Sarge kept up their network and constantly added new people to the town. They were always welcomed additions, hardworking good people. If I had to credit anyone for the town becoming something more, it would have been them as much as the mayor.

Kelso stayed in office for more than twenty years before he finally stepped down to retire. His son took over the store. He retired with his wife into the house we sold them. It surprised no one when his eldest son ran for and won the race for mayor. He continued his father's work on the town, steadily following his plan for it. Kelso lived long enough to see his dream come true, finally one day the pan was finished. A fully developed town sprawled across the once empty land. Mayor Kelso is listed as the founding fathers who designed the town. There's even a statue for him in the city park.

Bess and Percy ran the restaurant together until they both passed away. Bess went first and most of us believe Percy died three days later of a broken heart. They were buried side by side in our family plot at the ranch. Their tombstones declaring them as loving grandparents to Gertie and Thad. The children visited them regularly before and after they passed.

Our daughter Bess to no one's surprise married Mark, Rodger's adopted son, forever linking the two families. They have six kids, one per year for the first six years. Complications with the last child brought that to an end but they never missed a step. Taking in two orphans when their parents died from the fever.

As a wedding gift they were given the deed to her namesake's eatery. Bess had left it to her in my care until she was ready. I'd paid to have the small building taken down and built a larger hotel. When they took over it quickly became one of the premier hotels in town. Their dining room was the best in the county and the territorial governor was known to eat there when he could.

Thad attended college in Denver, becoming the family lawyer when he graduated. Ten years later he was appointed to the bench, eventually rising to the state Supreme Court. He married Constance who he met at law school and raised five children. He had stayed at the Swift house during school, eventually buying the property after graduation. He wouldn't let me pay for it but did allow me to finance the purchase.

Independent from the day he was born.

Reese worked as a US Marshal until he was killed. He cornered five bank robbers, killed two but the other three shot him to rags and left his body for the scavengers. By luck a passing drummer found his body and brought it to the office in Denver. He was buried with honors in there. It took me four months to find the last three and bring them in. They were the only hangings I ever attended.

We never reconciled with her parents and they died alone in Chicago without ever knowing their grandchildren. Gus told me years later when we had dinner in Denver that he had met them at the station the day they returned. He introduced himself and then politely informed them that any further action against us would have dire consequences. To quote him 'They turned whiter than my shirt, muttered some apology and faded from sight like unwanted apparitions.'

Mary passed in her 63rd year sleeping peacefully the night after a family gathering. Her last day on earth was surrounded by the entire family, including two great grandchildren. Somehow we both knew it was coming that night. When I kissed her goodbye and promised to see her soon she told there was no rush, she'd be waiting.

Now a week later I can see her emerald eyes calling me to join her. I'd known my end was coming long before she passed. The doctor called it cancer but the name hadn't mattered. What had was her not knowing anything was wrong. It was about the only secret I managed to keep from her. She had gone without ever knowing I was sick.

The day after her funeral I told Gertie and Thad, they've been by my side ever since. When Chance, Thad's oldest boy, came to say goodnight I knew she was there. When he left the faint smell of lavender and roses filled the room. She had come to welcome me home just like always.

The End

An introduction to Book Three in the Stone Cold series..

Catching up.

That first drive was a rough lesson. I'd expected it to be hard, but I had no idea how grueling it would be. You can't truly understand what it takes to drive half-wild longhorns two thousand miles until you do it. The older hands had warned me. Hell, Max even took the time to talk to everyone who hadn't previously made the drive before we left. He'd been honest and had reminded us how many drovers never saw the end of the trail. The only thing he could promise anyone was a decent burial, and even that came with caveats.

I'd done my learning fast. There was no room for anyone who couldn't pull their weight on the drive. Max was a better boss than most, and even he kept the number of hands to the barest minimum. Every hand on the trail cut into the profits. More than one drive never made it to the railhead because too many punchers died along the way. That first year left its mark on me.

During a midnight stampede, a panic-stricken steer had left a jagged scar on my thigh to remember him by. Two drovers died in that night of madness, all because one steer got spooked by God knows what. It was like a tide of horns rampaging out of the darkness, crushing everything in its path. You only had two choices if you wanted to live. You could out run them or get out of the way, and neither was easy in the dark of night. Turning them hadn't even been a possibility until they tired themselves out.

Another puncher died from a rattlesnake bite during that first drive. The damn thing was curled up so it was invisible underneath his saddle. He'd bent down to pick it up after chow and forgot to kick it first. The viper managed to sink both fangs into his cheek before he could jump clear. Knowing how it would end, he put a .44 caliber bullet through his head before the pain kicked in.

The brutal heat washed over us from dark to dark, there was no escape. If trailing a herd across Texas was a taste of hell, I needed to change my ways. The sun mercilessly scorched a man from above, and the body heat rising from his horse took care of the rest. Riding nighthawk was no better. The heat from two thousand head turned the cool breeze that swept across the open land into a hot wind. Cutting through the herd was like standing too close to a campfire. On cool nights, steam rose off them like mist in a mountain valley. It made watching over the sleeping herd damn near impossible some nights.

The dust and stink added to the misery. Everything smelled like beefs and sweat. River crossings helped wash the sweat away, but then the smell of wet animal stepped in to overpower everything. Minutes after the crossing, the dust that covered beast and man turned to mud. For the rest of the day, it washed down in every rivulet of sweat. The grit itched and chafed, adding a new circle to my personal hell.

From the Bar C to Dodge City, everything we ate was seasoned with dust. Coffee had a gritty finish that wasn't from the grounds. The food was edible only because Smythe knew his craft. Even then we ended up spitting out sand between bites more often than not. Jose and I had it better than most, our position ahead of the herd kept us out of the worst of the dust and heat. But as Jose had predicted, our good luck ended at Waco.

We rode into the dust of another herd a few miles ahead of us. After that, it was a constant dance trying to keep the two herds separated by at least a day. Drovers didn't dictate the pace of a herd, they simply guided it in a direction. Aside from that, the herd was either moving or stopped, there were no other options. The mossy-horned lead steer set the pace. No one wanted to bring thin beefs to market, not after all the effort it took to get them there. As fate would have it, the lead steer for that first drive was Lucky and he was faster than most. He'd led drives for Max before, and for a longhorn, he was fairly calm and steady.

The second year cleared up any lingering doubts I might have had as to how hard the trail could be. We lost three hands to stampedes, two in a fight with a war party, and one more to Kansas rustlers. We also lost nearly four hundred head along the trail. Some died from heat and dehydration since a spring drought that year had left more than one watering hole dry. Then some more went to rustlers wearing 'Kansas Livestock Inspector' badges. The rest were lost in stampedes, trampled to death under a thousand hooves.

Dodge City's rowdy nights claimed another two hands before we finally left for the return trip home. The returning crew had barely enough men to get the remade to the fort. Only Jose, Chet, Max, Smythe and I made it home. The rest were buried in unmarked graves along the Western Trail. That was the first year the drive didn't follow the Chisholm Trail. Supposedly the new route skipped part of Kansas, but I wasn't sure it was any better. Max had spoken with some other ranchers about problems along the old trail, and they had suggested the new route was better. Two of them had lost their whole herd to the Kansas live stock inspectors. Adding insult to injury, they also had to pay a bond to get their hands out of jail.

Max was done with the drive to Dodge City after that trip. Cattle prices had stabilized and he could get a fair price in Fort Worth at the new railhead. Next year, he planned on picking up drovers in Uvalde for the shorter drive. It wouldn't be as profitable but he was tired of burying hands for just a few dollars more. I had to tip my hat to him, the man could see change coming and adapted faster than most.

We didn't need any new hands for the winter, so Trent met us in San Antonio with a wagon. It was a weary group that rode south to the ranch after picking up supplies. Not long after we arrived, Jose and I made our way to the cabin to prepare for another winter riding the line. That winter passed just like the last one, freezing cold but in good company.

Riding the line tightened the bond we shared, but things were about to change for both of us. Jose had met a beautiful señorita in Uvalde last year. Whenever he was able, they had attended church together in the hope of obtaining the padre's approval for their marriage. A wife and a home were things he never thought he'd have. I knew this drive would be his last and I sure didn't blame him. I could feel the topic weighing heavily on his mind, but I didn't want to bring it up until he was ready to talk about it.

The snow was melting and spring was fast approaching when he finally brought it up. The weather had broken at long last and we'd been out riding the line that day, both horse and man relishing the freedom. I'd even taken an early spring buck just after noon, and now our cabin smelled like smoke and cooking meat. The venison steaks were the first fresh meat we'd had in weeks.

"Amigo, you know about me and Cassandra?" He asked tentatively.

"Figure you're about to get married an' settle down." I caught the stunned look on his face as I glanced over my shoulder. The last of my New York accent was fading and some of the south Texas drawl was creeping in.

"You are not mad, amigo?"

"Amigo, do you think I'm going to hold a grudge 'bout you getting hitched? Hell no! I'm happy for ya." I turned to face him, skillet in hand, with the heart and liver still sizzling away. The steaks were almost done, I'd pull that skillet off in a minute. "Sides, three years an' ya still can't cook."

"Amigo, if we are being honest, neither of us has learned to cook." He laughed, spearing a piece of heart from the hot skillet I'd set in the middle of the table. "Will you come back from Fort Worth?"

"No, I still want to see the ocean. I'll go west at the end of the drive, maybe head for Los Angeles."

"I should be going with you, amigo."

"No, you should be marrying that breathtaking woman before she comes to her senses." I smiled at the man who'd shared some rough trails with me. "You love her an' I want to come back here to find the fearsome man I've ridden into hell with bouncing a baby on his knee."

"Amigo, when you get that hacienda we will come. I will be your Segundo."

"No, you will come as mi amigo."

"Only if you hire a cook." He chuckled, breaking the tension.

Made in the USA
Monee, IL
24 May 2025